Quests
and
Quandaries

ALDA YUAN

BOOK ONE

OF

THE FLOATING ISLES

The Floating Isles Series
Quests and Quandaries
Portents and Poor Sense
Riffraff and Royalty
Saints and Sinners
Tyrants and Troublemakers
Book 6 – Untitled but taking suggestions
Book 7 – Unwritten but taking suggestions

The Immortal Warrior Series
The Black Knight
The Olympians

"This is what she spent time doing instead of participating in family time so it better be good."

— *Parents*

"The books are just thick enough to hide a phone if you cut holes in all the pages."

— *Some monster*

"*Meow?*"

— *Artemis the cat*

DEDICATION

This book is dedicated to the carbonate-silicate geochemical cycle. But please, would it kill you to kick things up a notch? I know nearly 8 billion people who would really appreciate a more effective carbon sink.

CHAPTER ONE

Only halfway through the fourth course,[1] I was bored enough to start thinking about pegging a drumstick at Emir Withercox. A perfectly justified sentiment, trust me. Though old as the nearest mountain range and about as wind weathered, he still had a powerful voice and absolutely would not stop bragging about his many conquests as a young lad.[2] Jak hissed to get my attention from across the table. When I looked over, he glared at me. "Don't do it."

"I have no idea what you're talking about," I said though he wouldn't believe me. Perhaps he saw me eyeing the plate of aerodynamic turkey legs lying between us. Or perhaps he knew me well enough to guess I wouldn't keep my promise to behave. I strove hard for the title of the most ill-mannered princess this side of the Zah River. I had a reputation to uphold.

Still, Jak suffered quite a lot in his self-appointed role as my minder. He often predicted that his thick black hair would go prematurely white on my account. I resolved to wait until at

---

[1] Slices of something or other. Most likely walrus in peanut sauce for interested parties.
[2] All a load of crock. I once spent an empty afternoon guiding his childhood best friend out of the woods the old man lost himself in. He made it worth my while in funny stories.

1

least the seventh course before I started trouble. Then he could tell himself and everyone else he'd been a good influence. Until then, I amused myself coming up with new nicknames for some of the more colorful members of our dinner party. The old ones felt stale already. I'd been calling Xerxes Ironclad for a long time. It was doubly appropriate since he neither took off his clunky plate armor nor opened his mouth.[3] Precisely so, his nickname survived the last cull. Surely, I had enough time to come up with something else clever.

Before I started seriously on this task, I noticed some strange activity. I sat up fully straight for the first time during the meal and stared at the dark cloud swirling into existence above my father's head. Without even thinking, I shouted, "Everyone under the table," before following my own advice.

Jak and I dived at the same time. Our heads collided in sync with those of the pairs of diners to our right and left. Even as I rubbed at what would soon be a bruise, I demanded, "Didn't we time this feast to avoid spontaneous storm clouds? Remind me to ask my mother to fire the official weather scryer."

"To be fair, he said they were *unlikely*," Jak remarked.

"If that's the extent of his abilities, I dare say I could be a weather scryer too," I shot back. "So would a monkey with a dart board."

"He actually has one in his office. A dartboard, that is. It covers the window."

"There's the problem then," I said. "He can't even look outside to judge the weather. Then at least he could give us instantaneous updates."

After a pause, Jak glanced up at the bottom of the table we huddled beneath. "Aren't storms normally noisy?"

He was right of course. I eased myself out from under the table and peered at the patch of dark clouds still hovering in the air. Now that Jak's comment shook me out of my initial shock, I saw it couldn't be a storm cloud. After all, it swirled counter

---

[3] A couple more I'm particularly proud of: Piccolo, Kill-more Trout, Moonshine.

clockwise.[4]

As I got to my feet, the cloud flashed bright red. I stumbled back into my chair, unsure what this meant. When the light faded, the cloud disappeared as well, leaving a small and rather rotund creature holding an oversized wand in her left hand. I recognized her kind right away and did not like how she looked at me. Sure enough, she noticed me staring and her delicate face lit up with delight. As she fluttered in my direction though, I vaulted over my chair and tore down the length of the hall, heedless of the stares following my passage.

Who cared what they thought? I had a questing fairy after me! I dashed past a woman who convinced her neighbors to donate all the untouched portions of the third course of curried chickpeas, barreled through a cloud of steam from a small table-side pool prepared for a guest who couldn't be far from hot water long. I nearly collided with the two men struggling under the weight of an enormous clay pot with the next course as I reached the curtained doorway at the end of the room.

After plunging into the hallway, I ignored the servers demanding to know what I did and ducked under the arms of my long suffering weapons' master when he tried to get me to stop.[5] I shouted a half explanation as I went down another hallway and lunged at an open door, elaborately painted in half a dozen colors. I caught it by the handle and swung myself inside, pulling the door closed as I went, a rather impressive maneuver when you consider the long trailing dress I wore. The door slammed shut with a boom, followed closely by a smaller thump as the questing fairy hit the frame.

The fairy chattered at me angrily from the other side of the thick slab of decorated wood but I ignored it. I didn't care if she had a mission. I only cared about not becoming her latest victim. I backed away from the door and watched it warily as I heard a pop like an oversized bubble bursting. When nothing happened,

---

[4] Everyone knows spontaneous weather events come out of the ether clockwise.
[5] It had been a long time since he could hope to keep up with me. And the man lived a tragic life even before he came to us.

3

I sighed in relief, only to immediately release a curse in alarm when the fairy appeared next to my head.

She struggled to lift her wand and bring it down over me so I moved out of the way. I slid aside, falling into a stack of pillows and knocking them everywhere. The ashes coming off the fairy's glowing wand floated harmlessly to the floor.

My relief didn't last long for she pumped her oversized wings and came hurtling in my direction. I grabbed the first thing I could get my hands on, in this case a silken duvet, and tossed it over the fairy. I wrapped her in the cloth and twisted the end a few times to prevent her from getting out.

As she rolled across the floor to extract herself, I scrambled to my feet, tripping over the end of my dress and ripping it. I considered for a moment, took out the dagger at my side and cut it the rest of the way around so the dress ended above my knees. Satisfied, I went to the door and wrenched it open.

The second I did, the fairy appeared and bonked me over the head with her wand before leaving in a self-satisfied huff. The end of the wand released a huge cloud of ash to fill my lungs. I could feel the sneeze working its way out and tried to clamp down on it, knowing what would happen if I gave in to the itch. I struggled but finally released a sneeze so mighty it knocked me back into the room.

My head hit the wall and my vision swam. The jagged pieces of sky peeking through the arched window went in and out of focus. Finally though, I blinked away the dizziness and looked down to see a fine layer of ash covering my whole body. Groaning, I rolled over, did my best to shake it from my hair and pulled myself to my feet. I coughed up the ash in my throat and was about to spit when my parents appeared in the doorway. Thinking better of hawking a gob of spit on their slippers, I turned to face the window and aimed out instead. I immediately heard a shout from below. I looked out and spotted one of my cousins glaring up at me. It looked as if I missed her. So no need for her to get so riled up. Her girlfriend apparently agreed with me because she grimaced at me. Maybe having to jump out of the way with such speed put creases in her leather outfit. "Don't worry!" I told her. "You're still prettier than me."

4

I withdrew my head and turned to look at my parents, as well as Jak, who arrived panting with exhaustion. Ask him to run more than two dozen steps and you might as well get ready to load him into a cart to get him home.[6]

"What happened to you?" Jak wanted to know. "Looks like something exploded in your face."

"If I wanted someone to state the obvious all the time, I'd get myself a Logorrhea Lizard," I told him.

"For the love of the gods, what did you do to your dress?" my father asked.

"Tried my hand at fashion design?" I suggested. "That's a career you'd approve of, right?"

My parents exchanged a look but apparently decided to let the joke go. But only because they had other, worse concerns.

"So, a questing fairy, huh?" my mother asked.

This question seemed so unnatural given the circumstances,[7] I immediately suspected foul play. I looked at her, then glanced at my father and it became clear they set me up. "*You* sent her for me, didn't you?"

"Now listen," my father said.

"I am not in the mood to listen," I told him. "Right now, I'd like to holler for a bit longer. Jak, you knew about this too?"

"I have nothing to do with this!" Jak protested. "I don't even know what's going on. Questing fairies aren't supposed to exist."

"Sure looked real enough to me," I told him. "So is the headache she gave me. Now why did you do this?"

"It's our way of breaking the news," my mother said. "You're going on a quest."

"You had her come in the middle of my birthday dinner?" I asked.

"You've never made it past six courses before so we figured it

---

[6] This actually happened on more than one occasion. We toiled under the same teachers for years and one punished us by making us run laps around the palace. Since I usually got us in trouble, I really had no right to complain about having to help Jak. It didn't stop me.

[7] I, for instance, upon seeing someone in such an ash covered state, might ask after their health.

wouldn't matter," my mother said.

This gave me some pause. I couldn't exactly claim different. Perhaps they knew me better than I thought. "Fair enough," I finally conceded. "Why are you trying to send me on a quest? What gives?"

"It's family tradition. The eldest child, or in this case the only child, must go on a quest. It is a condition of inheritance. Besides, how else do you think your father found a princess to marry him?" my mom wanted to know.

"You want me to save a princess and marry her?" I asked. "Two days over the Zah River will be enough if the stories about them all being in distress are true. It would rather jam up your plans to market me to Prince Narcissus.[8] I've always said Daya's a better candidate though I wouldn't wish such a fate even on her."

"Rahni, can you take this seriously?" my father demanded.

"I think I'm giving it exactly the amount of gravity it deserves. You're the ones who sent a fairy to dump ash on me in the middle of the dining hall," I pointed out.

"No other way to make sure you obey," my mother said.

"I'm not going anywhere. Those princesses can grow up and drag their own asses out of trouble," I said.

"Think about this," my father said, his voice strangely tinged with worry. At the time, I didn't think much of it. Sultan Osman was nothing if not a worrier, which is precisely what made his job so perfect. He could worry all day.[9]

"Listen to your father," my mother urged me. "You always wanted an adventure."

"Maybe when I still tottered about at knee level. You know

[8] Not his real name. I use the nickname because his real name is somehow more obnoxious.
[9] We had an epidemic of rabidly racist elves who liked to put on red hoods and find sentient wolves to kill. This might have been more a problem if the last group of Hoods United, also red hood wearing, didn't already run most of them off. Something about the red hood obviously gave people an intense hatred of canines. Meanwhile, a conflict might be brewing in the lands to our south. Then, a madman off in the woods somewhere kept killing other people's horses for no apparent reason.

what though? I grew out of it. I absolutely refuse to go on this quest," I declared. "That's final." In retrospect, these words were ill advised. I might as well have challenged fate to find a way to screw me over.[10] Yet even I didn't think it would come back on me so fast. I felt a searing pain in my upper left arm and clapped my hand over it. The pain faded as quickly as it appeared, leaving behind no scar but a thin band of goldish metal. Only, it wasn't gold.

---

[10] An expression, you understand. Few people in this day and age still believe in fate. Or at least, I hope so.

CHAPTER TWO

Even my mother looked a little guilty about the dirty trick they played on me. I didn't need them to explain. It hadn't been a questing fairy at all but a fairly good odds-mother disguised as one of her less dangerous cousins. Any time one appeared, there were fairly good odds of being subjected to a curse.[1]

"You cursed me?!" I shouted, probably loud enough for the whole palace to hear.

"We only meant it to trigger if you absolutely refused to go on the quest," my father tried.

"But you knew she wouldn't cooperate," Jak pointed out.

"That's what we feared. Do you think we enjoyed setting a curse on you?" my mother demanded.

"You must have enjoyed it a little bit," I said, strangely devoid of anger as soon as I accepted being stuck with this quest whether I willed it or not. "Admit it, the idea of having me do what you said for once tickled your fancy."

"Any hope this episode might affect your maturity has been well and truly dashed," my father said. His busy mustache jumped up and down as he spoke, as it always did when he grew

---

[1] Hence the name.

agitated. "Understand though, we didn't do this lightly. There's no other choice. You have to go. It's very straightforward, truly. As long as you keep to the Inviolable Rules of the Eigen States, you will be fine. You have more training than I ever did. My father liked to throw people into such situations without preparation as a test of character. Shame you never met him."

"I don't think it's a shame at all. Every story you've told me of the man makes me glad of it. He'd hate my guts and the feeling would be more than mutual," I said.[2]

I went too far for my father got all flushed in the face and began to roar. "Rahni Gazi, if you don't take that back, I'm going to-"

"No," I shot back before he could even finish scrambling for an appropriate threat. "What else are you going to do? You already cursed me."

This gave him some pause, enough for my mother to stick herself into the fight brewing between the two of us. Good thing she did. I don't know his excuse but I definitely wanted to pick a fight. All this talk of curses stirred me into the sort of mood where even Jak did his best to steer clear.

"Why don't you and Jak go to the audience room while your father and I apologize to the dinner guests?" my mother asked.

"They're probably gone already and making off with all the food too," Jak remarked. "The chance to poach meals is half the reason so many people come to anything Rahni is present at. Last solstice, someone made off with an entire lamb. I talked to someone earlier today who came all the way from Maug. Maug! That's at least two magic carpet transfers and a balloon over the Lagoon of Rumbling and Bubbling Doom."

"Good to know my notoriety has spread to the other side of the lagoon," I said as I brushed past him and went in the direction away from the audience room. I needed a quick wash and a new outfit, not to mention some time to think this over.

Jak followed me, watching warily in case I decided to take my displeasure out on him. It wouldn't be the first time so I didn't

---

[2] Maybe I was still a bit angry, come to think of it.

9

take too much offense.[3] Since I was certainly in no mood to relax, I walked right past the warm room in the bathing complex and stepped into the pool. I waded in and put my head under the spout so the water could run through and clean my hair.

When I finished, Jak brought me a shirt and some pants. A wise choice since neither of us knew what else might happen today. He also brought me my daggers and beloved kilij. Some days I liked gliding[4] about freely in my dresses as much as any princess in the Isles but today, the weight of a sword on my belt comforted me.

Once I strapped everything into place, I looked up to see Jak looking at me with some concern. "Okay," I said, "I know you have something to say. Go ahead and spit it out."

"You'll take me with you, right?"

My anger faded a bit to guilt at the earnest expression on his face. For as long as I could remember, Jak desperately, and I mean desperately, wanted to go on a quest. In fact, he constantly went out in search of one. Most quests came from fairies or curses but some came at the ends of thunderbolts. So Jak used to race outside in the lightning storms until someone gave him a couple good clonks on the head to show him what might happen to little boys who chased storm clouds and impossible dreams. He stopped trying to be struck by lightning after that but he never stopped hoping for an adventure to fall into his lap. It wasn't just for the sake of going on a quest. In the strange lands beyond the Zah River, miracles could happen and he needed one if he wanted ever to take back what he lost.

"I'm sorry Jak. I didn't even think. I'll tell them. The only way I'm going on this damn quest is if you get to tag along," I assured him. I waved him off before he could thank me. "Don't be ridiculous. If I have to go, you might as well get something

---

[3] To be fair, I only pushed him off the roof one time, when he callously made light of some true misfortune involving a broken clay disc. And he didn't even get hurt. I knew about the basin of water.

[4] You'd think this simply a figure of speech and mostly, you'd be right. But one year some seamstress a couple borders over had the bright idea of attaching propellers to a princess' dress. The results were less than desirable. Disastrous, even.

good out of it. Come on. Time to go face the music."

Apparently, word got out about the curse. Everyone we passed, guardsman to visitors filtering away from the main hall, peered at my arm, as if trying to see through my shirt to the band around my bicep. Finally, I got fed up and pushed my left sleeve all the way up as a group strode past. "Satisfied?" I called after them.

"We're going to have plenty of chances to pick fights soon enough," Jak told me.

"Just as well, I've been practicing my whole life," I grumbled back, my hand straying to the hilt of my sword. Now that I accepted having to go on this crazy trip, my mind skipped ahead to what we needed to make sure it went as smoothly as possible.

I only got halfway through a list by the time Jak and I arrived at the audience room. Both my parents stood outside the entrance. I expected them to wait inside, ready to pounce on me with their reassurances about the necessity of this venture and so forth.

"I went through all this in my day too," my father said to me as he put a hand against the door.

I noticed a strange look on his face again so the wave of smoke that billowed from the doorway didn't even surprise me. The cackle and the voice calling for us to come inside did. But I didn't start out of fear. Call it incredulity instead for I recognized the voice even through the affected accent and histrionic effects.

When I charged through the door, waving my hands to clear the smoke, I did feel a moment of doubt. The figure sitting on the other side of the room, bathed in smoke, really did look like a hunched hag crouched over a crystal ball. Then the smoke cleared a bit more and I saw a strand of blonde hair peeking out from beneath the pointy hat.

"Are you kidding me?" I shouted at the world in general and moved further into the room. I grabbed the hat on top of Brendan's head and ripped it off. Then I kicked him in the leg hard enough he leaped out of the chair, shucking the rest of his costume as he hopped around the room, howling in pain. Soon enough, the cloak, the mask, the hump under his clothes, even

11

the fake teeth he stuffed into his mouth fell away to reveal a
burly young man. This, of course, was our weather scryer. Why
he decided to put on this get up was anyone's guess. First
though, I had another axe to grind. "Jak, you did not remind me
to get Brendan fired for deficient scrying abilities."

"He got the lack of indoor weather right though," Jak pointed
out. "Seems a little unfair to light him on fire if he didn't even
get anything wrong."

Brendan heard the last bit and suddenly stopped hopping
around.[5] "Wait a minute. You can't fire me!"

"Want a bet?" I demanded.

"No!" everyone else in the room shouted in unison. They'd all
been on the receiving end of such a challenge.

Before I could get another word in, my mother interrupted
again.[6] "Rahni, stop fooling around and let Brendan do his job,"
she snapped.

"Is this a farce?" I asked. "Were you trying to fool me into
thinking some wandering fortune teller showed up to guide me
through my quest?"

"Not you," my father hissed. "The Board."

"Don't tell me you're actually scared of it. It's never paid us
any mind before, if it even has a mind," I said. At the mumbles
of concern this remark elicited, I sent glares in all directions. "If
you want me to do this, we're going to stop this silliness. Just
count yourselves lucky I'm cooperating that far."

"I suppose the fortune teller bit has fallen out of favor. Even I
think it's over the top," my father said.

"Not to mention potentially racist," Jak remarked.

"Agreed. Plus, you might have skipped all the cackling," my
father said.

---

[5] Which is proof I didn't hurt him bad. You wouldn't realize if you saw him
leaping around on one leg and keening tragically. His acting certainly
improved.

[6] She was really good at that. The power of interruption ran in her family.
Her grandfather once interrupted someone out of existence, though they were
standing on the edge of the Redlands so perhaps the victim simply got
swallowed up. No one had the guts to contradict him after.

Brendan sighed. "I do not get paid enough for this."[7]

Ignoring him, my father said, "I think we can move past the mentoring portion of this then. A lot of the traditional lists I consulted mentioned it only as an optional component anyway."

"The prophecy, however, is not optional," my mother said. "You'll sit and listen to that?"

"Is it anywhere near as awful as Brendan's disguise?" I asked.

Apparently taking this as the invitation it assuredly was not, Brendan spread his arms and started to recite the prophecy.

"Into the swirling fates you shall be cast,
With a magic sword in hand,
An old friend from years past,
And a creature long lost to the land.

One more you shall find,
Along the twisted way,
And to your band bind,
Unless you wish to stranded stay.

Boundaries both wide and deep,
You will cross and traverse.
In confusion long shall you steep,
Guided by rhymes just this perverse."

I started to laugh, so hard tears came to my eyes. At this point, things were so absurd I couldn't help but start taking them seriously. "Fine. The friend from years past is clearly Jak. I don't know about the rest. You figure it out if you're so eager for me to go."

"We have it figured out already," my mother said. "In fact, we've assembled all the parts mentioned in the first stanza."

"Stanza," I echoed with a snort. "Elevating it a bit, aren't you?"

---

[7] Not true in case anyone felt really sorry for him. For one thing, he got paid quite a lot considering how little he actually did. For another thing, humiliation came cheap. People did it every day for free, willing or not.

13

CHAPTER THREE

My scorn notwithstanding, we soon ended up in the
blacksmith's shop. Steam billowed through the room and no one
could hear anything but the mechanical whirling in the air and
the clank of massive gears turning against each other. We stood
clustered near the entrance and searched for any sign of Serge.

Finally, Jak cupped both hands over his mouth and shouted
the man's name at the top of his lungs. An answering shout no
one really understood came almost immediately and Serge
appeared out of the mist and smoke. He looked and dressed
unlike any other blacksmith. Though well muscled and as large
as you'd expect, he kept impeccably clean. His white coat, baggy
and long enough to nearly trail to the ground, didn't have a
speck of dirt on it. For though Serge might be a blacksmith, he
didn't practice his craft with his hands. Instead, he built
MACHINES[1] to do the work for him. No one else knew how
they worked. Half the time, Serge didn't seem to either, thus the
frequent accidents and why my parents detached his workshop
from the rest of the palace. Still, despite the hazards, Serge's

---

[1] Massive And Conveniently Handy Instruments Necessary for Easier
Smithing, or so he said. I thought it rather clunky but whatever he liked.

contraptions made very good swords and, when working, at a much faster rate than a person could.

Serge smiled at us in an affable manner and said something completely inaudible, drowned out by the thump and ring of metallic objects. If I looked at his face, I could have read his lips. But I fixed my gaze past him, at the steam swirling about the room. Every once in a while, I caught a glimpse of sparks rising into the air. As far as I knew, no one else in the Floating Isles had the barest idea how Serge did any of this.

Finally realizing we couldn't hear him, Serge waved us out of the main room and into his study. We filed into a cramped room but at least our ears didn't ring.[2] Papers littered the floor of the study and piled atop every surface. Diagrams with dizzying arrays of gears and metallic parts hung from nails off the walls. Since the room could hardly be messier, I didn't feel bad knocking a stack of papers to the ground to sit down on the only chair in the room.

"Happy Birthday!" Serge said to me as he rifled through his room for my gift. It took him some time but he finally remembered what I already realized, that he didn't keep any of the weapons he forged in this room. "Oh, sorry, it's in the armory. Come along please."

Serge led us toward the door we entered from and I saw everyone else looking at each other, bemused. He pushed his close fitting sleeve up to his elbow, opened up a panel next to the door, yanked out a metal pipe and started to crank it in a clockwise direction.

I knew what would happen so I grabbed a shelf to steady myself. When the room began to turn, my parents and Jak stumbled around trying to keep their balance, which I found more than a little amusing. Finally though, the room ground to a stop. Completely unfazed and oblivious to the expressions on my parents' faces, Serge opened the door, revealing not the

---

[2] Our teeth did clatter against each other once in a while as one of his contraptions pounded away rhythmically at a piece of metal. Made the whole ground shake. Yet another reason they gave him a separate building. Even I supported that decision.

smithy but what he liked to call the armory.

It was a small room, full to the bursting of weapons of all kinds. Various prototypes lay in piles on the floor, in many different stages of development. Some looked stranger than others. They ranged from daggers the size of needles to weapons that resembled shields more than swords. Jak picked up one of the latter, a behemoth of a sword with a blade the width of my waist and nearly five feet long. Though a truly hopeless fighter, Jak was abnormally strong[3] so he waved the improbable sword around like a twig. "Serge, can I have this?"

"You want that?" Serge asked, pausing in his headlong rush across the room to fetch my magical sword for surely that's what his gift would be. "Even I don't think it's practical. I made it solely for research purposes. I haven't even sharpened the cutting edge."

"That's alright. I'm tagging along on Rahni's quest. Only thing I can do to help keep away enemies is look intimidating. Hopefully, this sword will help," Jak said.

"Going to need a whole lot more than a big sword," I muttered but Jak refused to take the bait.[4]

Serge merely shrugged. He found a suitable sheath and I helped Jak strap the weapon to his back. However, this meant he could not actually draw the sword. The first time he tried, he got the sword stuck half out of the sheath and a band on his wrist caught on the hilt so he could neither keep drawing the sword nor push it back in. I laughed at him for a while before moving to help. When I finally detached his wrist from the sword and slid it back into his sheath, I remarked, "You know, maybe this trip won't be so bad after all."

"What, you like watching me make a fool of myself?" Jak asked as he unstrapped the sword to look at it. Intricate designs like the patterns of lace curled along the flat side of the blade and

---

[3] Something that ran in *his* family and wore away through time. His grandfather could purportedly move mountains with a sneeze. Even he only ever claimed to have done it once. He couldn't reproduce it at parties so who knows.

[4] Awfully smart, Jak was sometimes.

tilting it in the light gave a purple tint.

"Exactly, it'll be like any other day," I said.

Jak became so focused on the sword he didn't even respond to my comment. With a sigh, I pulled out a dagger, took the sheath from him and cut the upper portion off so he could pull the sword out without having to extend his arm all the way.

About the time I finished, Serge came back with a curved kilij in hand. I took it by the hilt and raised an eyebrow as I examined it. "This doesn't look any different from my old sword."

"That's by design. I know you're fond of it. If you leave your old one with me, I'll touch it up and get it back to you better than ever," Serge promised.

If this was his way of apologizing for his part in this, it worked. I pulled my sword out of its sheath and handed it over. Just as Serge promised, the new sword fit in my old sheath just right. "What exactly makes this a magical sword?"

"You'll find out when you need to," my mother said.

Perhaps she expected me to blow up again but I didn't even get angry. I didn't care about having a magical sword. I preferred to do my own work anyway. "Fine, we have most parts of the first stanza of the prophecy covered. What about the last?"

"Ah yes, a creature long lost to the land," my father said. "If Serge will show us out, we'll introduce you two to Keran."

"Will he try to eat me?" I asked, only half in jest.

"Definitely not," my father said with such confidence it made me suspicious.

This uneasiness only grew when my parents led us back to the palace and down into the basement. They used to be dungeons before an enlightened ancestor[5] demolished them in favor of living spaces for the poor and homeless. Then my grandfather[6] converted half the basement back into a dungeon, which had the effect of running off the other inhabitants,

---

[5] Not my grandfather. His part comes later.
[6] Told you he'd come up.

allegedly due to the smell.[7] My parents undid his changes in turn but found it a hard task.

They did their best to send the various captives back where they belonged but my grandfather collected, and collected was definitely the right word, far too many 'specimens,' as he liked to call them. Some of the creatures were sentient. Some nowhere near it. All, understandably I think, rather disliked the accommodations we offered. None put any effort into making our lives easy for us. They raised a racket day and night that kept the basement empty of all but the crankiest guards.

We heard the echo of many voices as we filed down the stairs and into the basement. The guards lurched up from their seats, more in surprise to see anyone coming down than in an effort to show us respect.

"Oh please, don't get up on our account," I declared, doing my best to make it more awkward for everyone involved.

Unfortunately, this didn't work because Ila was amongst the guards. She looked up from where she still sat and grinned. "I hear you're going on a quest?"

"How did you know?" I asked. "Who came down here to pass you the news?"

"I didn't need an update," Ila said.

I thought for a second and came to my senses. Of course Ila knew. My parents must have come down here to visit whoever had the bad luck to accompany us on our voyage. They always trusted her with the secrets they never told me. Usually, I didn't blame them. This time however, I did.

Ila saw realization dawn and chuckled. "Getting slow in your old age. Imagine how far behind you'll be by your eighteenth birthday."

A comment like this from anyone else would make me bristle but I only stuck my tongue out at her. I'd known Ila longer than even Jak and some of my first memories involved tottering after her. She treated me like a younger sister and I let her, half in awe of her self-confidence. These days, I could go toe to toe with

---

[7] The screams of the unfortunate probably didn't lend much to the atmosphere either.

her, with insults and with blades alike but I let her get away with a lot more than anyone else could hope to.

Ila got to her feet and clapped the guard next to her on the shoulder. "I'm giving you the command. Don't screw it up while I take our royals and the squirt where they need to go."

Jak sighed at the nickname and looked at her reproachfully. "I don't suppose it at all matters I'm taller than you now?"

"Not on your life," Ila told him as she led the way.

Back in my grandfather's day, such familiarity would have warranted at least a drawing if not also a quartering.[8] My parents and I tended not to take ourselves as seriously, mostly because we were not assholes.

"Any clues?" I asked Ila. I knew her well enough to see she ran through several jokes before giving it up and responding with a firm shake of the head.

I knew better than to ask my parents for clues. They seemed determined to play their tarot cards close to their chest, so close I hadn't even seen any yet, a shame because I liked to get creative with the interpretation of fortunes. You could really find out a lot about a person by reading their reactions to a made up future.

We walked through hallways with disjointed décor, constructed in a patchwork of styles from years of rebuilding and demolishing. Finally, we came to a room at the furthest reach of the basement. My mother knocked on the door and for a long time, we didn't hear anything but the keening of the tree creature a few doors down.[9]

I stopped thinking about the tree as a section of the door swung out. A wolf's head came through the opening and he turned his baleful eyes up to look at us. "You've finally come to take me out of this place? Hold on a minute and I'll try to work up the energy to open this door."

---

[8] There's some scholarly quibbling on the subject of whether this should really be known as a quinting since there are often five horses involved. Everyone seemed to agree quartering sounded better.

[9] A couple of years ago, we tried to find out where he/she, if it had gender, belonged but to no avail so it stayed until the restoration specialists figured it out.

"This delightful fellow is Keran," Ila said as she grabbed the doorknob herself and opened it, revealing a room devoid of furnishings behind the wolfhound.

Keran sat back on his haunches and looked at all of us without enthusiasm. It'd been some time since I saw one of his kind but the shape of the face, rounder than that of an average wolf and the color of his coat, a distinctive shade of silver-grey, gave him away. This was not to mention his size for he measured half again as large as the biggest wolf.

The way he crouched now though, with his ears drooped down, his spine scrunched up and his head lowered, made him seem much smaller. "Well," I remarked, "you look about as excited as I feel. We'll probably get along."

"I don't know nearly enough about you to come to a similar conclusion," Keran said.

"You're going to get to know both of us pretty well," Jak said. "Who knows how long this quest is going to take?"

"That's what I'm afraid of," Keran said. "I haven't left this palace for some time. I don't feel ready for an extended trip into the Eigen States."

"Don't get me wrong," I said to Keran before I turned to my parents, "but aren't you stretching the elements of the prophecy a bit here? I don't think sentient wolfhounds have been *long* lost to the land. It's been approximately six months. And if Keran has been hiding out in our basement the whole time, his people haven't even been lost."

"Technicalities," my mother said.

At this, I threw up my hands. "I couldn't care less. I thought you were a stickler for the rules."

"Keran is the best we've got," my father admitted.

"How do you feel about that?" I asked Keran. "Honored?"

The wolfhound released a theatrical sigh. "Not so much. I'm not even sure I want to tag along."

"But we talked about this," my mother protested. "This is the best way for you to reunite with your people."

"At this point, should I even want to? There are times when I rather enjoy my solitude. I can see you're about to get upset. That sort of thing gives me a headache so I'll fulfill my promise and go," Keran said.

"There's the unbridled enthusiasm we're missing," I declared. "I dare say we are ready to embark."

"You're not planning to leave right now?" my mother asked.

As it happened, I didn't plan to leave without further preparation but I couldn't resist. "I don't see why not. The sooner we get going, the faster we can get back. I'm looking forward to the midsummer's night celebrations. Maybe I'll be grateful enough to be back, I won't ruin the feast."

"And break your streak?" Ila asked.

"True," I admitted. "It's settled then. We'll leave now to get back in time for me to continue my feast crashing."

"Actually, we expected you to leave in two days," father said.

Keran reacted to this first by letting out a huff. "And listen to the tree creature keen for another two nights? Have I not suffered enough already?"

"You might as well come out of the basement and stay in the palace proper," I told him. "Surely we have rooms set aside for quest companions or some such nonsense."

CHAPTER FOUR

As it turned out, we did not. In fact, we did not have *any* extra rooms available for we passed them out to the various guests and moochers who came to watch me disrupt my own birthday dinner. When we discovered this, Ila asked, "Keran, how do you feel about broom closets?"

"I don't suppose anything is really beneath my dignity at this point. I accept this arrangement," Keran answered.

Naturally enough, we headed to the nearest broom closet. When I opened it however, we found a young woman inside, shaking a bowl of small bones. "Look, you didn't even have to dress Brendan up. We had a fortune telling witch here all along," I said.

The young woman glared, threw a bone at my head and slammed the door, after which she shouted through the wood, "I'm not a witch and you can stay out of my closet."[1]

"I've never seen her before," my father remarked as we moved on to find another closest.

---

[1] Rather rude since technically speaking, she was squatting in *our* broom closet. Then again, I did call her a witch. Though that's an honorific in many circles.

"Me neither," Ila said.

"You mean to tell me our palace is so porous anyone can get in?" I asked.

"What are you going to do? Fire me?" Ila asked.

"Definitely not the route I'd go," I told her. "Where am I going to get people gutsy enough to set you on fire? I'd have you discharged. Lightning is much faster anyway."

"I'll keep that in mind," Ila said as we reached another broom closet.

As soon as she opened it, Keran exclaimed, "Good grief," and did his best to hide behind us.

He didn't move fast enough for the resident of this particular closet already caught sight of him. The man levered himself out of the makeshift bed he constructed out of cleaning supplies and dead branches and took an eager step toward Keran before noticing the rest of us. He bobbed short and respectful bows in all directions. "You've brought the beast to the right place. I used to be an honorary member of the Hoods so I know what to do. If you step aside, I can destroy the horrid beast in moments."

No one seemed to know how to respond so I gave the man a big smile. "Gee, thanks so much for taking care of our little problem. Before you get started, might I borrow a broom?"

The man blinked but then grabbed the only broom and handed it to me. "Here you go."

"Many thanks," I told him, right before I jabbed the end of the cleaning implement into his stomach. He fell back into his bed as I slammed the door shut again and stuck the broom through the handle to keep him from getting out.

"Good thinking," my mother conceded as the man started to beat his fists against the door.

"Not all my good work. Imagine that, this broom closet actually had a real broom," I said. "Don't see that every day."

"You know, I've never thought about the high ratio of broom closets to brooms in this palace," Jak mused. "Do you suppose there's a principle governing the relationship?"

"Maybe if you work out the equation, you can get it named after you," I suggested.

"Is there a broom closet in this palace not already inhabited, by a member of the Hoods no less?" my father demanded.

"In my defense, he was an honorary member. I would have rooted out a full-fledged member by now," Ila said.

"Now I'm reassured," Keran said.

"Nothing more out of you," Ila told him. "Best remember who kept you alive this half year. The rest of you go ahead. I'll take care of the screaming idiot here."

Rather than try another closet and this time perhaps be confronted by a dragon who wished us to buy a timeshare,[2] I suggested Karen sleep in the corner of my own room. I had enough space and I thought we should get used to one another before we set off.

Despite the early hour, I decided to turn in since it had been a long day. As I drifted off to sleep, I indulged the thought of not going on this quest after all. Jak would be disappointed but could some curse really force me to do this? Immediately, I felt the band around my arm heat up, enough so I noticed.

No longer sleepy, I sat up in bed and tugged at it, trying to push it off my arm though I knew it would not work. No one ever cursed me before, through magic at least, but I knew how it worked. So it didn't surprise me when, far from sliding neatly off my arm, the band of mysterious metal tightened around my flesh. Perhaps it knew my attempts were halfhearted, for it only tightened enough to prevent me from wrestling it free.

I gave up before long and collapsed back onto the bed, determined out of necessity to go through with the quest, which did not mean I had to be happy about it. And I certainly was not happy about it the next day when I woke up. It didn't take me long to remember the events of the previous day. Shock that my

---

[2] Oh they were tricky, those dragons with their tag team tactics. I'd seen them in action before. One flattered while the other pushed until their victim couldn't help but sign on the line. Some of their other tactics were a bit more unscrupulous. They advertised these time shares as great investments but when you actually got there, it would often turn out to be located right next door to an active volcano or a troupe of unpleasant knife throwers eager to use you as target practice. And by that time, it would be too late to back out of the contract. And you already paid for the time so you were damn well going to use it, daily shower of knives or no.

24

parents went out of their way to curse me hit me all over again. I brushed it away for I had more important things to do.

When I sat up, I jumped at seeing Keran perched on a table and looking at me. "You're not going to watch us sleep this whole quest, are you?"

"Depends if there's anything more interesting to do," Keran said. "I woke early and didn't think it wise to leave the room, lest I run into our friend from the closet again."

"Surely Ila sorted him out by now. Still, you're probably right. Who knows what other mad dingbats we've let into the palace? Honestly, it's a wonder we don't face attempted assassinations left and right," I said.

"I heard about one incident a while back," Karen commented.

"I set her straight before her sword even left its sheath. Turns out she thought we banished her mother to the Lonely Isles of Solitude and Exile. I told her she got the wrong kingdom."

"But your mother did actually exile her," Keran said.

"Certainly. The woman tried to raise the Ancients from their Slumbers.[3] Can't have people running around thinking that's acceptable. I didn't want to break the news to her daughter so I sent her to Hitten. They can deal with her."

Keran snorted and hopped off the table with surprising grace. "You'll be a good queen one day, I think. Or a horrible one, depending on your mood."

"Gosh, you know me so well already. I did say you and I would get along." I got off the bed and considered the wisdom of going to the baths. I didn't know how long I'd be away from the comforts of home so I decided for it. The position of the sun told me I already slept to noon so it didn't matter so much if I wasted a bit more time.[4]

I took nearly an hour, soaking until Keran asked whether there might be a portal in the water I planned to take to the

---

[3] No one seemed to quite know which Ancients she actually wanted to raise. In the end, it didn't matter. They were, down to a deity, bad news. They already had their chance to ruin the world and nearly succeeded too. No need to give them another.

[4] It's not like I had plans, other than brooding over my bad luck. I could as easily do that while floating in warm water.

Eigen States. "I hope you'll torment Jak as much as you're attempting to bother me," I told him as I sank down into the water one last time.

"I'll make sure of it," Keran said.

"Maybe together we can drive him crazy within a week or two." A dress would be more comfortable in the heat so I decided to hold off on the leather armor until tomorrow. I did take my new sword, for magical or not, I might need it. I didn't think anything would happen today but I'd been known to be wrong.[5] No part of me wanted to be caught in a situation like yesterday where I had no choice but to run.

"No guards then?" Keran asked as we headed out.

"What do you need guards for? You have me."

"And you know how to use the sword?"

"You'll have to find out."

"I'm going to get myself killed."

I ignored this ringing endorsement of my skills and strode out of the baths, only to run into the guard posted outside. "Poor Yorik, you always get the worst jobs. My parents sent you to fetch me?"

"Also to make sure you didn't run off," Yorik admitted, lowering his gaze.

"Don't worry. Even I'm not foolish enough to try and defy a curse," I told him. "You can tell them I'll be in the tulip gardens."

"You'll be where?" Yorik asked, confused.

"The tulip gardens. It's the one with the flowers and walkways. You know it," I told him. I left him with that and turned on my heels, heading toward the garden as I said I would. I didn't look back but I knew he was shaking his head.

---

[5] Though I am struggling to come up with an example. There was that one time I thought I might like a pie dish better than kanafeh. It was a sad day for all.

CHAPTER FIVE

Jak found me lying on my back on a patch of grass and watching wisps of clouds float by. He made me proud by seeing right through to my purpose for coming here. "Did you get it?"

"Of course I did," I told him, patting my belt.

"You don't really think you can get away with this, do you?" he asked.

"Probably not," I admitted. "But I'm sure as hell going to give it a shot."

"I expect nothing different," Jak said as he sat down next to me. Addressing Keran now, he asked, "Did you sleep well?"

"As well as anyone can with a mortal enemy in the castle. That man and I have something of a history. He chased me halfway across the country before I got away and slunk to the palace. Perhaps he came here looking for me," Keran commented.

"Oh, he did. I asked Ila about it this morning. You won't be hearing from him anymore," Jak said.

"Exiled too? One of these days, they're all going to band together and make us sorry," I said.

"That's the topic of the next Regional Council, isn't it, the

27

creation of a new place of exile?" Jak said.

"What? They're going to make a lonelier island?" I asked with a laugh.

"Probably not so far from the truth," Jak said. After a time, during which I continued to stare at the sky and contemplate the world, Jak struck up a conversation with Keran, asking him why he stayed here in Savay when the rest of his people fled.[1]

"They didn't just flee the nation," Keran said with a sigh. "They faded into the mists. They're not quite dead but they no longer exist in a real sense either. Or at least, that's what I think I know."

"That's why you're coming along then, to get them back?" Jak asked.

"If anything can bring them back, it will be a successful quest," Keran said, his tone holding little excitement.

"You know, I never thought to ask yesterday. What can you do?" I levered myself up to rest on my elbows.

"Good question," Jak remarked. "It's Rahni's quest so she's the one to cut and slash her way through enemies. I'm the wise friend and mage."

"Don't listen to him," I told Keran. "He can do only a single rotten spell and not a useful one at that. I won't even dignify the wisdom comment with a rebuttal."

Keran thought for a long time before he answered, "Sarcasm and cynicism?"

"I've already got that covered," I said. "Anything else?"

"I don't suppose this will ever be useful but I can swallow coals," Keran said.

I responded with a grunt. "I suppose you can stand around and look pretty. I can't and Jak *certainly* can't."

"Part of that sentence is true," Jak muttered, which earned him a tulip to the face. I stopped there because these flowers

---

[1] I wondered myself but refrained from asking because I knew Jak would do it for both of us once curiosity got the better of him.

were expensive, a currency onto themselves.[2] Starting a fight here could only end badly. No to mention expensively.

We bantered back and forth a bit more before I suddenly got to my feet. Without telling the others where I wanted to go, I headed to the stables and saddled a horse. "Be back in a couple of hours," I told them before riding off. I came back from the marketplace promptly, but not quite alone. Inside my pocket lay a tiny green lizard with the power of speech.

Though young, it shouldn't take her very long to learn the human tongue. The merchant I bought her from named her something incredibly ingenious, like Liz. I decided to call her Naga instead. At the moment, Naga was sleeping. She would need the rest for I expected her to get to work on our behalf quickly. I bought her to remove from Jak the burden of pointing out every new bush and tree we passed. I also hoped she would learn some colorful curses and provide a running commentary during fights.

My parents did not seem impressed with this idea when I presented Naga. The little lizard blinked up at them and I swear the cheeky thing bowed. "Your Majesties," it said, making all of us jump.[3]

Even I didn't expect the voice to sound so human. These lizards were supposed to be little more than biological recording devices. Naga took every voice she heard, every word uttered in her presence and synthesized them to make a new voice all her own. Just because she possessed the power of speech didn't mean she had any more intelligence than the average dog. Still, it was impossible to not at least entertain the possibility of sentience.

"You don't think this affects the prophecy, do you?" my father asked. "She can't be the fourth member of the party."

"No, the prophecy is quite clear," my mother said.

"Is it though?" I cut in.

---

[2] They were pretty enough but anyone who paid more than a nominal fee for them must be plain out of their minds. But hey, they gave us money so why complain?

[3] Some of us, such as Keran, more than others. The fur on his back raised up like a startled cat. It made him look twice as big but also, somehow, kind of adorable.

Ignoring me, she continued, "The fourth member will not become a part of their band until they are in the Eigen States."

I didn't tell them I didn't intend to step foot on the opposite shore of the Zah River for a while. Most likely my plans would be turned upside down. Best not to let anyone but Jak know yet.

Having settled between them that my decision to add Naga to our group would not ruin anything, my parents started to clarify some of the conditions of the quest, as if saddling me with it in the first place wasn't punishment enough. My father brought out a map and slid it across the table to me.

The Floating Isles, as one might presume, look like a collection of islands crowded together. Some were actually islands, of the sort that generally comes to mind upon hearing the term, small and sparsely populated. Others were completely surrounded by inlets narrow enough to be rivers, seas small enough to be lakes. There were scientists who spent their entire lives arguing the whole was really a single continent. Anyone who bothered to look at a map would be struck by the fact that they were probably right. However, no one seemed in a hurry to adjust the name.[4]

As for the first half of the name, well, some worlds are round and hang in midair from nothing at all. Our world is flat and is suspended by way of massive wires.[5] Presumably, someone suggested the Hanging Isles and had their suggestion summarily rejected. And rightfully so, if you asked me. What a horrendous name that would've been.[6]

In any case, the chunk of land Jak, Keran and I would set off

---

[4] I understand the plural form is considered more poetic.

[5] What we're suspended from is not something anyone has been able to figure out to academic satisfaction. A lot of silly theories have been refuted however, mostly by application of just a small bit of that precious commodity called common sense. Some fellow way back suggested the sun as a candidate and this was actually widely accepted until some smartass set up a demonstration of all the ridiculous consequences of truly being suspended from the sun. I'm told he made a killing as a comedian of sorts touring with his machine.

[6] If perhaps a more appropriate one given what certain parts of the Isles got up to in their spare time.

for the next day lay nestled in the middle of the Isles. It was hardly the first map of the Eigen States I'd seen but I examined it closely anyway. Any map including the Eigen States had unique characteristics. Most maps didn't change. Once the cartographer's pen left parchment for the last time or the print blocks separated from the page, the lines and names of nations stayed put. These maps could become obsolete, faded with time, torn up into a thousand pieces but the lines stayed where you placed them.

Not so with a map including even the slightest corner of the Eigen States. Borders shifted all the time, whole nations disappeared and reappeared, cities became towns and villages transformed into sprawling metropolises, all within the span of a few moments.

Even as I looked at the half of the map taken up by an enlarged drawing of the Eigen States, a small city named Ome expanded to fill a massive swath of land only to be chipped away at the edges and suddenly fall in on itself like a tumbling pillar of sand. The pieces of the vast empire splintered down even further, absorbed by expanding countries or left as miniscule autonomous regions. Meanwhile, a range of mountains walked itself across the page while a coastline pulled itself straight and then caved in again.

As a kid, I spent countless hours watching the developments in the expansive map hanging in the main hallway. My observations and the copious reading my parents forced me to do on the subject told me only two lands remained consistent in each iteration of the map. Always, there existed a territory labeled Fairyland and an adjoining twin, the Evil Empire. No one could tell me why these two always remained when so many others came and went. Even they grew and shrank by turns, though always in tune with each other. As I watched, one seemed to grow larger than the other. It must have been only the trick of the light though for when I looked closer, they were once again perfectly matched.

Just like every other time I looked at such a map, I wondered how it worked. It wasn't that the shifting map represented events in real time but it wasn't completely untrue either. For

31

anyone living in the Eigen States, time passed in a linear
fashion, same as it did for us on this side of the Zah River. And
if you crossed over and came back, you'd find the same amount
of time passed on both sides. Yet for the areas you had no
contact with, anything might have happened and any amount of
time might have passed. It was as if the very act of laying eyes
on an area, being within the confines of one of the shifting
countries on the other side of the river, locked it into a normal
time sequence.[7] If you weren't observing them, seas might fall
and rise in the space of a single breath. Everyone you
remembered might cease to exist or come to not yet exist. Yet
when you returned, they would be there, as if nothing changed.

No one understood the mechanics behind this phenomenon. I
sure didn't. Just thinking about it for an extended period of time
made my head hurt. I once heard Serge refer to it as a quantum
effect on a macro scale but as I had no idea what that meant
either, this did not help. All I knew was the practical effect, that
a map of the Eigen States was worthless until you stepped foot
inside them, at which point at least your immediate area might
settle down and behave properly.

So when I asked, "Where do we go?" I knew it was a useless
question for of course place had little meaning in such a rapidly
shifting landscape.

Just as I expected, my parents shook their heads. "We have
no idea, but couldn't tell you anyway," my mother said. She
wound a strand of dark hair around her finger.

"The map will show you when the time comes," my father
said.

"Of course. What is it? The usual then? Four heroic deeds?" I
asked.

"Four?" Keran asked. "I thought the magic number was
three."

"Where have you been?" I wanted to know. "Four is even."

"I don't see what that has to do with it," Keran said with a
shrug. "Fine, we'll find four to perform. I can't imagine it will
hurt us to log an extra even if you're wrong."

---

[7] Or at least normal relative to you. As normal as it could ever get.

"Don't lose the map," my father urged with some force. "It has a protective charm on it. I traded a great deal of tulips to hire a traveling mage to perform the necessary spells."

"I did think the garden looked a bit bare," I remarked. "What kind of spells cost us half the flowers in the place?"

"Well it is waterproof now," my father said.

"Wow," I responded.

"The most expensive feature is on the back of the map. The Rules are inscribed there," my mother said without the slightest change in expression.

I flipped the map over as she instructed to see the four rules my parents drilled into my head from birth. I always thought them paranoid for the days when people regularly fell into mysterious dark holes and ended up inside the Eigen States were long gone. Chiang took care of that particular problem years ago. Only now, as I stared at the rules on the page, did I realize they had been preparing me for this moment.

The Rules were simple, more reminders to jog your common sense into gear than anything that might be helpful in the moment.

The Four Inviolable Rules of Staying Alive in the Eigen States
One- Keep Your Head![8]
Two- Be Aware of the Hair[9]
Three- Also Be Aware of the Heir[10]

---

[8] Some of that pure common sense I mentioned. People were quite fond of beheading on the other side of the river, mostly because it was the only truly irreversible maiming. Loss of a limb or two could be handled, even powered through in a fight and then fixed afterwards with an Echinoderm spell. Nobody knew how to reattach a head. Not for lack of trying, I might add.
[9] Magic is a lot more common and cheaply gotten on the other side of the river so anyone can be under glamour. The only way you can tell is by looking at their hair since no glamour spell ever hides the real color of someone's hair. As usual, no one knows why.
[10] This third rule hung on the fact that the rules of chance bent around anyone of royal heritage, by blood, adoption, or self declaration even. The more such people, the better the chance of the most unlikely things, perhaps good but mostly ill, befalling you. With me a princess and Jak a dispossessed heir, we'd be a walking pocket of improbability resistance.

Four- There Are No Such Things as Inviolable Rules[11]

"You paid through the nose for someone to write out the four rules I can recite backward and upside down in my sleep?" I asked.

"Of course not!" my father declared, making the mistake of taking me seriously for the umpteenth time in his life.

My mother proved more sensible and gave me a look. She didn't mean for it to convince me to give up my adversarial stance because that would make her more foolish than my father. And Sultana Malhun was certainly not foolish. "The rules will glow whenever you are in danger of running afoul of them."

"You mean to tell me we have to walk around with the map spread out in front of us at all times? I think I prefer to die," I told them.

"I'll hold the map," Jak said.

"As much as I'd enjoy the looks you'd get, I do want to live through this quest. You really think we're going to last long if we walk through The Darkest of Fells, looking like tourists?" I wanted to know.

"The map will become warm to the touch should danger arise," my father assured us. "There's no need to march around with it aloft."

I offered no verbal cooperation but I folded the map up and handed it to Jak. "Now, maybe some clarification on what you want me to do? I presume we're not going on a jaunt to tag a tree in an as yet unidentified location and come right back."[12]

"As a matter of fact, you need to retrieve an elixir," my father said.

I waited for more clarification but none came so I prodded, "And what do we need the elixir for? What does it do?"

---

[11] The last never required any explanation, even when my father first presented them to me as a girl. In a land of so much uncertainty and shifting magic, even the laws of physics might not stay put from second to second, so of course we could be sure of nothing.

[12] Unfortunately, such a thing could not be dismissed as crazy. People used to be forced to go on such quests on the regular.

"The elixir is endowed with a powerful renewal spell," my mother said.

"Well that sounds passably vague. Is it anything we couldn't hire a mage to whip up on demand?" I asked. "What do we need to renew?"

"Nothing," my father admitted. "We really don't need it right now. It may become useful for future generations, or at least that's what your grandfather told me. In fact, I had to fetch the same sort of thing back when I went on my quest. There's a stash of them in the deepest layer of our vault."

"Deepest layer?" Jak asked me under his breath.

"Don't ask me. I didn't even know we had a vault," I whispered back. I didn't question the statement because I had a more important point to clarify. "Let me get this straight then. I'm going on a quest only because of a curse in search of an elixir absolutely no one needs."

"Pretty much," my mother said.

"Bloody perfect," was my only response.

"Your supplies are being prepared as we speak. The three of you have an appointment with the One Way Mine Tunnels first thing tomorrow morning," my mother said, charging ahead.

"Great," I said. "I'm excited. We're going on an adventure. I'm going to go rest up while I still can." Before I could go, my parents stopped me.

"We are sorry about this," my father said, looking and sounding his most earnest. "We'd never subject you to this or put you in danger unless we couldn't find another way."

"Don't want to hear it," I told him. "I'm sure you're right about this being a last resort. This might even be good for me in the long run. But I sure as hell am not going to thank you for it now. Just leave me be and hope I don't get myself killed along the way."

My father seemed ready to continue protesting but mother stopped him from saying anything he would regret. I resented them right now and so I didn't want to listen to them talk about their reasons. But I was also resigned, in part because I understood their decision.

I might play the fool at times and mess with convention so

much it sometimes seemed a profession but I knew some matters had to be taken seriously.[13] Which was not to say I thought this quest a serious matter. Quests into the Eigen States had been a popular method, in days long past, to test the mettle of anyone who aspired to power. The youngest of a brood might set off to make his fortune and come back to compete with his older siblings. More often, the child of a penniless farmer would find herself in the Eigen States and come back with new powers or a fortune of her own. Some nations used to send heirs off, like my parents sent me, to ensure they were up to the task of governing. It seemed a particularly foolish way of testing. Anything I needed to know about governing a country I should learn from interacting with its citizens, not traipsing off to a land of dreams.

It never crossed my mind our nation might still have a law requiring heirs to go on a quest. Certainly no one ever whispered of it in my presence, something I found hard to believe, almost harder than believing we still observed such an archaic process. I couldn't say why but I trusted my parents enough to know they had reasons. I just didn't know why they would set a curse on me instead of explaining.

This pissed me off more than being sent on a fool's errand, not that I would tell them so. I'd much rather everyone think me a spoiled brat who didn't want to leave the comforts of home. Surely, this also said something about my character but I didn't think too hard about it.

With his longer stride, Jak caught up not long after I left the meeting room. He walked next to me and ducked through the door to my room before I could slide it closed on him. I thought about kicking him out but realized I'd have to open it to let Keran in. I left the door open wide enough for the wolfhound to slip in and went to my weapons closet. I grabbed a brace of matching daggers and dumped them near my bed so they'd be within easy reach the next morning when I dressed for the journey. I went about my preparations in silence as Jak watched me with a frown. Keran, when he padded in, went back to his

---

[13] Or at least mostly knew. Results vary.

corner to curl up and nap.

"Aren't you going to say something?" I asked Jak.

"I had no plans to open my mouth until you calmed down."

"That obvious?"

"I daresay your parents had some idea of your anger. They probably mistook the reason for it."

"They usually do," I remarked.

"To be fair, they have the weight of evidence on their side. Which is not to say you have no right to be angry," he added with some haste.

I considered him for a while before collapsing onto my bed. "Being angry won't help me focus tomorrow. Time enough when we get back. I'll probably have new things to be furious about."

"About time you see sense," Jak said.

"Oh I always *see* the sensible path. Rarely do I take it though."

CHAPTER SIX

When Jak came to my door bright and early, he found me already dressed, armed and ready to set off. Keran also declared himself prepared after he put on his armor. My parents asked the tanner to make him a set. It wrapped around his torso and even came with flaps protecting his neck. Though designed so he could shrug into it on his own, even without opposable thumbs, Jak and I helped him into it before we set off.

My parents came to see us go, accompanying us to the deepest portion of the palace,[1] underneath the dungeons. The hallway opened up into a cavern of sorts. It was what every five year old pictured a cave to be, with torches flickering against the smooth rock and glinting off the pillars of stone growing into each other.

A track with a rusted metal cart ran down the middle. Stepping out of the hallway and into the cavern meant passing through a force field separating the Rift and the One Way Mine Tunnels from the rest of our world. In a motif that must be tiresome by now, I didn't know how it worked, only that it did.

---

[1] I looked around but saw no vault on the way down. Goodness knows where they stuffed it if I never noticed it in all my years worming into every nook and cranny.

It ran through many of the realms on the continent this side of the Zah River, which would make it very useful if not for the fact it only ran in one direction, toward the River itself. Whoever built it and laid spells on it went to a lot of trouble for a system that only did one thing.

Now that the hour had come, I didn't bother hesitating. I walked up to the cart and vaulted in. Naturally, there were no straps or safety features of any kind save some handholds on the inside of the cart. I scooted to the front and lay one hand over a rusty bar while Keran hopped in and sat behind me. Jak clambered in with less grace and let his massive sword clang against the side of the cart.

"You better secure that sword," I told him. "I have no interest in being sliced in half."

Jak sighed but did as I asked and then nothing remained but for Ila to pull the lever and send us careening in the direction of the Zah River.

"Good luck," my mother called out as she and my father backed away.

I paid no attention to them and simply nodded at Ila, who threw the end of a rope over the lever. She pulled it tight and backed up along with my parents to the other side of the force field. "Bring me a keepsake or something."

"Fat chance," I yelled back at her.

Laughing, Ila gave the rope a violent jerk. The lever swung into place but for a moment, nothing happened. Then the cart started to vibrate and a buzzing noise built. Keran groaned and lay down on the floor of the cart. I gripped the bar a bit tighter. The noise continued to grow until I felt sure I'd be deaf when it finally died down. Meanwhile, source-less light filled my vision so I could only squint at my surroundings. The light exploded outward from its undefined source as the cart blasted forward, screaming along the track.

The light faded much faster than it came as we launched out of the cavern and into a narrow tunnel. The track went straight for long enough we became complacent. Though the ride was by no means smooth since the cart clattered and shook as we sped forward, it seemed safe for me to release my death grip on the bar. At which point, the floor suddenly dropped out from under us. The cart went into free fall and I lunged toward the bar so I could hold on with both hands. When the cart hit the rails again, the impact knocked me into the side of the cart.

We burst free of the darkness and into a large cave, illuminated dimly with the same source-less light accompanying our departure. I stuck my head a bit above the top of the cart in order to look ahead, only to see the ground drop away in a cliff not far in front of us.

Before I could shout a warning to the others, we shot past the edge of the cliff and continued on, still sliding along the rails, which floated in midair without support. Hesitantly, I stuck my head over the side of the cart and looked down past the rails. I couldn't see the floor of this vast underground cavern, only a red glow down in the darkness. Looking at it made me think about our precarious position so I sat back down.

Jak tapped me in the shoulder and wordlessly pointed ahead. I suspected what he meant to direct my attention to so I didn't turn to look until our cart almost reached the beginning of a break. The rails disappeared and only resumed far off in the distance, gleaming in parallel lines. Now, no one in their right mind would call me a mathematical genius but it didn't take one to realize we'd never make the distance. Improbably though, we did, sketching out what must have been a very strange curve through the air.[2]

No sooner had we crashed back onto solid rails than I noticed the next trial in store for us in the form of a rather large loop de loop. There didn't seem to be any reason for it other than to make our lives more difficult. I couldn't see why else someone would go to the trouble of constructing the track like this.

I thought for sure we'd all be flung from the cart and fall to our deaths before my quest even started. I grabbed Naga, stuffed her inside a pocket and yelled incoherently for Jak to make sure Keran didn't fall out. When we did pass through the loop though, the whole thing was anticlimactic. The world whirled

---

[2] Think of the usual parabola but with a straight length right at the peak. No doubt physicists world over would hate it. I certainly did.

around me for a moment but none of us were otherwise affected despite having been thrown upside down.

"Why not make the tracks flat?" Jak shouted as his teeth clattered together, echoing my own thoughts. "What is with all these jumps and spirals? They're not logical."

"They're barely physically possible. Why are you bothering about logic?" I demanded. That shut him up. Or perhaps the effort of holding on to both the cart and Keran at the same time kept him quiet. After a while, I got tired of seeing impossible visions flash by faster than my eyes could track them. I also got tired of glancing ahead and seeing the loops and impossible jumps our cart would need to make to reach its final destination. So I put my head down and closed my eyes. After a while, I became so used to the rhythm of our trip I almost fell asleep. Not a great sign for the rest of the quest.

Our cart slid to a stop so gently I didn't realize we arrived until I wondered why it became so quiet. When I opened my eyes and looked around, we sat in the middle of a cavern almost exactly the same as the one we started off in, down to the pillars of stone and shallow pools of water. I got to my feet shakily, with a hand on the side of the cart to steady myself. As soon as I stood, I saw something different from the cavern underneath my palace. A rocky slope lay ahead of us and at the top was a large square of light.

As soon as we climbed out of the cart, it went shooting back along the track the way we came, so fast it seemed as if the ground sucked it up through a straw. The opening above us began to close so I dashed up the slope, calling for the others to hurry. Keran actually got to the top first as it was much easier to crawl up on all fours. I came right on his heels though and hauled myself out with plenty of time to spare.

Jak had problems, being less than spry for his size.[3] He didn't panic though, struggling up the slope and pulling himself from rock to rock steadily. When he got close to the top, I grabbed his hand and gave a heave to yank him up over the edge.

By the time he pushed himself to his feet, the opening in the

---

[3] Or any size.

ground completely disappeared, leaving no trace behind. "I guess we're not going back that way," he remarked.

"Jak, have you not listened to me at all? I told you, it's no longer your job to state the obvious. That's why I brought the lizard along. Naga, you should have chimed in earlier," I told her.

From where she stuck herself on my shoulder, Naga looked at me with reproach. "I shall need to acquire more data before I am ready to perform my function."

"Don't get sassy with me. Or else I'll leave you here. You wouldn't like that would you?" I asked.

"I must remind you that you are speaking to a creature with only the semblance of sentience," Naga told me.

"I don't buy it. You're not telling me a barely sentient being can be so irritating. I know I set myself up for a joke so no one say a thing," I warned.

Jak raised his hands. "Don't look at me. I don't want to lose my head before we even cross the Zah River."

At this, I smiled. "But of course you know, I have no plans to cross the River."

"I can't see what else you plan to do," Keran said. "If you've found a way to complete the quest whilst skipping a trip into the Eigen States, I will fully support it. The thought of risking my life for some misplaced sense of glory isn't something that stirs my blood."

"No promises," I told him. "But I do have a plan."

From where we emerged, it took merely an hour of walking to get to the edge of the Zah River. At first, I went along with some confidence in my scheme. As time wore on though, I thought less and less of our chances. I had a feeling this quest would not go smoothly if we let ourselves step foot inside of the Eigen States, which is why I planned this work around. But I also assumed the quest would find a way to reassert itself no matter what I did. I just hoped we wouldn't lose the boat or else Frey would never let me borrow the thing again.[4]

---

[4] No chance of losing it completely of course. It was unceasingly loyal to Frey. I tried to steal it as a kid and actually succeeded. Didn't realize at the

When we reached the banks of the Zah River, I felt severely underwhelmed. Given that this represented the border and barrier between our everyday world and the Eigen States, I expected an impressive body of water with a torrential flow. Instead, we faced a lazy river not much wider than the one winding past a small mill. One could shout easily across the space from one shore to the next. In the end, it didn't really matter. As long as the boat could float on it, that's all I cared about.

As we got close to the water, a puff of smoke appeared out of thin air and hit us directly in the face. We all reeled back, though only half in surprise.[5] At this point, few things could surprise me any longer. All the stories of my childhood came back to me and I knew precisely what I would see when the smoke cleared to reveal a dark figure. And lo and behold, a frightening creature with a protruding jaw and gnashing teeth loomed out of the smoke. He had scaly limbs and a tail whose end trailed in the water.

For a minute, the ugliness of this guardian of the threshold kept me silent. Then I realized I'd seen the mask before. When I stomped forward though, Brendan held his hands up to stall me and took a half step back into the water. "Wait, wait, don't hit me again. I'll take it off." He shed the costume quickly and seemed quite pleased with himself despite my seeing right through his disguise. He probably didn't think he could get away with it without another kick to the shins. I was not about to grant him victory just yet.

"What are you doing here?" I demanded, jabbing my finger into his chest at each word.

He took another half step back to get out of range. "You know. I'm the threshold guardian. I've come to test your purity before you proceed on your journey."

---

time he let me take it for he knew the boat would return itself to him before the day ended.

[5] The other half being alarm in case the smoke carried poison or otherwise toxic materials. Couldn't be too careful, especially on a quest.

"Excuse me? Purity?!" I demanded.[6]

"It's a pretty standard procedure," Brendan said. "I need to make sure you are eligible to go on the quest."

"You sent me on it!" I protested.

"Just a formality," Brendan said cheerfully. "Consider it an administrative necessity to clear your provisional acceptance."

"What is this? A wyvern credit scheme?"[7] I demanded.

Brendan actually laughed at that. He didn't look quite so happy a second later when I gave him a hard shove into the water. As he sputtered and flailed before realizing it didn't even come up to his chest this close to shore, I walked away and brought a paper boat out of my pocket. I laid it in the water and called out a complicated, guttural word Frey told me to use. I was no mage, unable to do even a single spell. The magic causing the small paper boat to unfold came from the object itself. Still, I felt a thrill of excitement watching the paper boat grow bigger and bigger. The edges folded out piece by piece, building into the hull of a sizeable ship. As the ship grew, the bottom started to change, darkening and hardening from flimsy paper into wood.

After the paper folded up to form the rim on all sides of the boat, it started to build the mast and then the sails, moving faster all the time. To top it all off, half a dozen oars clattered into the bottom of the boat. I wasted absolutely no time jumping on board. I gave Jak a hand up while Keran gazed morosely at the boat. He didn't protest[8] though before backing up a few steps and taking a flying leap onto the deck.

As soon as he landed, I went to unfurl the sails. Truth be told, I didn't know how to sail a boat. Just as well then this ship could steer itself. As soon as I released the sails, we started to float

---

[6] Out of incredulity and anger of course. What a boorish idea. Purity.

[7] Unlike dragons, wyverns had no natural propensity for math. But their similarity to dragons allowed them to set up elaborate schemes where they tricked people into thinking that they were in the good hands of their more mathematically gifted cousins. To be fair, the two species were nearly indistinguishable to most people. Even dragons and wyverns themselves often get confused though few would admit to such a thing, unless of course, it was to their financial advantage to do so.

[8] Out loud, that is. His drooping ears were quite expressive.

gently down the river.

"Wow," Brendan said. "That's amazing. How did you get your hands on it?"

"He owes me a few favors," I shouted back.

"What exactly is your plan?" Brendan wanted to know as he followed us downstream from the shore. "I take it you don't mean to cross the River."

"Not if I can help it," I responded. "I have no interest in wandering aimlessly through the Eigen States searching for dubiously good deeds to do. We're going to follow the river until we complete those four tasks. Then we get in, fetch the elixir and get out without lingering about."

"I admit that's rather clever," Brendan said.

"I don't really need your approval," I told him.

"It's too bad we can't allow it," Brendan said.

"I don't like that," Jak said. "I don't like that at all."

"It's probably bad luck to say this but what can he do from shore?" Keran asked.

I hesitated before answering but finally said, "Nothing, I think. He's not even any good at predicting the weather." Since it'd become a habit for the world to prove me wrong as often as possible, I released only a sigh when Brendan suddenly hurtled a spell against the side of our boat.

The water around us was no longer calm and flat. The surface began to undulate and darken as if an isolated storm appeared around us. I watched the water in despair, having no way to stop it from happening.

"This is bad," Naga chimed in.

"Hey, good job!" I exclaimed, brightening for the moment, in time for a huge wave to loom up and swat all of us overboard.

CHAPTER SEVEN

The water carried us to the other side of the river, depositing us neatly in a line about ten feet away from shore. I swallowed a whole mouthful of water before I managed to get my feet under me. When I spun around, I saw Brendan call up another wave to bring the ship back to his shore. Even as I watched, he made the ship fold back into its original size.

"I'll give this back to Frey," Brendan yelled across the river as he held the folded up boat aloft.

I responded with a rude gesture[1] and dragged myself toward shore.

"Don't lose that map and you'll be fine," Brendan told us and then disappeared.

"I had no idea he was such a good mage. You think I could get him to teach me?" Jak asked as he stood up and shook some water free of his head.

"We're holding a grudge against him. Don't even think about

---

[1] Trust me, you don't want to know. I learned it from an Oversized Eagle Rider. It's hard to scream at each other with the wind roaring past. Instead, the community developed a vast vocabulary of signs and gestures. Predictably, most were incredibly vulgar.

it," I told him as I took another step in the direction of shore. I was still cursing Brendan when I finally stepped out of the water. Thoughts about how I'd make him miserable when we got back so occupied me, I didn't at first notice the changes taking place.

When Keran stepped out of the river though, I noticed something very strange. A crescent of white fur appeared on his forehead, which until now bore nothing but an even stretch of dark fur. Only then did I look down at myself and see I wore a dry cotton dress instead of the pants and leather armor I put on this morning. My hair sprung free of the braid I spent a lot of time on last night. Dread washed over me even as Jak patted the new leather breastplate now on his body.

"Take out the map. We need to take a look at it," I said.

"It's no big deal. At least our clothes are dry," Jak said.

"Easy for you to say. You got something out of the deal," I told him.

Jak dug the map out of his pocket and snapped it open. Given my parents' and then Brendan's insistence we keep it safe, I was glad to see our dunk in the river didn't harm it. Maybe it was a good thing they paid for it to be waterproof after all. My relief faded very fast when I took the map from him and located our position. While most of the Eigen States continued to change and shift in the usual way, the names and borders in our immediate region remained stubbornly stuck to the page. And just as I feared, we landed ourselves right on the shores of Fairyland. This discovery upset me so much, I flopped to the ground.[2]

Keran could not see the map so he cleared his throat and asked for an explanation. When Jak told him where we landed, Keran nodded a couple of times before admitting, "I have no idea what it means."

"It means we're doomed," I said as I sat up and dumped everything out of my sodden pack. I needed to change into my spare set of clothes before we continued. I wouldn't be caught in

---

[2] Probably unwise given the wet state of my hair but I couldn't bring myself to care.

a place as dangerous as Fairyland with skirts long enough to lift me up like a glider when I went to do a backflip.

"You're being a bit melodramatic," Naga quipped as she struggled out of my pocket. She also bore a new white crescent moon on her forehead.

"Granted," I said as I attempted to explain this to Keran. "You'll notice we've all undergone a transformation. It happens sometimes when you leave the Zah River and emerge in the Eigen States on a quest. It's a dumb way to say you've arrived in an unfamiliar land. In this case, our clothes have transformed to reflect our supposed place in this society. Appearance matters most here in Fairyland." I tugged at the material of my current outfit. "Look at me for instance. Fairyland has adjudged me and assigned me the role of a peasant. Meanwhile, the land seems to think Jak is a warrior. That's almost rich enough to convince me to forgive it for mistreating me."

"What about me?" Karen asked, looking down at himself. The leather armor we helped him into this morning looked precisely the same.

In answer, I lifted Naga off my shoulder and pointed out the moon on her forehead. "You've got one of these too. Seems Fairyland considers both of you animal familiars."

"Oh come on," Karen exclaimed. He strode over to the water so he could see himself. He rubbed at the mark with a paw but this did absolutely nothing.

"I'm sure it will come off as soon as we leave this place," Jak assured him.

"Which, if I have anything to say about it, will be as soon as possible," I said. In line with this, I abandoned my previous plan to dry out my clothes and change into them. Happily, I still had my weapons so I used a dagger to make some adjustments to the dress. I made a slit along the side and cut it short enough it wouldn't hinder my movement. Then I strapped all my daggers on belts on the outside of my clothes. I felt ridiculous and looked it too but at least this way, I wouldn't be as defenseless as this stupid place thought to make me. Finally, I tied my hair back to get it out of the way. The last thing I needed was to be done in because I couldn't see during a fight.[3]

While I did this, Jak took all of our clothes and wrung the water out as best he could. He went through the rest of our supplies and tossed out the food too sodden to eat. Then he repackaged everything into one pack and slung it on his back. So at least one good thing came out of this.

Before we struck off across the landscape, I made sure to loosen my sword, even if the motto of the place was, "Good Always Prevails."[4] Even if Fairyland really was the sort of place good always triumphed, there would be plenty of people ready to do us ill. Plus, I didn't trust its motto. Supposing we were lucky enough to be counted within the ranks of the good, something of which I was by no means certain, I didn't trust the magic to give us a hand. Much more likely for it to dig a dagger into our sides and wrench it about to screw with us. Brendan's trick earlier with the wave only reinforced my leeriness towards any magic I did not control.

"We'll stop at the first village we see and buy some armor and dry clothes for you," Jak promised.

"And if we're lucky, passage out of this place," I said, without any real hope. "Does the map have anything we can use?"

Jak squinted at the spot where we came ashore and shook his head. "It's not detailed enough to help us there. Heading east is the shortest way out of Fairyland."

"Might as well get going then," I said. "The sooner we start off, the faster we get to leave."

If only it were that easy. Not long after we left the banks of the Zah River, heading east as Jak suggested, we stumbled into an ambush. We were all still a little discombobulated from our dunk in the River and hadn't really gotten into the mindset necessary to survive in a place like this. Or else we surely would have noticed the problem before we walked into it.

---

[3] It's doomed many a heroine, though not as many as you'd think with all the descriptions of flowing hair and trailing curls or whatever. In any case, I have no desire to be added to the list that does exist.

[4] Even if I didn't have the phrase drilled into me from a young age, the first road sign we saw had the words underneath the place name. As if people came here on vacation or something.

We found a trail leading away from the River and followed it east, hoping it might take us to a town or a city. At first the path curved through uncultivated plains so regular and unchanging they might as well have been painted into place. The light beating down from above soon dried our hair but didn't feel harsh enough to make us curse the lack of shade. In short, everything was perfect. Too perfect.

The track led us into a forest. As I later realized upon reflection, the trees started to grow closer and closer together, throwing the path into greater shadow as we went. If I'd been paying even the slightest bit of attention, I would have recognized this as the sort of region with a high incidence of ill luck and figured out a way around. As it was though, I didn't look at my surroundings until Jak cleared his throat and held up our map. He tapped the first rule. I saw it pulsing and glowing reproachfully as if disappointed we got ourselves into trouble so quickly and failed to heed it earlier.

A dozen short figures came tumbling out of the bushes and assembled in a semicircle. They shared green, wrinkled skin and were identical down to the extra sixth toe on their left feet. Matted black hair covered their heads and ragged tunics served as their clothing. All held various copper weapons in their hands and a few even bared their teeth at us. If I had any doubt about their identity, the capital letters spelling out the word Goblin and then a number on their shirts would have given it away.[5]

---

[5] Now you and anyone else with the requisite amount of sanity might wonder how we could read it. After all, we passed through who knows how much distance underground before arriving in the Eigen States. What odds of us not only speaking the same language but that the goblins called themselves goblins? Worry not because some ancient misguided mage performed a massive spell to eliminate all the confusion of languages. People continued to speak their individual languages and write their own scripts but we all understood each other fine. If I had such a large concentration of magic to spare, I'd have done something else with it. It's said this mage aimed to eliminate violence between nations because she thought language differences caused discord. It seemed astonishingly naïve to me. Wars and violence between groups happened now, as they always did, for the simple reason that people were often assholes. Being able to communicate just meant they could tell each other so.

"This could have been avoided," Naga remarked.

"Oh shut up," I told her. Though I knew the answer, I went ahead and asked the goblins anyway, "What do you want?"

"Well, you are on quest right?" Goblin Number Five asked.

"No?" Jak tried.

"You have an improbably large sword on your back," Goblin Number Eight pointed out.

"Fine, we're on a quest. But it's mine, not his," I said.

Goblin Number One pulled out a thick, dogged eared manual and flipped through it a few times before looking up at me in confusion. "I don't see anything in the Storybook about serving wenches leading quests. Even immodestly dressed serving wenches."

It took a massive effort of will to avoid exploding in a fit of anger at this comment. It wouldn't help because these goblins were locked into their roles. I dredged up everything I knew about Fairyland to try and come up with an answer to move our conversation along. On the bright side, if these goblins identified us as an adventuring band, then Fairyland must put us on the side of good. These goblins had the misfortune of being on the losing side so we'd probably end up fighting them whether we willed it or not. Better to get it over with quickly.

"Should we tell them what you are?" Jak whispered as he sidled closer to me.

I thought it a bad idea given our third Inviolable Rule.[6] Of course, the land itself already knew my identity and Jak's as well. Still, announcing it out loud seemed like inviting doom down on our heads. Even if good triumphed, there could still be inconvenient maiming and deaths before victory.

"She's a princess," Keran said, taking the choice away from me.

"Oh," Goblin Number One said with a nod of understanding as he stuffed the manual back under his clothes. "You're a princess in disguise then. Best one I've seen in years. When we're finished here, you must tell me how it is you turned your skin this light brown color. Walnut dye perhaps?"

---

[6] The one about being aware of the heirs. You remember.

51

"Uhh... no," I said.

"Back to your original question," Goblin Number Twelve said, shooting her companion a glare. "We have the task today of mildly inconveniencing you before you carry on with your quest. If we're really lucky, we'll be able to inflict a lingering wound to teach one of you an important lesson further down the line."

"Is this a joke?" Keran asked.

"That's a question you'll be asking a lot before we're through," I said.

"I assure you we are most serious about our work," Goblin Number Four said, puffing out his chest to make certain we took his point.

Keran ignored this and turned to us. "This can't be right. None of this makes any sense."

"Just think of it as being air dropped into a middle of one of those stories involving princesses being kidnapped all the time and needing rescue. There's a sort of logic there. Not one I like but you've got to pretend for now," Jak told him.

"I don't think I can," Keran said. "Look at them. Are the dozen of you out of your minds? You have numbers stitched onto your shirts. Is it for us or for yourselves? You all look exactly the same to me. Is it so you can tell each other apart?"

"We need them because we can't see much in these disguises," Goblin Number Four said as he pulled his own head off. Or rather, he pulled off the top of his disguise. It took some twisting and yanking but he finally got it. The goblin still had green skin but it was smooth and unblemished. His dark hair was slick with sweat but fuller and healthier than the coarse strands on the mask. His eyes were brown and warm, nothing like the red pits on his disguise. In general, his features were fine and delicate, beautiful in fact.

Goblin Number Nine started tugging at her own mask as well, muttering, "If he gets to take his off, I don't see why I have to keep it on." This goblin too, turned out to be beautiful, with large brown eyes like the other but blonde hair.

"I'm very confused," Keran said. "I thought you said appearance determined everything. If goblins actually look like this, why are they stuck here, waylaying travelers?"

"I have no idea what's going on," I admitted freely.

"What have I told you about going off script?" Goblin Number Twelve demanded of them.

"But Daisy-" Goblin Number Four began before she made a gesture to cut him off.

"No names!" Goblin Number Twelve hollered at him. "Not after the bastard from the Parnassus School."[7]

"None of us are real mages so you don't have to worry about curses," I told her.

"And glad of it we are," Goblin Number Twelve or Daisy rather, said to me. "I don't trust mages."

"Me neither," I agreed.

Daisy looked at us for a time before tugging off her own mask, having come to a decision. She tossed her mask into the bushes and shrugged out of the rest of the suit. Once this followed the mask into the dense forest, she stood before us in her natural form. The weariness she carried told me Daisy was probably in her middle years. She was rather plain, with nothing of the beauty of the first two goblins who revealed their faces to us. Certainly though, she did not look grotesque. "You folks seem decent enough. I don't think any of us really wants to fight you. I'm getting tired of it, truth be told."

Goblin Number One, the largest of the goblins at about four feet tall, pulled off his disguise last. He still clutched his manual and looked at Daisy in astonishment. "We can't abandon our roles. It says in the Storybook we have to attack them!"

"Sod it," another goblin said, this one with bright blue hair arranged in spikes. "For once I want to not attack travelers at first sight. Every time it's the same thing. We hear the alarms go off, don our suits and come down here to wave our swords about ineffectually and get our arses kicked halfway to the next

---

[7] Nasty, nasty group of mages, let me tell you. They sold their services to the highest bidder but without applying any moral compass. So they put down insurrections for tyrants and killed off anyone who drew the ire of their less scrupulous rivals. You might have to sell half the country off to pay for their services but of course there would still be people willing to use them.

moonrise. It's all so tiresome. I'm tired of being evil."

"Jabir has a point though," one of the older goblins commented. "What if the Board catches wind of this rebellion? What if it pays us a visit?"

"It has plenty of more important things to contend with, I'm sure," Daisy said. "I'd be happy if it did pay us a visit. Then we could finally get some answers."

"We'd like some while you're at it," Keran reminded her.

Somehow, all of us ended up sitting together on one side of the road, introducing ourselves. As each of the goblins reported their name, I saw as much variety amongst them as among any sizeable group of humans. That some of them should have short brown hair and others flowing hair dyed a bright red made perfect sense to me. Or at least it would if we were anywhere but Fairyland. As far as I knew, goblins here were supposed to act as dastardly as the storybooks said. They weren't supposed to have their own independent thoughts and resent their lot in life. That they didn't immediately accost us already surprised me. Everything after confused me utterly.

When we introduced ourselves, I asked again for someone to explain. In accordance with my parents' orders, I spent countless hours studying each of the states appearing and disappearing off a map of the Eigen States. Fairyland and its counterpart featured so largely in those lessons such that before today, I might have said I knew precisely how things worked here.[8]

"Things have been changing around here of late. Oh the princesses still get themselves into trouble and the knights still have to hack and slash them out. Aye, the beautiful peasant girls still just *happen* to be long lost nobles and all the dashing princes still get the girl in the end. But something is different; the balance is off kilter. Not everything falls into place according to formula," Daisy said with a snort to emphasize the point. "Used to be all goblins were born as ugly as the masks we wear now. And hell, to hear my parents speak of it, everyone seemed perfectly content to go out and snatch up wayward travelers. Some of them were even successful. Then something happened.

---

[8] Now, of course, I realized I knew jack shit.

Some of our people began to question why we were doing this when we knew we would lose. And then they started to ask why we wanted to hurt people at all. About the same time, the young goblins being born had finer features, smoother skin and much better hair.[9] The process was slow but it did not go unnoticed."

"Indeed not," Naga commented.[10]

"In any case," Daisy continued, "at first we thought it might be our own fault, that we called down this change by our questioning. But we soon found this change happening everywhere. Things were being thrown awry. Princesses would sometimes be kidnapped by princes and rescued by dragons or worse yet in terms of the order of things, save themselves. For a time, everything and everyone ran amok. But then the monarchs got together to restore order.[11] They codified and distributed the Storybook you see Jabir with. It tells us what we're supposed to do, what we need to look like. That's the way it's been for some time."

I tried to process this information but my mind reeled in utter disbelief. This challenged everything I learned. If I was wrong about something so basic as the character of Fairyland, what did that mean? How could this process have been occurring for so long and we knew nothing about it on the other side of the River? Could fifty years pass here while one passed back home? If no one crossed from one side to the other? I had a feeling this might be the crux of the mystery but I would not be solving it here.[12]

"Why don't you leave then?" Jak wanted to know.

"Were it so easy," Eve said with a sigh. "We've got an aging population of grandparents at home, many of whom are as enthusiastic about pulling travelers to pieces as they used to be.

---

[9] I could attest to that.

[10] Apparently, she didn't quite yet understand her job description only included insulting enemies. Come to think of it, maybe my fault since I never told her.

[11] Their own order, of course, with them on top.

[12] I resolved to at least ask Serge when we got back. He knew all sorts of strange things he shouldn't. It made me suspect he lied about his origins. Well that and his contraptions.

Then we have fools like Jabir who have turned a bureaucratic set of rather oppressive laws into a holy book. Can't leave without them, can we?"

"If there's one thing that hasn't changed since the days when the Storybook might have described reality, we're a clannish people. Few of us would deign to move without the rest of the tribe," Daisy said. "Give it another few years though and I suspect the younger generation will be fed up enough to do as you say."

"I'm thinking about it already," said Carol, the goblin who sported spiked hair. "Only thing is we don't know much about the world outside our forest here."

"Can't be a bad method then, to stop adventurers and ask for a chat instead of a fight," I mused. "I dare say you could learn a lot, more than from your Storybook."

Jabir seemed rather indignant at this comment but the other goblins thought it a great idea. So they started with the three of us. There was nothing unusual in my story and they didn't even blink when I told them I came from across the Zah River. Apparently, plenty of adventurers from the Floating Isles still ended up here, along their track.

Once we finished, Daisy got to her feet and thanked us for our time. "Now perhaps we can do you a good turn. Where are you headed?"

"No particular destination," Jak told her. "We have to complete four heroic deeds before we find out where we must go."

"No offense but my main object is to get out of Fairyland as soon as possible. Preferably while giving the Evil Empire a wide berth." The look on Daisy's face told me I should cast my hopes aside. "Let me guess, we'll end up there no matter what direction we go?"

"It's a way of keeping the balance," Deidre said. "Everyone who enters one way must go out through the other."

"Sounds great," Naga chimed in. Everyone stared at her.

"Are Logorrhea Lizards supposed to develop sarcasm?" Jak asked.

"Apparently," Naga replied, looking at us without the

slightest bit of guile.

"That aside," I said slowly. "Can you direct us to the nearest village where I can get some decent leather armor? Mine disappeared after we crossed the river and I don't have any dry clothes to replace this impractical outfit."

"I doubt we have anything big enough to fit," Daisy said, sweeping a critical eye over me.

"We have enough gold, I'm sure, to buy some ourselves," Jak said. "Wait, they still accept gold, don't they?"

"Worst comes to worst, you can always slay their neighborhood monster for them," Ron suggested.

The goblins all disappeared into the forest after giving us directions to the nearest village with a monster problem,[13] leaving us to our own devices. Once they left, Jak chuckled. "I dare say this is going to be an interesting adventure."

We hadn't gone fifty steps before one of the goblins, Uma, crashed back onto the road and ran after us. When she arrived, she thrust a copy of the Storybook into my hands. "You'll probably need this. Mostly everyone still follows it to the letter. It only describes Fairyland. You'll be on your own once you get to the Evil Empire." She ran off before we could properly thank her and I hefted the book.

Flipping through it, I saw precisely what I expected, what amounted to a volume of bureaucratic jargon supplemented by diagrams and pictures of improbably ugly villains and impossibly beautiful heroes. "I wouldn't be surprised if everyone in this cursed land has self-image problems. Look at those muscles. And the sheen on those horns. You'd have to shine them for hours."

"Remarkably high incidence of pale skin and blonde hair too," Jak remarked as he looked over my shoulder.

"Want to take a look?" I asked Keran but he waved me away with a paw.

"I bet I can tell you what wolfhounds are supposed to look like. Teeth too big for their mouths and consequently too big to be of any use? So much slobber they should be dehydrated

---

[13] And who knew if it would be a real monster at this point.

within half an hour? Hair so matted you'd think it never rained here?"

"Remarkably accurate," I admitted when I found the entry. "If it helps, these are only for regular wolves. I can't find anything specific for your kind."

"Oh, I'm not supposed to exist. Much better," Keran said. He sulked while Jak and I talked over our options. This didn't take so long for they were really few and far between. No matter how we sliced up the situation, it'd be a week of walking before we got to the border between Fairyland and the Evil Empire. Our best bet to get out as soon as possible would be to get our hands on some horses.

CHAPTER EIGHT

The village, when we finally happened upon it after following a less traveled fork in the road, may as well have popped right out of the entry in the Storybook for a picturesque small town. Small huts with thatched roofs stood in rows within the clearing, still here and there dotted with the vestiges of tree trunks not completely dug out of the ground.[1]

Men and women walked about calmly and didn't seem as if they were being terrorized. Just as I wondered whether to start doubting what the goblins told us, one of the women spotted us. Or rather, she spotted Jak for she came sprinting in our direction, her arms raised in supplication. "Everyone, we are saved! An adventurer has come to slay the Beast!"[2]

All in all, her display was so comical, I bit back a laugh. My mirth died once she and the other villagers gathered up to welcome the hero and his 'serving wench.' I swear, sometimes I feared for the state of originality in this world.

---

[1] Completely unrealistic. I didn't know of any other farming villages that just left wood in the ground.
[2] Probably should be a few more exclamation marks there but I'll spare everyone the enthusiasm.

I cleared my throat to catch their attention. "People, it's my quest. Direct your supplications over here. And make your pleading particularily pitiful. No keening though. I can't stand that."

"It's *your* quest?" the mayor of the town asked. "Are you sure?"

"Do you want a beast slain or not?" I demanded in turn, which shut them up but did nothing to dislodge the disbelief on their faces. I brushed away their halfhearted apologies and asked for some information about this monster they wanted to be rid of so badly

"It's massive," shouted one villager.

"Covered with fur," another called out.

"Teeth the size of daggers," someone said.

"Of course," Keran muttered with a sigh.

"He's snatched three children in the last week," the mayor explained after she waved everyone else into silence. "He hides in a cave to the west of our village."

When the rest of the village looked as if they might burst into pleas once more, I took charge, bludgeoning them into silence with imperious looks and well placed orders. Soon enough, I had something approaching my old wardrobe back. I found the shirt I acquired to be a bit loose but not so much it would interfere with my movement. The trousers fit just right though I raided the closets of several homes before I found what I needed.

Before we went off to confront this monster, we also extracted some food from the villagers and a promise to provide two horses when we came back triumphant, as we surely would. Or at least, that's what the Storybook said. I didn't know where exactly it said parents should not try to rescue their own children but I refrained from commenting about this.

The villagers cheered for us as we plunged into the thick of the forest, heading due west. It felt like backtracking to me but it would be worthwhile if it actually counted as a heroic deed. At this point, I no longer knew. It sure sounded heroic. I thought my problem with this place would be its reliance upon stereotypes. The forces of evil wore black and sported horns. The forces of good all emitted rays of sunshine. The girls would be delicate and frail as the porcelain super original authors liked to compare them to. The heroes would be as brainless as a bull on a testosterone fueled rampage.[3] Now nothing was as it seemed. Sure it resembled the real world a bit more but hell if I understood it any better.

"A bear like creature they said," Jak mused as he flipped through the book. "All I see under bears is they should live in threes and build inviting cottages. Also conveniently not eat anyone who sneaks into their homes. As long as they're beautiful of course. Ugly people and oh great, those with darker hued skin, are up for grabs. That's us I guess."

"On both counts?" I asked, to which Jak did not respond.

He continued flipping and made a noise of discovery. "I think I've got it. We're hunting the Beast, with a capital B. I suppose he does rather look like a bear. With a larger set of teeth."[4]

"Is there a word for being prejudiced against sharp teeth?" Keran wanted to know. "It's not our fault. We don't have hands like you humans. We have to do everything with our mouths."

"You need to stop being so sensitive and give us umm... a paw here. Tell us if you smell any monsters or children nearby," I told him. "I thought animal familiars were supposed be barely seen, never really heard and only really useful during the climactic battle when their sudden death enrages the heroine."

"Well, he's not one," Naga popped her head out of my pocket briefly to register that opinion and sank back in.

As it turned out, we didn't need Keran's grudging help after all. We heard the laughter of children from far off and slowed down. I traded a glance with Jak and he shrugged, communicating his own confusion. We should have known better than to take what the villagers said at face value. At the time, I figured if their monster liked to snatch children, he or she must not have been affected by the changes coming over

[3] With about as much sensitivity for people around them.
[4] In case anyone wondered, these looked about as unrealistic as any other set of teeth pictured in the book. The illustrators must have a thing with teeth. The pictured heroes sported teeth gleaming bright enough to cause problems on a dark night. Every villain meanwhile, had horrible teeth. Did a sugar addiction perhaps come with evil?

Fairyland.

Though the laughing children prepared us for the unusual, we all still stopped and stared upon seeing the Beast, who looked so frightening on the page, rolling on the ground with three children under the age of ten jumping on top of him. They giggled as they poked him with sticks and he pretended to cower with fear. When the Beast rolled over, he saw us and froze. He gently pushed the children aside, got to his feet and lunged in our direction, baring his teeth, which were, in defense of the villagers,[5] indeed massive and frightening.

Instead of hacking at him though, I let go of the hilt of my sword, backed up a few paces and held up my hands. "We're just here to talk!"

The Beast pulled up short and let his lips come down over his canines. He looked at us quizzically, not sure what to make of us. Fair enough, since I didn't know what to make of him. Certainly though, I didn't intend to kill him. Unlike the goblins, every bit as smart as humans,[6] the Beast seemed to have difficulty stringing words together. He wasn't the brute the Storybook made him out to be but he would not be winning any poetry prizes either. He thought for a long time before pointing at the sword at my belt and asking, "On quest?"

Leave it to him to figure out the obvious. I smothered a sigh and nodded at him. "You'll have to return the children, I'm afraid."

"No," the Beast said, shaking his head vigorously. "They stay."

"They have to go back to their parents," Jak said, to which the Beast only shook his head more forcefully.

"We don't want to go back," declared one of the children, a boy who looked about eight.

"We ran away on our own," a younger girl said. "Our parents are boring, always worrying about monsters. At least he plays

---

[5] Not to mention the Storybook illustrators.
[6] If even the comparison should be made. Sure, we'd been one of the most dominant life forms for a while but we made a huge mess of things on a pretty regular basis.

with us and pays us attention."

"I think we've seen everything," Jak said.

"Probably not a good thing to say," Naga commented before I could get around to it.

As the children glared at us, I took a couple moments to turn the situation over. It took some work to get my mind wrapped around what happened here. Even as I groped my way toward an equitable solution, a rival band of adventurers crashed into the clearing. I could tell immediately they were also on a quest because they all carried weapons fashioned into inefficient shapes and came lumbering into the situation like idiots.

The group numbered a half dozen, with five young men a bit older than me as well as a young woman perhaps my age. The boys were all well muscled and wore armor designed less to protect them from injury and more to show off those very muscles. The girl carried a sword like one who didn't know very much about how to use it. I thought she might be one of those girls whose effectiveness in a fight was talked about very much but then belied by the sheer amount of times she needed rescuing. At some point down the line, someone would realize her beauty meant she could never be just a miner's daughter or whatever else her cover story entailed. If their story followed tradition, the leader of the questing band would win her heart and her lost kingdom along with it, after an appropriate amount of hacking and slashing through enemies. If looking to defy convention, perhaps she'd fall for his best friend instead and the leader would get a consolation prize of some sort.[7] If *really* audacious, maybe both at the same time,[8] leading to much agonizing and terribly tragic angst.

When the leader opened his mouth, I cast my vote pretty definitively for the second option. He waved his sword not at the Beast but at us. "Back off. This is our heroic deed. Get your

---

[7] Invariably, the 'prize' would be a girl because surely completing a quest should earn you the love and undying affection of some random person. Probably some unfortunate girl they encountered in the latter part of the quest. Perhaps also turning out to be a princess or heiress of some sort. You're getting the picture I'm sure.
[8] Ye gods, the sheer variety of outcomes!

own."

Left to my own devices, who knew what sort of impolite response I might have come up with? Happily, Jak read pretty fast. He sent the whole troupe a serious look. "How can it be your heroic deed when you haven't even Registered yet?"

"What?" the leader asked, momentarily baffled by such a ridiculous statement.

I'll admit, this misdirection impressed me and I granted Jak an appreciative nod. While our rivals puzzled over his statement, he said to me, "Parts of this can be fun."

While Keran rolled his eyes, I recognized his comment as an attempt to reconcile his own excitement at finally having set off on a quest with my obvious displeasure, I patted him on the arm and gestured at the rival group. "Just keep at it and I'll go talk to the Beast. I'll jump in when everything falls apart."[9]

"I'll stick with you," Keran said.

"Safer that way," Naga agreed.

Jak held up the Storybook and jabbed his finger at a page somewhere in the middle of the book. "It says right here you have to Register your acceptance. We came from the village east of here and they asked us to eliminate the Beast. So this is our deed after all."

"Okay, listen," I said, addressing the children more than the Beast, who curled his massive paws around them protectively. "These fools I'm going to have to fight off in a minute? They're the reason you need to go home. If you don't, more are going to come and hurt your friend. They're going to want to chop his horns off and bring them home as trophies. Doesn't that sound gruesome and unsanitary?"

"He can fight them off," the girl said. "He's already done it once."

"We're going to fight this group off for you. But there will be more and sooner or later he won't be able to run them off. Either he'll end up killing one of the idiots who call themselves heroes.

---

[9] As it surely would, not because of Jak's negotiation skills though I doubted those as well, but because this group just seemed too blockheaded to really parley with.

Or much worse, he'll be killed himself. I know you don't want that," I said.

"No, we don't," the oldest boy finally said. After a whispered exchange with his friends, he said, "Fine, we'll go home."

The Beast might not be able to say much but he understood the result of our discussion. He began keening in a low voice painful enough to make Keran lie down and try to cover his ears with his paws. I winced as well and shouted for the Beast to stop it. "Look, I know, you like kids? How about I offer you a job?"

It soon became pretty clear the Beast didn't understand the concept of a job.[10] So I explained it to him even as Jak continued to argue with the band of heroes. Finally, I got across I wanted the Beast to leave Fairyland, swim across the Zah River and go to my fortress where he could be assigned to help out at an orphanage or to take care of my many cousins.[11]

"He'll have to leave," the girl said, glaring at me.

"You'd be bad friends indeed if you'd rather he die to stay with you," I said.

Unlike their parents, these kids seemed a commonsensical lot.[12] Though they didn't like it, they obeyed and went along home after bidding the Beast an emotional goodbye. For his part, the Beast looked at me as if trying to see whether or not I meant to deceive him with talk of a place with rooms full of children to play with. "Look, I promise you this exists. I don't know how else to convince you."

"Perhaps allow me," Keran said. He got up and padded over to the Beast. At some unspoken signal, the Beast got down on all fours and looked Keran in the eyes. When he got up again, the Beast turned and headed west immediately. I reflected as he walked away I couldn't be sure he knew how to navigate to my home. I gave him directions but I didn't know if he could read

---

[10] And why would he? A modern innovation, this idea of a certain kind of labor defining who you are. I didn't entirely know how I felt about it either.
[11] Unlike my parents, who never even got around to producing a spare for their heir, their siblings birthed enough children to populate a village. That would a real pain in a generation or two.
[12] Which spoke well of the future of the village. If the changes were all like this, they had my full support.

road signs. I couldn't call him back though because I had problems of my own to take care of.

"It's getting away," one of our new friends observed.[13]

"Can't we all let it go?" I asked of them. "The children are on their way home. The Beast won't come back here. Everyone can go home happy. The deed is complete."

"That's not how you do it. We have to *kill* the Beast. That's not how any of this works," the leader said.

I laid a hand on the hilt of my sword and made sure to put myself between our rivals and the Beast retreating into the forest. "I'm afraid I can't allow that. Fight me if you want but don't say I didn't warn you'd lose."

"Are you trying to pick a fight?" Jak asked as he walked over to join me.

"What, not obvious enough?" I asked in turn. "I know they're obtuse so I'm trying to be as clear as possible."

Meanwhile, the other group of adventurers discussed their next step. They took so long even in the extremely unlikely event they managed to beat us into submission, it would be too late to track the Beast down.

"You leave us no choice but to challenge you to a brawl," the leader of the rival group declared. He tugged off his leather glove, reeled back and chucked it at my head.[14]

I whacked the glove out of the air with the flat of my sword and burst forward, happy to be doing something I understood. Perhaps the other side expected me to respond with some ritualistic phrases. My headlong charge took them aback. By the time they scrambled into motion, I already kicked the leader in the leg and knocked him out with an elbow to the neck.

Which is precisely when I spotted an enormous sword coming at my head. This would be Jak of course, flailing ineffectually in his usual way. It wasn't so bad when he had a

---

[13] Perhaps they too needed a lizard like Naga. Though for their sake, maybe one a bit less sarcastic. They wouldn't understand.

[14] His aim, incidentally, turned out to be truly awful. Honestly, if you're going to pull something so unnecessarily elaborate, at the very least you could try doing it well.

practice sword in hand. Not so much the case when his weapon could split stone in half, not to mention my head. To avoid a permanent end, I leaned away from his sword. The blade swept past, only just clearing my head. When I levered myself up again, I gestured for Jak to retreat. "Let me handle it."

Shaken from his near miss, Jak agreed. He backed away from the fight, holding the flat of his enormous blade against his chest. Whether he meant to protect himself or protect other people nobody could say. I pressed forward.

The girl flew at me next, with such ferocity I reevaluated my earlier judgment. Then when her sword struck my blade, she nearly dropped it. I couldn't help laughing at her, even if she did look appropriately chagrined. I didn't let my amusement slow my blade because I slashed it at her before she could recover her grip. Her sword tumbled through the air and her gaze went not to me but to the sword as it flipped over and over.

I wasn't about to let such laxity go unpunished and so her inattention earned her a blow to the chest that knocked her to the ground. Her remaining companions presented about as much trouble for me. Their leader clearly got his spot on the strength of his looks alone for the rest of the group proved a bit smarter. They came at me together, spreading out far enough I couldn't keep all of them squarely in sight at the same time. I knew better than to underestimate my enemies but after a day full of frustrations, I saw no reason to deny myself a chance at enjoying this.

So I let them think they had me cornered. I let them see me back up and let them think my rapid takedown of their other members came from luck alone.[15] And as soon as the first bit of relief leaked into their expressions, I struck. The young man closest to me went down when I dug my fist into his stomach. The one who swung his sword at me fell to the ground when I hooked a foot around his leg and pulled. He crashed hard and the ground knocked the breath right out of him. One more hurtled at me and tried to ram his shoulder into my chest. I stepped to the side and gave him a push, sending him sprawling into his

---

[15] Some extraordinary luck, if so.

friend.

Seeing them all momentarily incapacitated, I took a few steps back to let them recover before they gave it another shot or retreated. Confirming my opinion these young men weren't entirely stupid, they picked each other up, helped their friends to their feet and ushered them away. Naturally, their nominal leader proved the most recalcitrant. Though stumbling over himself, he thought it best to try and launch another attack. One of his friends grabbed him by the shoulders and pointed him in the opposite direction and in his confusion and dizziness, he continued charging forward. It was all I could do to prevent myself from laughing out loud.

Once they were gone, I turned to my companions and noticed the incredulous look on Keran's face.[16] Clearly, he didn't believe me when I told him to leave the fighting to me.

"Fine job," Jak praised though Keran interrupted before he could say anything else.

"Unbelievable," Keran said.

"We're traipsing through the country with a manual clutched in our hands telling us how to act. There's magic floating about that allows a paper boat to become real and you're confused years of training lets me get the better of a few idiots?" I asked.

"It's not that," Keran said. "It doesn't seem possible for you to be that strong given..."

"What, given that I don't seem to have much muscle? We have in our party a lizard that can speak, a mage who can only perform one spell and a wolfhound that can swallow coals. And you want to bring logic to the argument that I shouldn't be able to fight as well as I can?" I asked.

"You may have a point," Keran admitted.

"Besides, if there's anything I do approve of in the manual, it's the part about the heroine[17] always winning in a fight,"[18] I

---

[16] You might think incredulity would be hard to convey on a canine face. And you'd be right. But he managed it. Probably had a lot of practice.

[17] I mean the Storybook itself probably only mentioned heroes in keeping with its usual sexist nature but I assumed the principles applied to me too.

68

said.

"Alright, don't let it get to your head," Jak said. "We still have a lot of work to do."

"I would've thought you'd be happier about this," I said. "One heroic deed down and only three more to go."

"I'd be happier if I knew for sure this one counted," Jak said.

"By Fairyland standards, definitely not. But I don't think we're bound by those. We'll be fine," I said.

"You're in a good mood," Naga commented, right before Keran could say the same thing.

"A good old fashioned fight is something I understand. After everything, it's good to see something making sense," I said.

I carried this confidence back with us as we returned to the village. Once there, we found out the kids I sent scurrying back already did most of our work for us. They convinced their parents we killed the Beast and drove off his human accomplices. The little girl even told the adults his body scattered into dust as soon as he perished. Their creativity rather astounded me and I could help thinking some hope remained for this accursed land after all.

When we left the village, both Jak and I rode on horses as white as snow.[19] In fact, the issue of how such a remote village got their hands on and were willing to give away such expensive horses rather bothered me.

"I asked the mayor while you raided their food stores," Jak said when I made the comment.

"Don't think I've overlooked your reproach. It could be a long time before we get our hands on some truly good stew. The Storybook can mandate all it wants about proper questing diet but I'm not spending hours stirring a pot while we should be on

---

[18] Not quite true of course. You could lose a fight. But only if you were meant to learn some important lesson from it. I clearly had nothing to learn from those goons.

[19] Almost unnaturally so. I swear they practically shone, which might make sneaking around hard.

the road,"[20] I told him.

"In any case, the horses come straight from the stables of the nearest palace or castle. Used to be such horses would spontaneously appear in villages whenever a hero passed by and did a heroic deed for them. Apparently, horses no longer come out of thin air so they have to be bred," Jak explained. "People are very upset about it." The costs of upkeep is a perennial issue at the Regional Council. Apparently, local records diverge wildly.

"Everyone here is out of their minds," Naga said.

"Exactly what I've been saying," I agreed.

---

[20] Not that I would spend hours stirring a pot even if we didn't have somewhere to be. There were few things I hated quite so much as cooking. Okay fine, there were a lot of things I hated more than cooking. But still.

CHAPTER NINE

By nightfall, we reached the edge of the forest and emerged into rolling pastures. We made camp though, in the shadow of the trees so the light would not attract all manner of creatures. The only good thing about Fairyland was the ease with which we could set up camp. The magic keeping goblins locked into their roles might be breaking down but some things still worked fine. Just kick a few sticks into a pile, smack some rocks together above them and boom! a fire.[1] No need for kindling or even extra fuel to keep the fire going. The wood burned but was not consumed, an unsettling but very convenient phenomenon.

It might well be a magical fire but it emitted plenty of warmth so I cared little about its exact nature. I flopped down next to it while Jak moved about, sticking branches in the ground so we could lay our damp clothes across them and let them dry out for real. The sound of the fire and Jak shuffling about lulled me to sleep and I didn't wake until something skittered over my face.

I started and sat up to see Naga glaring up at Jak, who

---

[1] Can't imagine this didn't lead to rampant forest fires. It's a wonder anyone built anything out of flammable materials.

apparently dropped her right onto my face. Perhaps in anticipation of my wrath, he already ducked to the other side of the fire and busied himself looking innocent. Instead of getting angry, I only smiled, scooped Naga up and put her back on my shoulder. "I suppose it's good at least one of us is enjoying this trip."

"Sorry," Jak said.

"It's alright. You don't have to keep apologizing. It's not your fault I'm stuck out here. Incidentally, what is your plan?" I wanted to know.

"I have no idea," Jak said. "I've spent so long hoping for a quest to come around, I don't think I ever put thought into how going on one would help me. Perhaps I as a boy, I imagined the simple act of taking on a quest would give me the strength and the allies I needed. Maybe I thought I'd do a few good deeds and the universe would repay me for it. Silly, isn't it? And yet, I can't help but believe it a little, even now."

"I'm not going to lie and say it isn't wishful thinking. But what the hell, we're in a land where fairy tales come to life. Why shouldn't yours have a chance? I'll keep on the lookout for anything that might help you," I said.

"The important thing is to help you finish your quest," Jak said. "That's an achievable goal."

When I laughed, he raised an eyebrow at me so I explained, "Look at us, being so supportive. Especially me. I don't even think we've gotten to the part of the quest where we're supposed to discover other dimensions to our companions. As if such trips actually have a transformative quality or something."

"I'm not convinced they don't," Jak commented. "I suppose we'll only know at the end."

"I know where I'm putting my money," I told him.

"You might lose that bet," Jak said.

I started to protest but Keran interrupted to say, "I'm afraid I'm not too clear on how this whole quest is meant to help you. Or me for that matter. Rahni, your parents told me I might be able to bring back the rest of my people. You have a goal, to fetch the elixir and return alive. How do we determine our goals?"

"I'll tell you what I know. Given how much things have changed in Fairyland, don't take it too much to heart," I said.

"It's more than I know," Keran said.

"The gist of it is things have a way of working themselves out in the Eigen States. If you manage to survive, you'll come out with a resolution, one way or another," I told him.

"What? That's it?" Naga demanded on Keran's behalf.

"Doesn't sound like an answer at all," Keran muttered.

"Look, I don't like it any better than you. But it's true. There's something in this whole process of setting off on a quest, some magic inherent in the act of taking one on perhaps," I said.

Keran sighed and buried his face into the crook of his arm, apparently too upset at the world to offer a reply.[2]

"He'll probably be in a better mood in the morning," Naga remarked though she punctuated it with a yawn.

Naga was very wrong. Keran woke up no happier than when we went to sleep the night before. He loped along after the horses but hung his head almost to the ground, paying no attention to our surroundings, to say nothing of enjoying the way wind came through the perfect grass.[3]

I did my best to keep my spirits up, not just for the sake of my sanity but because we really had something to be happy about. With these horses, we'd get to the border of Fairyland in half the time. Plus, I made the decision, seeing as we had sufficient supplies to see us through a few days, to avoid heroic deeds at all costs. None of us wanted to encounter another situation like with the Beast. All things considered, he turned out to be an easy case. After some initial misgivings, I felt sure my aunts and uncles, not to mention anyone else with unruly children, would thank me.

What if we encountered a dragon next time? I could just imagine the lecture Fin might bestow upon learning I invited a

---

[2] To be honest, I understood the impulse. Sometimes, it all got to be a bit much.

[3] Incidentally, who made sure the grass didn't grow past shin length and kept it all so green? Another mystery of Fairyland. They were starting to pile up.

dragon into the kingdom to set up financial services to compete with his own bank.[4] Much better to avoid the problem altogether. That always worked, right?

For a couple of days, perhaps to everyone's surprise, it did. We kept to the main roads and camped there. We avoided any and all population centers and greeted anyone we met with polite but distant salutations before moving on.

Everything went swimmingly until the third day and I started to hope we might actually make it out of Fairyland no worse for the wear. Which only goes to show even cynics like me needed to temper their expectations about this place.

Over the course of the morning, the road narrowed. I noticed this but saw no solution other than to keep pressing forward and hope for it to open up once more. For if the road continued on like this, we would stumble upon a heroic deed sooner or later. Lo and behold, we soon saw a sizeable town ahead. Unlike the village where we performed our first deed, this properly deserved the label of a town. A few buildings even topped three stories. The streets might be paved with cobblestone.[5]

I didn't want to find out. I thought about suggesting we gallop past the town to avoid any misconceptions and avoid being pulled into anything. But then a child darted out into the road and I reined my horse in. As we discovered soon after we left the first village, these horses didn't just stop when I called for halt. No, they dramatized everything. When I pulled gently on the reins, the horse reared up onto her hind legs and pawed at the air a few times while I hung on and glared at her mane.

At this point, I felt almost accustomed to her antics.[6] The

---

[4] And this didn't even take into account the legal mess given the ironclad clauses in our contracts. Just thinking about it made me shudder. Even worse than Fin's displeasure would be the suit he might bring against us. I was sure he would hire someone from his cousin's firm, Twenty Lawyers Under the Sea, made up of marine dwelling dragons. I'd met his cousin once and she was a lovely dragon. It was just that she tended to bring massive storms wherever she went.

[5] Which, incidentally, seemed a horribly exhausting way to pave streets.

[6] She also really liked to neigh in an unnecessarily dramatic fashion and toss her head. She did this at unpredictable intervals, sometimes making

first time, I nearly fell right off the saddle. Who would've thought she needed to rear up on her hind legs after I directed her to the side of the road and made it very clear I wanted a simple halt? Keran tried his best to talk the horses out of performing in this way but they didn't even understand his request. They'd been trained too well. Or too poorly I suppose, depending on how you viewed it. I know how I viewed it.

In any case, I bounced a little in the saddle when my mare brought her front hooves back to the ground. The child paid us no attention and ran off shouting at the top of his lungs. Only when he'd gone a distance did I process what he said and groaned out loud.

"You heard it too?" Jak asked.

"Can't we pretend we didn't?" I asked in turn, which got me nothing but a glare from Jak. Of course, I never seriously considered moving on without further investigation. We could hardly allow a witch burning to take place on our watch.

And so, we found ourselves in a town square watching several townsfolk wrestle a young man up to the platform. "Mmm, that's strange, isn't it? Jak, what does the Storybook say about witches being attractive young men?"

"There is a rather homophobic section about "effeminate" men likely being warlocks," Jak said.

"Oh great," Naga said.

"I think it's pretty clearly a witch burning. If I have to hear the phrase one more time, I think I'll have to bite someone," Keran said.

"Better save it for later. We might soon find ourselves in a situation where you can put your aggression to good use," I told him. "But if this *is* a witch burning, what's going on?"

"Don't know. Witches are only supposed to be Certified Old Hags with at most one relative to protest their execution or sinisterly beautiful young women. Not sure what that's supposed to mean but I think we can be certain he doesn't fit the bill," Jak said.

---

conversations difficult and ruining a number of jokes that relied upon precise timing.

75

As we talked, the townsfolk deposited the young man in the middle of a pile of wood and backed away. Another man walked up with a torch held high and signaled for silence. He got it eventually but not quickly enough for his tastes if the foul expression on his face meant anything. When everyone finally quieted down, he started off on a prepared speech.[7]

Having laid out his argument for why this young man should be cast into a fire and roasted into a crisp, he swept his gaze through the crowd and made the traditional challenge. "Whomsoever knows of a reason why this burning should not take place, speak now or forever hold your peace."

I thought for sure it would be up to us to save the day but a voice rang out from the crowd before I said a thing. "Stop, I beg you in the name of She Who Represents All That Is Holy!"

"A bit of a mouthful," I commented. "Suppose it prevents cursing using her name. By the time you finished, you'd forget what you were angry about."

In the meantime, the thin and sickly looking man who interrupted the proceedings struggled to the front and held out his hands to the crowd, "Please, everyone, you must listen to sense. This man has done nothing to deserve this fate. Search yourselves and find the good inside each of you. I know you'll see this is wrong."

"Get out of the way!" someone shouted at him. "You're going to block my view of the burning."

"At least take off the hat," a woman said. "That's so rude, don't you know?"

To his credit, the man, who looked to be a priest of one order or another given his tattered robes, didn't even flinch. He pressed forward gamely, appealing to every sense in the book[8] but getting nowhere. The longer he stood there talking, the more the crowd yelled at him to shut up and get out of the way. I

---

[7] Most of it turned out to be pretty stock so I won't bore you with the details. Suffice to say there were a lot of 'unnaturals' and 'abominations' being thrown around.

[8] Really though, every sense in the Storybook. Not a very long list, as you might imagine.

feared they might seize the priest and toss him into the pyre along with their so called witch.

I stepped into the middle of it and got their attention by shouting and waving my sword in the air.[9] Once I had their attention, I explained, "My companions and I are traveling adventurers with the luck to stumble onto your charming town. I'm afraid we don't quite understand what's going on here. You say this young man is a witch?"

"No question about it," said the man with the torch. "He sank when we threw him in water with irons."

As this sounded like a rather astounding piece of stupidity, I turned it over a couple times. When I accepted the man was being perfectly serious, it took me some more time to suppress my instinct to call him a fool. "I think you've got the instructions wrong. Witches are supposed to float because the water rejects them. Ordinary people sink when they have irons weighing them down. Heck, sometimes ordinary people sink without chains. Haven't any of you swum before?"

The nearest pious woman looked scandalized by the very thought. "Such frivolous activities are the domain of the Dark One. Water is her element."

"Okay, we can work with that," I said. "If water belongs to the Dark One, wouldn't her servants *not* drown in it?"

Probably to prevent anyone from actually thinking this over, the red-faced man with the torch, who seemed the most eager to get started with the burning, though much of the townsfolk followed him closely in terms of enthusiasm, waved my words away. "There's no time for dithering about. The time for questions and interrogation is over. The sentence has been handed down. We have only to execute. We cannot afford to hesitate."

When most of the townsfolk nodded, I knew we would have to take drastic measures. I exchanged a glance with Jak, who nodded in support of the next obvious plan of action. Clearing my throat again, I said, "I have no choice but to call for a Trial

---

[9] I tried some tamer methods first but those got me nowhere so I defaulted to flailing.

by Fire[10] to get some of our questions answered."

The entire crowd groaned even as the would be victim sighed in relief at the stay of his execution. The man with the torch fumed but could do nothing for such a challenge, once issued, could not be ignored. He stuffed the torch into the hands of an assistant and started pointing at people in the crowd to come forward and help him. With nearly a dozen people working together, it didn't take long for the trial to be set up.

When they brought out a bow and some arrows, they offered them to Jak instead of me even though I called for the Trial. I stalked over, snatched the weapons out of their hands and went to the line drawn out in the ground. I eyed the target and tugged at the bowstring a few times to get a feel for it. It seemed serviceable. Which is all I really cared about at this point.[11]

Before we started, one of the townsfolk walked over to me with a small green hat. I took it from her and poked at the lone feather sticking out from one side. "What is this?"

"You're to wear it," the woman responded, baffled by my confusion.

"Why?" I demanded.

"Nobody really knows why. We just do it," Fran said.

"Fine, as long as you don't randomly burn people to death to conform. Oh, wait, I guess you do," I said. It was an off hand dig so I didn't expect her to get so red in the face and practically dash off. I looked at Jak but he shrugged so I let it go. There were more important things I should be focusing on, such as who the townsfolk would send out to be my opponent.

When Matthew, the man holding the torch, sent himself out against me, I nearly purred in delight. Perhaps Jak was right after all. Quests could be fun. Wiping that look off this man's face would be the best thing I did in quite a while, knocking out the would be hero the other day included.

---

[10] Okay, I'll be honest. I only knew to call for it because I made Jak give me a brief summary of the most important parts of the Storybook. I couldn't be bothered to read it myself. All the bigotry disguised as morality repulsed me too much.

[11] Well that and getting all of us, supposed witch included, out with as few burns as possible.

Before we got started, the man reminded everyone of the rules.[12] The Trial by Fire didn't proceed quite like any other trial. The two sides competed not just with arguments and words but by firing arrows at a target.

Only the person who hit closest to the center of their target could ask a question in any given round, of the defendant, in this case the unfortunate young man now uncomfortably tied upright to a post. I had no argument in mind to get him out of this situation. In truth, I doubted any argument would convince the townsfolk not to kill him.

I called the Trial partly to get some answers as to how he ended up in this situation. I also wanted to diminish the immediate danger by getting him away from the pile of straw and wood. More importantly though, we needed a good opportunity to get him out of this unscathed. It was one thing to encounter a small band of fighters and drive them off. It would be quite another to try and fight off an angry mob. I had no idea how to extract ourselves. My current plan consisted of keeping them all talking as long as possible, or at least until they messed up enough for us to take advantage.[13]

Matthew waved a hand at me, indicating I should go first. Not having any reason to be shy, I stepped up and nocked an arrow. To let him think he had a chance, I sent the arrow a little to the right of the center. The crowd murmured and Matthew seemed slightly taken aback.

He took his time with his shot, lining it up and straining his muscles as he let his body settle into the correct form. I resisted the urge to make a quip, figuring our relative performances would make my point for me. And our new friend did not disappoint. His arrow did hit the target but struck the edge and hung off the straw material by a single strand. The officiator moved to measure the distances even though everyone knew the result. Matthew cut him off with a short gesture.

Rather ungraciously, he gestured for me to ask my question.

---

[12] Also written on page 394 of the Storybook, at least according to Jak.
[13] Not so far fetched as it sounds, incidentally. People are remarkably fond of providing just those sorts of opportunities.

Perhaps the townsfolk thought I'd try the tack the priest used but if so, I disappointed them. I simply looked over at the young man and asked, "What's your name?"[14]

This question startled him too and it took him a moment to properly organize his thoughts. "Proctor," he finally responded. "Old town stock. Born and raised right here."

I nodded at this, raised my bow and shot off another arrow, letting it hit the target a half inch closer to the middle. This time, Matthew's arrow flew right over the top of the target, giving me the opportunity to ask my next question.

"So Proctor, how did you end up in this situation?" I asked.

"Well, I won the lottery," the young man said.

"Excuse me?" Jak asked.

"You're not allowed to ask questions," the official scolded him.

Instead of arguing the point with him, I took the next shot and when given the go ahead, repeated Jak's question.

"It happens every ten years," Proctor explained. "Everyone in the town gathers round and picks out a slip of paper. The winner is the one who pulls the slip with a red dot on it. They get to be tested for witchcraft. As you might imagine, given the rigged nature of the test, every winner is a witch."

"Only proves the worth of the lottery," someone in the crowd called. "It sniffs out the witches, it does."

The situation looked a lot worse now. If these townsfolk did this before, selected one of their number to sacrifice, they would be all the more rabid about continuing it. If they already committed a horror, they needed to continue or else risk realizing they did it for no reason but their inability to stand against evil. And it was evil, even if that should never win out here in Fairyland. In any case, if activities like this truly counted as good, I'd rather be evil.

As much as I might hate these people, cursing them under my breath didn't help us rescue poor Proctor. Hoping Jak would

---

[14] Mostly, I just wanted to know. But also, I thought reminding the townsfolk he did have a name might snap them out of their insanity. Rather naïve of me, in retrospect.

come up with something, I kept Proctor talking. I asked him inane questions, about his childhood to his future plans, really anything to keep him talking. And because I never gave Matthew a chance to speak, he couldn't even protest my non-tactics.

CHAPTER TEN

The crowd soon ran out of patience as I did nothing to further anyone's case. The tension grew until I feared they might thrust us into the pyre if we didn't figure out something soon. Fortunately, the town temple burst into flames.

I didn't turn to look.[1] To avoid letting this chance slip through my hands, I pulled back the arrow I already nocked and fired it not at the target but at Proctor. He practically squeaked while the ropes holding him to the column loosened. Another couple of arrows did the trick and let him shrug the severed ropes off. I looked on with some pride. "Always wanted to do that," I said to no one in particular.

While the rest of the crowd went off to take care of the temple, Matthew was not fooled. He tossed away his quiver of arrows and whipped the bow at my head. I ducked and stabbed him in the ribs with the end of my own bow. As he crumpled to the floor, I ran toward Proctor, seized him by the arm and yanked him along as I ran down the street. Jak and Keran caught

---

[1] Well maybe just a glance, enough to see it went up like tinder in a completely unnatural manner. Must be something about the carbon content of their trees.

up with us as Matthew let out an angry shout and called for the townsfolk to follow us.

Naga climbed out of my pocket and skittered to my shoulder to take a look. "Not good," she said before she crawled back. In my other pocket, the map pulsed with warmth and I could see the glowing of the warning on the back. The stupid thing could shut up. I didn't need it to tell me we were in trouble.

"Can you run on your own yet?" I asked Proctor.

When he hesitated, Jak grabbed him, threw him over his shoulder and ran ahead of us. Keran put in a burst of speed as well and pulled ahead of me as well.

"Might be a good idea to go faster," Naga said.

I looked behind me to see a massive mob of people with torches, ropes and pitchforks. "What the hell? Where did they get all that stuff? Also, why pitchforks?" Naturally, no one answered these questions. They were too busy running for their lives, something I had to work on as well.

Fortunately, angry mobs never seemed to win against the heroines and heroes of a quest. No time to check in the Storybook but I was pretty sure. I'd find out soon enough because the crowd began to gain on us. The prospect of having to fight them off drove me to run faster, enough so I pulled ahead of Keran and Jak before letting them catch up to me.

"This was a terrible idea," I said as we continued running.

"We just need to get to the edge of town," Jak responded as he panted like a dog.[2]

"Don't tell me angry mobs pull up at the edge of their towns and stop chasing you," Keran said.

"Page 451," Jak told him as he huffed and puffed.

Subsequent events proved him right. About the time we reached the outskirts of town, Jak tripped on a rock and went tumbling. Proctor flew off his shoulder and rolled an impressive

---

[2] Really though, his performance so far impressed me. Sure, he seemed ready to collapse but at least he kept moving. On an average day, he'd have fallen over on his face halfway down the road. Though come to think of it, if he couldn't run so fast but for the murderous townsfolk on his heels, I'd rather not see him beat any more speed records.

83

distance before staggering to his feet. He tottered around before falling into the dirt again.

"You get him and I'll haul Jak to his feet," I told Keran.

The wolfhound sighed but went to do as I asked. Meanwhile, I grabbed Jak by the arm and pulled him up. He limped for a bit before he could set both feet on the ground and only when we started running again did I think to look back. The whole crowd stood and watched us leave them behind. They stood even with the last house and held their pitchforks and torches high for no practical reason I could see. Just about every other person had a coil of rope in his or her hands and I wondered again where exactly they hid all these implements earlier.

"I think we can slow down," I said.

Proctor looked back at the mob and seemed about to call toward them but I hit him before he could.

"Don't push our luck," I said. "Keep moving."

"Sorry," Proctor responded and continued jogging forward. He didn't look back again until we went too far even to see the glow of the torches but I did. And I saw Matthew's gaze burning into me. Not fazed, I glared back and silently wished for him to fall into a well or out of a window.[3]

"What's his deal?" Jak asked when we ran far enough to justify slowing to a walk.

"You mean Matthew?" Proctor asked.

"Who else?" I questioned in turn. "He tried to brain me with a bow. Bastard."

"Probably the nicest thing he's done in years," Proctor said. "He's the most famous witch hunter in these parts. He makes the rounds and helps each of the towns organize their lotteries."

"What is up with these lotteries?" Keran wanted to know. "I confess I don't understand how anything works in Fairyland. But Rahni said the motto of the place is something close to good always prevailing. How come this Matthew has free rein to persecute and kill?"

"I guess it all depends what you mean by good," Proctor said.

"Even so, it takes some serious imagination to twist his

---

[3] Preferably with only a pile of filth to break his fall.

actions," Jak said.

"Not as much as you'd think," Proctor remarked. "You see, they're right. I am a witch." He clapped his hands and a forearm length stick appeared in his hand with a small flash of light. It was a silly looking thing with a quartz stone at one end and a rope wound on the other to serve as a grip. Proctor waved it in some complicated motion in the air and produced a small bat.[4] It fluttered in my face before disappearing in a puff of smoke.

"I didn't expect that," Jak remarked. "What else can you do?"

"I don't rightly know," Proctor answered. "I don't even really know why that spell produces a bat. Or what bats are good for. I don't have a lot of opportunity to practice. Ever since I figured out I was witch, I've tried to keep it quiet. You can imagine why."

"Doesn't explain why you're supposed to burn," I said. "You're not hurting anyone. I know it's a stupid question given where we are but seriously?"

"To be fair, it's long been a fact witches make a lot of trouble. I know a village not far away burned to the ground because a witch developed a grudge against the miller. Half a dozen people died," Proctor said.

"And what has it got to do with you?" I asked.

"Nothing but you've got to remember these people are scared of all the recent changes," Proctor mentioned. "Used to be the world was one way and one way only. You took the life you got and did what you were meant to do without protest.[5] No questions asked. Now there are choices. So of course people make some bad ones."

"You're being very cavalier about the whole experience," I said. "It's okay though. If you don't feel like condemning them, I don't have any compunction about doing it on your behalf."

"Me neither," Jak agreed with a firm nod. "Makes me want to rant like the priest did."

"Speaking of which, what exactly happened back there?" I

---

[4] Really small. Think about the size of a thumbnail. I thought it looked like a fly.
[5] I very much doubted this but I let him have the point.

85

wanted to know. "Where did the priest go? Is he the one who set the temple on fire?"

"He went off to do it while you kept the crowd busy," Jak said. "I told him we'd get Proctor out if he caused a distraction big enough. I think he did a good job."

"Very respectable," I said. "I'm honestly a bit surprised. I thought the clerics would be first on board with a witch hunt."

"Usually," Proctor said. "He's always been a little strange. Not the sort other clerics like to hang out with during their annual conferences if you know what I mean."

"They have those?" I asked.

"How else do you think they standardize their doctrines?" Proctor wanted to know.

"Divine inspiration comes to mind as an option," I remarked but even Proctor knew at this point not to pay attention to me in my contrary moods.

"Will the townsfolk turn their anger on him?" Keran wanted to know.

"Oh no, everyone is used to him. He's always agitating for one thing or another," Proctor said. "No one pays him any attention. I didn't either until the stuff he talked about affected me directly. That's always the way, isn't it?"[6] As we continued to walk, he snapped his fingers to make his wand disappear and caught me eyeing him. "What?"

"We need another member for our quest and it wouldn't be half bad having a real witch on board. I don't suppose you'd consider joining our band," I said.

"Definitely not," Proctor said. "You think I'm crazy enough to stay? You have my gratitude because you rescued me but there's no way I'm signing up with a quest. Some appreciation it would be if I got myself killed after the trouble you went to saving me."

"You know, I don't even have an argument," I said. "Fair enough. You need anything before you go? Can't give you a

---

[6] Sadly so, for most people. Me too. I don't exempt myself from the condemnation. If anything, it applies to me more than most. Royalty here after all.

horse because we've lost those now. Innkeeper is probably thanking his lucky stars right about now."

"Oh no, the Storybook is very clear. Those horses will only let questers ride them. She'll have to turn those over to the proper Author-ities," Jak said though even he winced at the pun.

"We only have what, one more day in this terrible place?" I asked. "Let's hope we don't have the misfortune to see any of these people."

"In my experience, such declarations only invite bad luck," Proctor said.

"In mine too," I agreed.

We parted with Proctor not too long after. He had a cousin in another corner of the land who'd been trying to convince him to leave Fairyland with her for years. Apparently, she didn't much like her prospects here. Really the absolute best someone like her could hope for was to be plucked off the street by an illiterate prince and plopped into a throne. And ruling a nation here in Fairyland was about the worst thing that could happen, next to being burned as a witch or hung from the gallows because you were an orphan.[7]

So it made perfect sense to me Proctor's cousin wanted to get out. The only thing that didn't make sense at first is why Proctor refused to leave earlier. Eventually, I figured that Proctor had a life and prospects here. He held onto them despite knowing he'd be found out sooner rather than later. Which just went to show people could be serious suckers.

Proctor told us he didn't need anything but we sent him off

---

[7] Well, maybe being made Queen wasn't the *worst* thing that could happen to someone here. But it certainly didn't seem attractive. You sat in a hard seat all day long in starchy clothes, prohibited by the rulebook your peers themselves drew up, from doing anything productive. On top of that, you had to worry about the next kingdom over raising an army because while no one could change things for the better, invading your neighbors was fine, as long as done by the book. Which basically meant loudly decrying they had been taken in by the wiles of the forces of darkness and betrayed the forces of good. Sure, someone could overthrow them, again in the name of good, but it wouldn't help you none if they chopped off your head already. See Inviolable Rule Number One.

with a portion of our gold anyway. After perusing his Storybook, Jak advised him to keep the money in his sock. Apparently, thieves and highwaymen had a bad track record with such spots. We waved away his thanks and told him to get on his way.

"All their unnecessary rearing aside, I rather liked the horses," I said as we continued on. "I'm going to miss them. Not enough to go searching for another heroic deed to do yet, of course. But still."

"That reminds me. Do you think rescuing Proctor counted as one?" Jak asked.

"I'm not really sure what standards we're going by anymore," I said. "If by Fairyland standards, I again say hell no. If by more sensible standards, though how sensible could any standards be, it's possible?"

"What in blazes is that?" Keran demanded. Had he been human, he would have pointed straight up. It took an explanatory word or two from him to get the rest of us to look at the sky. I saw immediately what he meant. It was hard not to notice the giant ball of flame rushing for us.

CHAPTER ELEVEN

As we scrambled away as fast as possible, Jak shouted, "Why didn't the map alert us?"

"Technically, it's not looking to behead us," I responded. "It wants to vaporize us."

"Much better!" Jak said.

The roar grew as the ball of flame continued to stream down. Keran dashed past the rest of us in a streak of silver.[1]

I could run a lot faster than Jak even if he was fleeing for his life but I wasn't about to leave him behind. I resisted the urge to look back to check the progress of the meteor or whatever it was.

It hit the ground a lot faster than I expected, so hard it jolted both Jak and me off our feet. I twisted through the air as I fell forward to land safely and roll back upright. Jak hit the ground like a sack of cornmeal and rolled against my feet as I turned. I half expected a good size circle of burnt foliage. Instead, I found the grass completely undisturbed. Only one thing changed. A double-handed sword now stuck up out of the ground.

---

[1] Someone clearly didn't feel too much concern about the other members of his band. His loyalty to the group left something to be desired though his sense of self-preservation seemed healthy enough.

Keran came trotting back, completely unabashed for having abandoned us as soon as the going got tough. He nodded toward the sword. "What's that for?"

"It's the answer to whether rescuing Proctor counted as a heroic deed," Jak said as he pushed himself up to his knees.

"Don't tell me, another magic sword?" I asked. "What do I need two for? Or maybe it's for you Keran."

"What luck," Keran said as he sat down. "Just tie it to my back. I'll joust with it."

I gave Jak a hand up since he seemed to be struggling. He staggered over to the sword, laid his hands on the hilt and yanked. It didn't budge, no matter how much he strained. After a couple minutes watching him struggle and get more and more red in the face, I pulled him away. "Leave it alone. We don't need the stupid thing anyway."

"You should give it a try," Jak said.

I scoffed at this. "If you can't do it, there's no way I can. You're far stronger than me."

"Just give it a shot. I have a feeling about this," Jak said.

No point really to argue so I went over and tugged on the sword, not hard enough to really strain my muscles but plenty hard enough to make me fall over when the sword slid out of the ground without any resistance whatsoever. I narrowly avoided hitting myself in the head with the pointy end and blinked at the sword when I sat up. I shook my head as I got to my feet. "Makes sense I suppose. It is my quest. Now what do I do with it?"

In the end, we tied it to *my* back. I would've been happy to leave it exactly where we found it but Jak thought it a good idea to keep it around, at least until we left Fairyland for good.[2]

"What is that smell?" Keran demanded as I fiddled with the straps to try and make the sword sit more comfortably against my back. Easier said than done for after all, it was a naked blade. The hilt dug into my shoulder and even if we wrapped most of the sword in Jak's spare shirt, I still didn't like the feel of it. I always carried my sword on a belt at my side so it would take

---

[2] As soon as possible, if I had my say.

some time for me to get used to moving around with this blade on my back. On the bright side, it proved to be a lot lighter than I expected. Maybe it came part and parcel with the magic.

"I don't smell anything," I told Keran when I transferred my attention away from the sword.

Keran made a face of disgust and looked at the two of us in disbelief. "Ugh, how can you not?"

I looked at Jak to confirm the nonexistence of any smell. We were still shrugging at each other when the smell hit us and we made identical faces of disgust. Only Jak though, recognized it.

"You're not going to like this," Jak told us as he looked around.

"I'm certainly not pleased at the moment," I said as I pinched my nose for unbelievably, the smell only got worse as time went on. And to top it off, the map started to pulse with warmth again. "Can't we get even a moment of peace?"[3]

"First rule right?" Jak asked as I pulled out the map briefly.

"Something in the Storybook about this?" I asked when I saw he got it right.[4] "Is it a giant skunk or something because if so, I'm throwing in the cowl, curse or no curse." The band still on my arm tightened slightly in reproach and I glared at it until it loosened, almost sheepishly. Great, now I was assigning sentience to armbands made of strange metal. Just what I needed.

"It's not a skunk," Jak told me as he suppressed a chuckle. "This is a Reek of Wrongness."

"I don't believe it. What, it lets you know whenever you're in danger?" I asked.

"It's the odor certain servants of the supposed dark carry with them," Jak said.

"Let me guess, ogres?" Keran asked.

We spun around and saw an ogre perhaps nine or ten feet tall lumbering in our direction. He looked precisely like the drawing in the Storybook. So either he was a really good at disguising

---

[3] But of course not. Who did I think I was fooling?
[4] Though it didn't really take a genius to figure out everyone wanted our heads.

91

himself or the changes taking place hadn't affected him as yet. As he drew closer, I found myself hoping for the former. Broad shouldered and stout, he looked strong enough to rip up a tree and fat enough to eat it as a snack after mushing us with it. Straggly blonde hair tied off in a few large braids knocked against his face and neck with each step he took. A war axe about the size of me hung from his hand and he swung it back and forth.

"Running might be a good idea right about now," Naga commented.

"I agree with the lizard," Keran whispered.

I seriously doubted running would help but wasn't averse to giving it a try. It might work. Heroines seemed to have pretty good luck when it came to the business of running from enemies. Unfortunately, we didn't even get there. A new wave of stench, just as pungent but carrying with it elements of musty cave air, hit us. We swiveled to see yet another enemy headed in our direction. This one stood as tall as the ogre but wielded a maul instead of a war axe. She had considerably more hair than the ogre and it sprouted all over her body. Her teeth bunched out of her mouth and I might have mentioned it if not for Keran's sensitivity on the issue.

"Troll?" I guessed.

"I think so," Jak said.

"Wait a minute. The sun is out. Shouldn't it be turning her to stone by now?" Keran demanded. When we turned to look at him, Keran did his version of a shrug.[5] "What? I couldn't sleep last night so I flipped through the book. Having to turn all those pages meant slow going. Whoever prints these things should really learn to be a little more considerate to those without opposable thumbs."

"You can register your complaint when we get back," I told him. "More importantly, Jak, do you have any answer for him regarding the sunlight? I'd like to know too."

"I have no idea," Jak admitted.

"What do we have you around for again?" I asked as I pulled

---

[5] He sort of tipped his head in a certain way if you're curious.

my sword out of its sheath.

"To carry your bags?" Jak asked.

"Right. Better keep doing good work then. I'm going to be occupied for the near future, I expect," I said.

"You're not going to fight them," Jak said.

"You have a better idea?" I wanted to know. "I'm very open to suggestions."

Neither Jak nor Keran had anything so I mentally prepared myself to be either chopped in half by an ogre or mashed into pulp by a troll.[6]

Then the troll and ogre spotted each other.

"Hey!" shouted the ogre. "I saw them first."

The troll scoffed at him. "I smelled them first."

"You can't prove that." The ogre frowned as he thought about it. "Even if you could, it means nothing."

Both the ogre and the troll pulled oversized versions of the Storybook out of their bags and started flipping through the pages. They started calling out page numbers at each other. At first, I turned from one to the other, waiting for them to finish their argument. Then I pushed Jak and Keran to get them moving, hoping we could get away before either of our enemies noticed.

The troll and the ogre stomped up to each other and ended up looking at the same copy, gesturing wildly and saying something about a Definitive List of Dastardly-ness[7] that would tell them who had first dibs on our entrails. I didn't plan to stick around to see what they decided.

We didn't get far before both parties realized we were taking advantage of their inattention. They nodded at each other, now in perfect accord. "Keep running," I ordered and tossed Naga at Jak. He caught her and she ran up his arm and into his breast pocket.

---

[6] Jury being out on which sucked more.

[7] Really an impressive list. It folded out from inside the Storybook and trailed long enough to brush the ground. The contents of the manual were all crap but the presentation was top notch. Leather covers and vellum pages or what I assume is vellum because nobody has quite explained exactly what that is.

"Can you handle both on your own?" Jak wanted to know as he skidded to a halt.

"Probably not!" I called back in answer as I charged at our enemies.

The ogre's first swipe nearly took my arm off but I sprang away just in time. The troll's maul thumped into the ground inches from my foot so I scrambled back. With my sword extended, I lunged at the ogre, slashing a superficial cut on the outside of his leg. He jerked and crashed into the troll. The impact took them both down.

The two pushed and shoved as they got to their feet and I hoped, for a moment, they might turn their anger on each other and leave us alone. Fat chance. For when the troll levered herself upright, she threw her maul straight at me. I flung myself to the right and rolled to my feet. I spun around to see the business end of the weapon hit the side of Jak's sword with a clang that seemed to echo in the air.

I dashed over to Jak's side for the blow knocked him flat. The maul lay next to him and his eyes were squeezed shut. Jak still had his sword clutched between his hands and I saw the massive blade now bore an enormous dent. "Can you get up?" I asked.

"I don't know," Jak said as he finally opened his eyes. "I can't feel my hands."

"No surprise," I told him as I pried his fingers free of the hilt of the useless sword.[8]

Shaking himself out of his daze, Jak seemed finally to understand what I wanted. He let go of the sword completely and let it fall to the ground. "I liked it."

"It must have liked you too. If not, you'd be dead," I said.

Jak got to his feet, grabbed the hilt of the maul that destroyed his sword and tossed it at the ogre. I dropped to the ground in case the thing got away from him but the weapon curved through the air in an impressive arc. The ogre lifted his war axe and swung at it. The cutting edge of the war axe bit into the maul and cracked its head in half. The war axe also broke down the middle from the impact. The vibrations from all this

---

[8] More useless sword that is, with the dent and all.

crashing together caused the ogre to topple over again. The flat
side of the broken war axe came back to clobber him on the head
and he dropped senseless to the ground. The troll was too busy
being upset over her broken weapon to take notice of us.[9]

We found Keran waiting for us not far off. "Good to see you
didn't run off completely," I told him as we all snuck away, as
quickly and silently as we knew how.

"Wasn't going to be much help in such a fight," Keran said
with a shrug. "What did you want me to do? Bite them and get
chopped in half? Besides, you told me to run."

"You did," Naga said. She leaped from Jak's shoulder back
onto mine.

"I really liked that sword," Jak said.

"Now you have a new one," I told him as I unwound the belt
holding the magic sword.

"It does cut through the air better," Jak admitted as he hefted
it.

"I bet it cuts through everything better," I said with a snort.
"Maybe you'll be more likely to slice an enemy and not me."

"You're not going to let it go anytime soon, are you?" Jak
asked.

"Of course not," I told him.

I dropped it for the moment though and Jak fitted the sword
into the sheath already on his back.[10] We continued onward,
moving at a fast clip but not in a hurried manner. All in all, I
was pleased, about as pleased as anyone could be after facing
down an ogre and a troll. We survived the encounter for one.
Plus, I no longer needed to lug around a second sword. So a win
for everyone except the ogre and troll who were thwarted in
their quest for a meal. I could live with that.

In a little bit, when it got darker, we set up camp. When we
woke the next morning, it'd be only a few hours walk to the

---

[9] By the sound of her keening, you'd have thought she lost her first born. Did
I mention how much I hated keening?
[10] It took some adjusting of course. The sheath had been designed for a blade
twice again as wide. You could probably take the leather and make half a
dozen sheaths for normal swords.

border. Sure, the Evil Empire wasn't exactly a honeymoon spot. Still, it would be better than this place, with its all too fake designations of good and evil making it harder, not easier, to parse right and wrong.

I half expected someone, perhaps the troll from earlier, to disturb our sleep. But no one attacked us, no one came at us with their false moralizing, no one stuck a copy of the Storybook in our faces and told us they needed to kill us because a passage said so.

I knew better than to think this meant we were home free and naturally, Fairyland met my expectations. The place seemed to be very good at that. Ever since we left our horses behind, we stayed off the roads, taking a straight course through the countryside. This meant weaving through trees and pushing our way through the undergrowth so we didn't expect to see people. And yet, not two hours after we set off the next morning, we nearly ran full tilt into another band. Keran warned us in time and we dropped to the ground, happy to avoid confrontation.

Lucky for us, this other group didn't mind announcing their existence to the world. They crashed through the trees, stomping and cursing enough to vie with a small army. When they came into view, I counted four people. Perhaps they were on a quest as well. One of the boys looked like a prince[11] and I saw the circlet on his head when he came closer. Their conversation made it clear they were on a hunt for a princess. They didn't want to bring her back and make her queen though. Rather, they wanted to hand her over as an offering to the demon[12] terrorizing their state.

"The land is peppered with princesses," one of the boys grumbled. "How come we haven't come across a single one?"

"We did a bit back," another said after a pause. "I saw a tower."

"Why didn't you mention it?" the prince demanded.

---

[11] Pompous, overdressed and prone to strutting through the forest without looking at the ground. You know the type.
[12] If it was even a demon that wanted princesses. Probably it just wanted to be left alone. If so, I sympathized.

"I figured we'd find something better. You know how it is with princesses locked in towers. They've always got some nasty creature guarding them. I don't want to have to tangle with any beasts."

The prince smacked a hand over his face. "Gaston, you're an idiot. This is a quest. Of course we're going to have to do some beast slaying."

"Oh all right," Gaston said. "I think I remember where. I can take us back."

"We'll compromise," the prince told him with a sigh. We go a bit further but if we don't find another princess soon, that one in the tower is going to be the one. Her lucky day."

"I spotted the tower too," Jak remarked once the group disappeared into the bushes.

"One last heroic deed here and then we're gone," I decided. "I'll make us run if I have to but we're leaving Fairyland today."

"I expected you to argue more," Jak said as he led the way.

"I want to get there before those four bastards," I told him. "If they think they can just march around, kidnap some poor girl and hand her over like a bartering chip, they've got another thing coming."

"That prince and his friends are going to get it," Jak said to Keran.

The wolfhound snorted at. "I think I know what that look in her eye means by now."

CHAPTER TWELVE

I set a rapid pace so less than half an hour later, we saw the top of the tower peeking through the trees. From a distance, it looked five or six stories tall. White stone made up the exterior and a purple flag flapped in the air above the highest point.

We approached with caution, aware Gaston was correct in at least one respect. Invariably, something nasty and usually tied to the task by a spell, guarded Princess towers in Fairyland. When we arrived at the edge of the clearing, we saw no guardian. In fact, we saw only a girl wearing an improbably clean silk dress sitting with her back against the base of the tower. We found her doing something very stereotypically princess-like, weaving a basket out of grass.[1] Caution, and Jak, urged us to wait before walking over but I decided to approach.

"Hey, are you the princess who lives in the tower?" I asked though I knew the answer. Whoever thought I'd string such a sentence together? I suddenly recalled my joke to my parents about rescuing a princess on this quest and swallowed a laugh.

---

[1] Even from this distance, I could tell it would be a rather useless exercise. That thing would barely hold itself together, much less serve as a container for anything else.

98

I wasn't laughing when the girl finally looked up. She surveyed our group, her dark eyes sliding right over Keran and I. She wore a vacant expression, absolutely devoid of interest. Then she noticed Jak and bounced to her feet. "Hi! I'm Jazmin. Are you a prince?"

"Not exactly," Jak answered after a sizable pause.

"I suppose it doesn't matter. You are here to rescue me right?" Jazmin wanted to know. Before he could answer, the princess turned her gaze onto me. "Is this your serving wench?"

"That's it! I never want to hear that phrase in relation to me or anyone else ever again," I shouted, taking an involuntary step. "I'm going to kill her." I moved forward in half seriousness, waiting for Jak to stop me. When he didn't, I turned to glare at him. "You're supposed to keep me from doing stupid things."

"I'm not convinced this counts," Jak said as he eyed her with suspicion.

I grunted at this. "You might have better judgment than I like to admit."

"I think everyone has better judgment than you give them credit for," Jak said.

I ignored him and turned back to the problem at hand. Fixing Jazmin with a serious look, I explained the situation. "We're not here to rescue you from your tower. It doesn't seem like you need it.[2] We're here to warn you about the four guys headed this way. They're bad news. They want to spirit you away and offer you up to a demon."

"I see," Jazmin said slowly. "I will keep an eye out but there's nowhere for me to go."

This sounded more sensible than I expected and I was about to comment on it when Keran said, "Maybe we can help. Don't we need another member for our group?"

"No way," I said.

"You said we needed one," Keran pointed out.

"Is it too late to find Proctor again?" I asked. When Jak

---

[2] Someone apparently messed up the bit about keeping her in isolation. Maybe they forgot to actually cast the spell and the enslaved guardian wandered off. It's happened before.

glared, I relented. "Fine. How do we induct her into the group? Anyone have a specter I can wave over her head? Should I do a chant?"

"You could calm down," Jak suggested.

I seethed in silence for a few moments before accepting things as they were. I didn't like it but then again, I didn't like much about this trip.[3] Adding one more to our number like the prophecy said only meant maybe getting out sooner. So I bit down on my frustration and turned to face Jazmin again. "Alright, here's the deal. You're going to join our quest. We are rescuing you after all."

"I don't see why I should want that," Jazmin said.

Something in her tone gave me pause and I rethought my approach. I looked again at Jazmin and stripped away my preconceptions. Was I making the same mistakes I hated everyone else in this land for constantly making? The thought horrified me. So what if this girl acted almost precisely as the Storybook said she would? Might she not also be pretending? And so what if she turned out to be exactly as the Storybook decreed she should be? Did she not deserve to be rescued and taken seriously, both as a victim and as an agent with her own free will?

So I took a deep breath, looked Jazmin in the eye and started over. "Look, we came here to warn you of the danger. My name is Rahni Gazi. I'm a princess too. My companions and I are here in Fairyland on a quest unrelated to you. We happened upon a prince and his men who wish to rescue a princess and bring her back as an offering to convince some unidentified monster to leave them alone."

"Wow, very calm," Jak remarked once I finished.

"I'll get the hang of it eventually," I told him.

Jazmin's eyes narrowed and she looked first at me and then at Jak. Before she could say a thing though, the four boys I mentioned burst into the clearing and started toward us.[4]

---

[3] And by that, I mean nothing at all.

[4] This is precisely the sort of behavior that gets so many so called heroes killed. Charging into a clearing without any prior preparation could be

"How did they make it here so quick?" Keran asked.

"They must have a Nick of Time with them," Jak said.

"Are we supposed to know what that means?" I wanted to know.

"Anyone named Nicholas has unnaturally impeccable timing," Jak said. "Which, as you might expect, has led to an overabundance of Nicks. Unfortunately for them, their timing can be both extremely good and exceptionally bad. So it's a wash."

"Of course," I grumbled. "Trust Fairyland to be overloaded with bad puns."

"Maybe we should all retreat into the tower," Jazmin suggested as she backed toward the door at the base of it.

"Is your guardian going to come out soon?" Jak asked. "Interesting nothing attacked us."

"Oh, she's long gone," Jazmin said. She didn't elaborate and we didn't have the time to question her. Once we ducked inside the tower and she slammed the door, I again asked what became of her guardian. Once more, our questions came to nothing for we heard one of the boys thump on the door. They shouted for Jazmin to come out, saying they only wanted to rescue her.

"We can talk to them from the top of the tower," Jazmin said as she headed to the stairs winding their way up.

We proceeded onto the balcony as quickly as possible, the better to observe the four young men still hollering below without being seen ourselves.

"Are you sure they don't want to rescue me?" Jazmin asked after she leaned over to take a look. "They look precisely how I imagined a rescue party would look. Perhaps better."

"They might look properly coifed and dressed but you can't trust them," Jak said.[5]

Jazmin seemed to waver, not knowing who to trust. Perhaps when she heard the new arrivals planned to deliver her to a monster, she thought they would look the part. Perhaps they

---

suicide, unless it was me and I knew I could handle any threats coming my way.

[5] Not really his most persuasive argument, I'll admit.

should all be dressed in dark colors and carry around cruel looking knives.[6]

In any case, the appearance of these young men, clean and well cut, made her doubt us. Though tempted to be frustrated, I understood how it must look from her perspective. All her life, she'd been taught to look at the world one way. A few words from us would hardly convince her.

"How about we get them to admit it?" I asked.

"It's not I don't trust you," Jazmin began.

"No that's precisely it. And I don't blame you," I said.

"You don't?" Keran asked.

"It'd be the first time," Jak muttered.

"Neither of you are helping. Why don't you make yourselves useful?" I asked.

"Tricking a bunch of block headed idiots into giving away their plans? Shouldn't be hard. Especially as they're the villains," Jak said.

"Are they?" Keran asked. "They're on a quest too. Maybe they're good. Certainly, they seem to think so."

"Too confusing to bother thinking about," I finally decided after we all looked at each other and shrugged to indicate befuddlement. "Let's get this done. Worst come to worst, we go down and bash a few heads. We've still got that." Not waiting for the others to confirm, I went back inside Jazmin's room and grabbed a vase. I plopped the flowers onto a table. Then I marched onto the balcony and poured the water onto the heads of the four young men below. They all reeled and stumbled about as if I threw hot pitch on their heads instead of water.[7]

"Give it a rest," I called down. "It's only water."

The four caught sight of me and exchanged glances. The prince finally cleared his throat and attempted a weak smile. "Are you the princess?"

---

[6] As far as I could tell, this meant curved and serrated here in Fairyland. I had a couple of daggers fitting the bill. I stuck them deep into my boots, both for safe keeping and my safety. A shame because they were quite useful for cutting bread.

[7] One even cried out "Argghh" in the most affected way you can imagine.

Instead of answering this question, I went back, fetched another vase and emptied it over him. Only when I reduced him to sputtering and frantically trying to brush his hair back into place did I respond. "The princess is not coming down to speak with you."

"Are you her protectors?" the prince wanted to know. "If so, we mean her no harm."

"Give it up," Jak told him as he leaned over the railing. "We know all about your plot to offer her up as a sacrifice."

At this, the prince fell silent but his companion Gaston gasped in shock. "How did you know?" As soon as he opened his mouth, two of his companions tackled him but the damage was already done.

"Sorry for doubting you," Jazmin said.

"Easier than I expected," Keran remarked. "I guess I'm wrong. Maybe they are the villains after all."

"I suppose even Fairyland wouldn't consider offering someone up to be eaten very good," Jak mused.

"I don't think that's at all the case," I said. "I think it's a case of Everything is Better for Princesses. Fairyland didn't do a damn thing when his fellow townsfolk wanted Proctor to burn to death for the sake of its version of good. If Fairyland is giving us a hand, it's only because Jazmin is a princess and that makes her special."

"That's messed up," Naga commented.

"I've only been trying to point that out this whole time," I said.

"Look, don't be alarmed," the prince below said.

"Please, share your logic. We'd absolutely love to hear it," I shouted down.

The prince sighed and addressed Jazmin when she finally leaned over the railing to look down at them. "Princess, please, let us come up and talk to you. I know our plan sounds unappealing[8] but we mean well. It works out for everyone. We finish our quest, our people are spared the tyranny of the monster that threatens their lives, and good prevails."

---

[8] I'll say. He should try getting eaten some time.

"I think you skipped over the part where I'm sacrificed," Jazmin said.

"Honorably," the prince remarked.

"But sacrificed," Jazmin pressed.

"You're fulfilling your purpose, just as we are. I don't see what you have to complain about. We'll almost certainly raise a temple in your honor. It might be a joint one with a couple other martyrs and it might take a couple decades to finish, but still," the prince said.

"I don't know how you can pass up the opportunity to get a *joint* temple," I said. "We better open up the door for them."

It took Jazmin a half second to realize I meant this in jest and she cracked a smile. "Perhaps we'd better." As she walked away, she told us, "Provoke them into attacking the door."

"She has a plan right?" Keran asked.

"We're going to assume so," I said as I went to find more things to throw at the prince and his friends. As it turned out, they didn't wait to be provoked. By the time I came back with my hands full of projectiles, I could already hear the sound of blades hacking wood.[9]

A huge crack echoed through the air when the would be heroes finally broke down the door. As they rushed inside the castle, Jazmin came back, bearing an enormous coil of thick rope. She tossed the entire bundle over the side of the balcony. It uncurled as it fell down the side of the tower. The end, wound around a small knife, hit the ground with a thump. Meanwhile, I took a closer look at the rope itself, finding it to be made of a coarse brown material. "Is this hair?" I asked.

"I tried a lot of other things out first. You wouldn't believe the amount of silk I've torn to shreds. In the end, nothing else really held the weight. It's not my hair, if you're wondering," Jazmin said.

I looked at her hair, so black it almost hurt my eyes and then back at the rope. "I wasn't but thanks for the clarification."

---

[9] A shame for everyone involved. I found some pretty good things to throw and a few well thought out insults. I made the most of it and threw everything over the side of the balcony anyway.

"I don't think I can get down," Keran said as he put his front paws on the railing and looked over it.

Jak sighed. "I feel as though I've become a packhorse. All for the cause." He picked Keran up and started to climb very slowly. By the time he got halfway down, I heard footsteps as our assailants reached the top floor. Two heavy wooden doors, one opening into Jazmin's room and one onto the balcony, stood between us. Still, I figured we should probably get off this tower while they were occupied.

I didn't fear the four young men after us. In a square fight, we could chase them up and down the staircase of this tower without breaking a sweat.[10] But all our talk of who counted as good and who evil, at least in the eyes of Fairyland, made me nervous. I certainly did not fit the bill as a traditional princess. And I got the feeling Jazmin didn't either, no matter she might look the part.[11] I needed no delays a few hours shy of the border of this horrible place.

"You go first," I told Jazmin. "I'll bring up the rear and hold them off if they burst through."

Jazmin grasped the rope and put one foot over the side before looking at the empty space beneath her. "This seemed easier in theory."

"You're not afraid of heights, are you?" I asked.

"No, just a bit afraid of the ground," Jazmin said.

"You'll want to get rid of those shoes," I told her, pointing at the slippers pinching her feet. I hauled her back over the balcony and demonstrated how to get down, by keeping her bare feet planted firmly against the side of the tower and taking it step by step. When she had the hang of it, I vaulted back onto the balcony. She moved slowly, almost painfully so while the prince and his friends worked at the door with vigor, I stood guard with blade out.

This door must have been a lot stronger than the one at the

---

[10] Their bones and their pride, would, of course, be a whole other matter.

[11] Well, mostly look the part. She did have dark hair instead of blonde and brown skin instead of white but the flowing dress and overabundance of makeup matched.

base of the tower for they were still chopping at it by the time I went over the side. At this rate, their weapons would be as dull as training swords.

I reached the ground not long after Jazmin and gestured for everyone to head into the woods. As soon as we entered the shade of the trees, Jazmin stopped and shook her head. "What?" I demanded.

"I can't go in there without shoes!" she exclaimed. "Who knows what I could step on?"

She had a point and Naga said as much. So I turned to Keran. The wolfhound shook his head as soon as he realized what I had in mind. "No way. I'm no animal familiar, the mark on my forehead notwithstanding."

CHAPTER THIRTEEN

Half a dozen threats later, Jazmin sat on Keran's back with a fistful of his fur clenched in each hand. She bounced up and down as we went through the forest and he made no effort to ease the ride for her. After the second time he nearly knocked her off his back by charging under a low hanging branch without warning, I hollered at him to stop it.

"You're the one who suggested she come along," I told him after grabbing him by the ear. "Right now, I like her better than you. I'm this close to tossing you off the quest and letting her take your place."

Keran grumbled but at least stopped trying to punish Jazmin. He even pulled himself together enough to apologize when we finally slowed down. I saw no evidence of the prince and his band on our tail so there seemed no need to thunder through the forest, attracting who knew what manner of enemies.

Once we slowed, Jazmin released her death grip on Keran's fur and pivoted back and forth on his back to take in her surroundings. She seemed endlessly fascinated by every detail of the woods and kept pointing out perfectly mundane things, entirely undeterred by our lack of enthusiasm. Sure, the wonder of the nature was great and all but I didn't know anyone who could summon more than a grunt of agreement at repeated observations on the appearance of lichen.[1]

After a while, I blocked out her voice and turned my attention to more pressing matters, such as planning out the next phase of our journey with Jak. "How long until we reach the border?"

"We can make it by tonight if we cut a straight line there," Jak said.

"We need to find a village and get our hands on some boots for our newest member," I said.

"Some less conspicuous clothes would not be amiss either," Jak commented.

I heartily agreed for her dress, while pretty, was not practical for travel.[2] The trailing hem already tore and bore mud from being dragged across the ground and scraped against rocks. Twice already, she got it caught in a bush with thorns, forcing us to hack her free, which probably left our pursuers a nice trail to follow. On top of all this, she stood out, all decked out in bright orange, against the brown and green backdrop of the forest. I called for a stop and forced Jazmin to change out of her dress and into my one remaining extra outfit.

Jazmin had a couple of inches of height on me but my clothes fit her. When she finished changing, she stood there, tugging on them and staring down at herself as if they were the strangest things she'd ever seen.

"Look, they're not strange garments," I said. "Don't tell me you've never seen trousers and a shirt before."

"Yes, but not on a woman," Jazmin explained. "I confess I didn't know what to make of you when you first appeared. I decided your strange dress must be because of your low station."

"You can refrain from making such confessions in the future," I told her. "Now let's get going. The sooner we get you

---

[1] Or no, I'm wrong. We had a famed scholar back home by the name of Cesar who spent ten years studying one species of fern. What he got out of that lengthy period of study perhaps no one, not even Cesar himself, could say. Maybe he'd be delighted by Jazmin's interest in the flora. We certainly were not.

[2] Or maybe for life in general.

some shoes, the sooner you get on your feet, the sooner I stop wanting to murder Keran for being uncooperative. So everyone wins."

Perhaps deliberately to spite me, Keran tossed his head like a horse and kneeled down so Jazmin could climb onto his back. Only when he pushed himself up and started trotting did I let him see me smile, a sure indication I conned him. He decided to take it with good humor and continued on without protest. When we did come upon a village, Keran even volunteered to go nick the boots and came back with a serviceable pair.[3]

Not long after we left the village behind, we walked into the middle of a mysterious mist. Since this was never a good sign, I suggested a hasty retreat. Then the mist cleared a bit, revealing a pond. The water was remarkably still and so perfectly reflective, I half doubted it could be liquid at all.

As we stood watching, the point of a sword pierced the surface of the water and rose up, slicing through the air. When the hand on the hilt cleared the water, I took a step back. The others noticed my surprise and saw the hand grasping the hilt a moment later.

The sword stopped rising in the air with the arm halfway out of the water. It took me a second to realize this must be a reward for another heroic deed. "Seriously, why don't they have a normal way to deliver magical swords? Maybe the only thing magical about them is the supernaturally annoying delivery process."

"What do you think it's for?" Jak asked. "Oh, for saving Jazmin?"

"Too traditional of a reason for my tastes but I'll take it," I said.

"I thought you weren't heroes," Jazmin said.

"We're not," I assured her. "Or at least, not in Fairyland terms. The story of how we ended up on this quest is long and sorrowful."

---

[3] We never did figure out how he managed that particular theft. I thought for sure he'd get caught in the act. A huge hulking wolf creature didn't exactly blend in.

Keran snorted in derision. "Give it a rest. You're not the one with a real sob story. I'll bet even Jazmin has a better one."

I didn't expect him to take me so seriously and figured he was still bitter about having to carry Jazmin around. His words made me think we never got a straight answer about what happened to Jazmin's guardian. Before I could explore this line of questioning, the sword drew our attention again. It swayed back and forth as the hand holding it waved impatiently.

"I suppose we should take the sword," Naga said.

"Who gets to wade in for it?" I asked.

"I've been abused enough today," Keran said. "Plus, it takes longer for my fur to dry."

"I don't have another change of clothes," I said, looking pointedly at Jak, waiting for him to volunteer.

Before we could sort it out, a woman surged out of the water, splashing us all. She marched toward us as water streamed down her hair and over her face. "What is it with you heroes?!" the woman demanded as she stomped through the mud, squelching. "It's as if you've never heard the stories. If the Princess of the Pond offers you a sword, you damn well take it!"

"You're a princess?" Jazmin asked, taking in her bedraggled appearance and the way fury twisted her face.

This didn't strike me as the smartest thing to say, what with the woman holding a magical sword. Thankfully, the princess didn't notice. She threw the sword at our feet and sloughed back into the water without another word.

I couldn't really blame her for being cross. I'd be too if I spent all my time in the depths of a pond, handing magical swords out like a shopkeeper with candy on the fairgrounds.[4]

I picked up the sword and found it completely dry. Is that what made it magical? There were worse special features.[5] "I don't suppose anyone wants to go back to the village to steal a sheath," I said. Upon which a leather sheath broke through the

---

[4] Presumably, they got more business out of the deal. I had no idea what she got out of distributing the swords. Certainly not a sunny disposition.

[5] Also more useful ones but at this point, anything that did no harm seemed good.

surface of the water and came hurtling at my head. I ducked in time. Jazmin didn't. We all heard a wet smack as the leather slapped her in the face.

I thought for sure Jazmin would want to go home after this latest round of abuse. I certainly would. She picked herself up and lifted the sheath from the ground. "She's rather rude."

"On the bright side, we're one deed closer to the completion of this quest. And you, my lucky friend, you get a magical sword. I don't suppose you know how to use it?" I asked. The look on Jazmin's face was all the confirmation I needed. "Never mind. Just don't stab yourself."

"Will you teach me?" Jazmin wanted to know.

"Look, Jak. She's more eager to learn how to defend herself than you are. Tell you what Jazmin, if we don't make camp too late, your first lessons start tonight," I said.

"You don't want her to teach you," Jak warned. "Rahni can complain but she's the reason I never learned to handle a sword.[6] She has no patience. No one learns anything from her."

"I'm a completely different person now," I told him.

"I'll believe it when I see it," Jak grumbled.

I had plenty of plans to prove him wrong but I didn't get to act on them that night. We were practically home free, down to our last half hour in this forsaken land when the prince and his crew caught up to us. We only just pushed our way back onto a real road amid the dying light when they came galloping up on horses every bit as white as the ones we received after our first heroic deed. The third rule on the back of the map glowed but not quite in time.[7]

The horses overtook us and blocked our passage down the road. The prince patted his horse on the neck absentmindedly before swinging himself out of the saddle. Neither he nor his friends looked angry, merely exasperated as if dealing with mere

---

[6] Sadly, pretty much true. I'm also the reason a couple of my older cousins gave up. Even as a kid, I got over-enthusiastic with a sword in my hand.
[7] Which sort of defeated the purpose. Why even bother if it couldn't tell me about a threat until it was too late to escape it?

111

children not yet mature enough to see the world their way.[8]

"Look where all this foolishness got you," the prince said. I hadn't caught his name but what did it matter? He didn't have much of an identity so what did he need a name for?

"If you'd come with us like we asked, there'd be no need for unpleasantness," Gaston said with a shake of his head.

"I don't know what you call being eaten but it sounds pretty unpleasant," I shot back as I pulled out my sword.

"You'll want to put that away before you hurt yourself," the prince said, with a note of genuine concern in his voice.

This part cracked me. All manner of insolence, every insult in the book I'd have borne to see if there might be a different way of getting rid of these four. If he sneered at me or employed even the smallest modicum of sarcasm, I could have shrugged it off. But this, this proof of his smugness, the arrogance he wore like a cloak, set my teeth to grinding and my palms itching. He really believed I couldn't handle the blade I held.

I wasted no time with words or protests. I charged forward and bashed him upside the head with the hilt of my sword. His eyes rolled back in a satisfying way and I did my best not to be too happy about it.

Once the prince fell to the ground, his friends attacked. His horse also lunged at me with his mouth wide open. I wasn't about to let a horse bite my ear off so I stepped out of the way and smacked his flank with the flat of my blade hard enough to send him scurrying.

In the meantime, the prince's companions got their act together. Two stayed to subdue me while the other charged at everyone else. I ducked under first one sword and then the other, reminding myself that to get too cocky might mean a tragic death. But it was one thing to remind myself and quite another to believe it because neither of the young men fought with anything approaching real skill.[9]

---

[8] I agreed with half the statement although not on the identity of the children.

[9] They flailed about more than anything. Which might work in a battlefield with chaos sweeping across the plains. It certainly didn't work with me.

They did, however, have the advantage of height from atop their horses. Their steeds were much better trained than ours. Perhaps these horses only worked properly for princes and their retinues. In any case, I neutralized their advantage with a couple slashes of my dagger. The saddle straps came apart and both young men tumbled to the ground. In the time it took for them to sort themselves out, I sent both their horses galloping away and checked on how the others were coping with their friend.

As I turned around, he had his sword raised above Jak's head. I lifted my hand to throw my dagger only to pull back when it became obvious they didn't need me. All of a sudden, a force field shimmered into existence in front of the young man's sword. His blade hit the force field and he tumbled from the back of his own horse.[10]

---

[10] Rather pinwheeled you know. Never seen anyone fall off a horse with less grace.

CHAPTER FOURTEEN

This had no resemblance to the one spell Jak knew so it confused me, to say the least. In the midst of my shock, the prince I whacked earlier got up and tackled me. My instincts reasserted control and I hit the ground with a roll that got me out of his reach. Unfortunately, I did manage to lose my grip on my own sword.[1]

I released a curse at the darned thing as I got back to my feet only to see the blade flying at me. At first, I thought one of the young men picked it up and threw it at me but it moved strangely, not like you'd expect a weapon to fly. So I reached out a hand and the hilt settled into it. After that, it took but a moment or two of work to make sure the three young men facing me down were unconscious.

With them down for the count, I turned my attention back to the last enemy still at large. In the end, I didn't have to lift a finger. Before I got close enough to grab him by the neck, a glowing hand appeared in midair and slapped him so hard he

[1] Something I would not be telling anyone back home when it came time to recount my adventures. They didn't need to know about such an inglorious moment.

spun around.

I watched the glowing hand warily until it disappeared and looked first at Jak. "You don't have anything you want to tell me, do you?"

"Not that I'm aware of," Jak breathed. I already knew his answer, if not from his repeated attempts to learn some magic, then from the astonishment on his face as he beheld the fallen young man.

I next looked at Keran, who rolled his eyes at me. Finally, I fixed my gaze on Jazmin and asked the question she'd been avoiding. "What exactly happened to your guardian?"

"I got rid of her," Jazmin finally admitted after a couple of false starts. Each time she tried to ply us with an excuse,[2] I waved a hand to dismiss it. She didn't seem happy to be forced into this admission and I thought I knew why.

"What was she?" I wanted to know.

Here Jazmin took another stab at lying her way out. "A woodland spirit. Really a dull thing. It didn't take much to talk her out of her guardianship."

"I don't think so. I'm not quite so dull as your imaginary woodland spirit," I said. "How about I give it a try? She was a giant of some sort. That's where you got the hair for your rope. Now you and I don't have to consult the Storybook to agree giants are highly territorial and stubborn as all hell. How exactly did you talk her into leaving? I'd like a demonstration of your powers of persuasion. You'll need them to convince me."

Jazmin sighed and slumped in defeat. "I used my magic. I couldn't tell you how. I don't have complete control, you see." She nearly cringed as she said it. Before I could assure her we would not react as her parents did, Jak interrupted.

"This is great," he said, all enthusiasm now with the initial shock passed. "Forget the sword stuff you asked Rahni to teach you. I've got all the magical knowledge you could ever need right here. I'll help you control those powers."

Jazmin looked at us in surprise. "You mean to tell me such

---

[2] She tried to tell us her guardian wandered off one day. Then she said her guardian tripped and fell into a giant hole. Right.

abilities are not taboo where you come from?"

At this, Jak finally saw past his own excitement and came to the same conclusion I did. "That's why they put you in the tower?" Jak asked.

"Part of the reason. But Containment[3] hasn't worked on me. At first, I thought my powers might disappear and I could go back home," Jazmin said.

"And that's why you jumped aboard our quest," I said. "It's your only way out. If not this group of buffoons, it'll be another who finally kidnaps you. Or worse, your parents will return and find your powers not confined out of existence."

"Does this mean you could have magicked yourself some boots instead of riding on my back?" Keran demanded.

"Don't tell me you're still sore over it. Plus, I don't think mages can produce things out of thin air. Jak?" I asked.

"Some mages can. It requires a fair bit of practice. If she tried it without proper training, she might have lost control and turned us into gnats or something," Jak said.

"I know who I'd volunteer," I muttered. Keran butted me in the ribs with his head for this bit of insolence. This led to a bit of a scuffle, which I dare say I won. When it ended, I turned back to Jazmin. "Look, I'm not going to lie and say your abilities don't pique our interest. They might smooth the path of our quest. But we aren't taking you along for your powers. So use them if you want. Forget them if you will. The choice is yours. We're not your parents and soon enough we'll be able to toss out this damn Storybook and the rubbish in it for good. Decide what you want and it'll be good enough for us."

I said the right thing because Jazmin grinned and gave us hugs. Even Keran got one and tried to hide a smile. After that, we continued down the road, eager to leave before the young men we left unconscious came after us again.

We saw the border long before we reached it. A shimmering

---

[3] According to Jak and the Storybook, this is a pretty horrible theory pedaled by some idiot hundreds of years back. Basically, it said magical powers and other 'forces of darkness' needed only to be contained (hence the name) to be suppressed. You can imagine how well this worked.

barrier started at ground level and ended somewhere up in the clouds. From a distance, it came in and out of focus for it was clear and seemed to undulate very slowly. The Evil Empire and Fairyland joined abruptly, as if each land had its end sliced off before being pushed together.

On our side, grass grew in lush and perfect patches. Unnaturally symmetric flowers swayed in the light breeze. The dirt road under our feet hardly kicked up any dust and proceeded along in pleasing curves. The trees by the side of the road seemed completely free of disease and grew without unsightly blemishes.[4]

Not so on the other side of the barrier. Chaos reigned. Trees crowded into each other, fighting for light of a very different color. The dirt road, once it entered the Evil Empire, wound haphazardly back and forth on itself, led over hills and under entwined branches.

We stopped short of the barrier and peered at the other side. Keran finally said, "Are we certain it's better there?"

"I've never left Fairyland," Jazmin added.

Even I hesitated a bit looking at the grim landscape. I knew the Evil Empire would be the reverse of Fairyland in most respects. For one thing, their motto was a mirror of Fairyland's. In fact, a sign by the side of the road promised that "Evil Never Loses." Still, I didn't expect the effect to extend so far. If Fairyland looked idyllic, the Evil Empire seemed caught in an eternal winter.

But it was all appearance and artifice, just as with Fairyland. "It's no use stalling. If we want to get anywhere else in the Eigen States, we have to cross through the Evil Empire," I said.

"I suppose we don't need this anymore," Jak said, hefting the Storybook. He turned around and hurled it in the direction we came. We all watched it curve through the air, flapping in the wind. Then it fell, disappearing amongst the treetops.

"Not bad," Naga judged, echoing all our sentiments.

With Jak's gesture to give us confidence, we pushed through the barrier. I took the lead. Since it was my quest, I figured I

---

[4] Or really any character.

should take the symbolic first step.[5] The dim light lent a haunted look to the land. The bare trees stood out stark against the sky. And though I knew it had to be my imagination, I couldn't help but see them as tendrils reaching up to claw at the clouds.

On the other hand, I saw no princes who wanted to deliver Jazmin to a messy death here in the Evil Empire. At least, not yet. Most likely I'd hate this place as much as I hated Fairyland within a matter of days.

It didn't take nearly so long. Before allowing ourselves to rest, we moved away from the border. To make sure the princes would not be able to find us even if they ventured here, we got off the main road. Unfortunately, that meant striking out through the undergrowth, which in turn meant dealing with supernaturally irritating brambles.

They absolutely blanketed the ground, forcing us to hack our way through. This rather ruined the point of leaving the main road. Even an idiot would be able to follow the trail we left. Finally though, we struggled to a relatively clear area and made camp. The problems didn't cease there. Though none of us saw any animals in our trip through the dead forest, the sounds of the night were louder than ever. All manner of creatures, their voices and calls distorted in a maddening manner, shrieked and howled and hooted. Nothing live even came close, convincing me these noises were but illusion, produced through magic.

Needless to say, no one slept well. Finding out we'd have to slough through a bog did nothing to improve my mood. I looked out at the wet mess and reminded myself for the umpteenth we had to do this.

I took one step into the bog and immediately sank up to my knee. Jak grabbed my hand and helped pull me out of the mud. "Oh hell no," I said. "We've got to find a way around this."

"Yes definitely," Jazmin added quickly.

---

[5] The whole questing business might as well be a series of symbols. It couldn't hurt to lean into it.

CHAPTER FIFTEEN

In the end, the land didn't give us a choice for we found ourselves surrounded by the bog. It crept up on us during the night. Jazmin tried demanding to be carried but didn't get far. It was a terrible time for everyone. So when I decided we would find the nearest road and use it, damn the consequences, no one raised a cry of protest.

By the time we stumbled free of the bog, we were all caked in mud. Keran got the worst of it for his fur took in all the water and the debris and tangled with it. But no one looked ready for a ball, let's just say. In fact, Jazmin came to the point of tears. The mud in her boots squelched and some of the water on her body flew into my face as she sat down. "I have never felt so disgusting in my life," she said. All of us joined her for a break and echoed her sentiment with silence.

When the mud started to seep into uncomfortable places, Jak nudged me. "Did you mean what you said about following the roads from now on?"

"I certainly did," I told him. "My lessons are coming back to me. The countryside of the Evil Empire is absolutely littered with bogs and swamps like this one. Not to mention epicenters of spontaneous weather activity. Except here, it's not a couple of storm clouds. You get Pockets of Darkness appearing in midair. I'd rather not find out firsthand what happens if you get sucked into one."

"Fair enough," Jak said. "Every single part of me covered with mud agrees with you. I'm just worried we'll stand out."

I gave him a look. "You mean you don't think every Evil Empire citizen walks around looking as if she took a two-month bath in a deep well of -"

Keran interrupted. "Is there a river nearby? I'd like to get this off me and I'm certainly not licking it."

"We're stopping at the nearest Inn and all getting cleaned up," I told him.

"I want a bath as badly as you do but we can't possibly go to an Inn," Jak protested.

"Why can't we go to an inn?" Jazmin wanted to know.

"Have you ever been to one?" I asked.

"Doubt it," Naga said. Even she had a healthy coating of mud and was busy rolling in the sparse grass. If it worked for her, perhaps I'd give the method a try as well.[1]

"I've only ever lived in two places," Jazmin said.

"Then you're going to need a primer on Inns," I told her. "Bear with me. Most of this won't make a slight bit of sense. It sure doesn't to me. But there's something called the Law of Inn-Verses."

"What does math have to do with this?" Jazmin wanted to know.

"If you asked my grandpuppy, everything," Keran grumbled. "Budding mathematician until some Red Hood cut him down in his prime." His voice petered off as he lost himself in his thoughts so Jazmin turned back to me.

"That's the Law of Inverses," I said. "This is Inn-Verses. Two words, sort of. Stay with me here. Each Inn in Fairyland and the Evil Empire is a universe on its own and has its own set of rules. Stepping inside one is like going into a different world. Some Inn-Verses are milder than others. You get a hint of green

---

[1] I could hardly look more ridiculous than I did now.

in your skin and lose it once you leave. You grow an extra toe on your left foot. Then again, you might step inside to see everyone transformed into miniature stars for the space of the night."

"Uhhhh," Jazmin finally managed after a while.

"If it's any consolation, you're not supposed to get it," I said.

"This is not a good idea," Jak said.

"She's going to do it anyway," Naga pointed out.

"I see it's come to this," Jak said. "Even a mindless lizard can out-reason me. It must be all the mud in my brain."

With Jak now signaling his reluctant agreement, we headed down the road with every intention of stopping at the first Inn. Unfortunately, Doomsday was a bit intense for our tastes. It had a huge clock on the face of the building and inside, time hovered at about two and a half minutes to midnight on the last day of the universe. I wanted no part of that so we moved on.

The next Inn appeared a lot less forbidding.[2] Which is not to say it looked inviting, this Rosen's Bridge. The bulletin warned travelers against the occasional brawl. That didn't bother me. Hell, even the ballrooms back in Fairyland saw those once in a while.

Before we went in, the innkeeper came around the side of the building and hailed us. He was some sort of dwarf, but not a standard issue Fairyland one with a big beard, big axe and maybe even some soot from a forge. There was a delicacy to his features and sharpness in his mis-matched eyes, one brown and the other grey. At this point, I'd become confused about who should look ugly and beautiful where so I pushed the matter aside.

"What happened to you lot? Get pushed into a swamp?" he asked as he beheld us.

"Neighborhood brats," I told him, remembering we were in the Evil Empire and doing the best I could off the top of my head. But apparently it made perfect sense to the innkeeper.

"I had a cousin who always used to do it to me," the innkeeper said, shaking his weighty head. "She grew up to do plenty of bigger and badder deeds though so who knows? Perhaps it's an indicator of Evil. Why don't you come around

---

[2] No enormous and threatening clock at the very least.

back and I'll hose you down? Don't want you tracking mud inside. You understand."

So we didn't get baths but we did get clean. Tiriaq, the innkeeper, didn't lie about having experience with this sort of thing. He even went back inside to fetch the special scrub he formulated to get the smell of the bog out.

Keran squeezed out of his armor and we hung it in the stables to dry. He spent the longest time under the hose and Jak even gave him a hand scrubbing once he finished himself. Finally, Keran was fully satisfied and Tiriaq led us to the Inn. As soon as we walked in, I liked the place. After spending a whole week looking at nothing but human faces or at best non-human faces made purposefully grotesque, it felt nice to be amongst more normal circumstances. People of all species mingled within the bar on the bottom floor of the Inn. The two trolls toward the back weren't growling like animals but rather having an animated debate with a human and a griffin.[3]

Lest I get too happy, the laws of this particular Inn-Verse intervened. The woman nearest the door looked at us with suspicion. "Are you on a quest?"

"Yes," I said.

The woman groaned with feeling and shouted over all the other conversations. "We've got some questers here."

"Come on," a dragon in the corner said. "I nearly lost a claw in the last one."

The adlet[4] next to him chuckled. "I'll go easy on you this time."

I watched everyone reluctantly getting up from their seats, pulling clubs out of their belts and finishing off their mugs. "Wait, is there time to explain?"

"Sure," said the woman. "Most of the time, this is like any other part of the world. But when a group of questers come in, we have to change our behavior. We've got to have a brawl to

---

[3] Smaller than you might imagine. About the size of a large dog but way sharper claws.

[4] Human-like torso and canine legs as if a werewolf paused in the process of transformation.

release the energy."

"That doesn't make sense," Jazmin said.

"Try to remember it's not meant to," I told her as I seized a broken off chair leg from the wall, in imitation of everyone else collecting a blunt weapon. "Just stay behind me and duck when I duck."

"I really should get in the habit of asking before I let people inside. Ah well, we're due for a good brawl. Will someone remember to smash all the barstools? I think you'll all agree we need new ones. Leave the walls alone if you can stand to. James and I just redid the paneling," Tiriaq said.

"Aye, boss, we'll keep it as gentle as we can," a komainu[5] said.

"How gentle can a brawl be?" Keran asked.

"I guess we're about to find out," I told him. I took another chair leg off the wall and tossed it to Jak. "I don't think anyone is going to come after you with a vengeance. Can't hurt for you to wave it around like you know how to use it."

"I think I can manage to survive a brawl," Jak told me. "I've had practice. You start them often enough."

Tiriaq went behind the bar and grabbed an odd cylindrical piece of wood with a grip at one end. It looked like a club but sanded down too perfectly not to have another purpose. I nodded at him as he came out from behind the bar. "What is that?"

"It's a bat," he told me.

It certainly didn't look like it had wings and echolocation to me but I didn't have time to ask for clarification. The woman who first questioned us looked around the bar. "Everyone ready?"[6]

"No use dilly dallying," the adlet said. She spun around and hit the dragon next to her right in the snout. And so, the brawl began. As far as such things went, it was a friendly affair. Assailants joked with each other and asked after families even as they broke bar stools over heads.

---

[5] Large, muscular and rather like a blocky lion if you're not familiar with them.

[6] This had to be the most civil fight I'd ever witnessed. We'd be breaking out the tea cozies, whatever they were, next.

An ogre, much smaller and more graceful than the one who assaulted us back in Fairyland, ran straight at me with a bar stool firmly in hand. I saw no anger in his gaze and he even saluted me as he brought the end of the stool at my head. I leaped out of the way and jabbed the blunt end of my chair leg into his stomach. He went down with an oomph and let the stool clatter to the ground.

I hooked a foot through it, tossed it up and caught it. The chair leg I handed to Jazmin, who gazed around in understandable alarm. I'd been in enough fights to know these people fought without real malice. I bet she hadn't so it must seem as if we would all get ourselves killed waving stools and chair legs with such force. She had Jak and Keran flanking her though so she didn't need to worry.[7]

While they retreated to the nearest corner, I took a few steps forward, looking to head off any threats. First came a slender spirit creature with oversized wings. I sent her off with a bop on the head. Next came a vampire so I pointed at the sharp end of another chair leg I picked up. He held up his hands and retreated. The ogre I jabbed in the stomach tried to get up so I walloped him in the back with the stool he so kindly delivered. When he struggled up to his knees, a tall elf with skin several shades darker than mine nudged him so he smacked into the floor. "Come on Onard, you know the rules. Take four solid hits and you stay down. I walloped you twice and so did she."

Onard muttered unhappily but he stayed down. Meanwhile, the elf bowed at me. "Name's Monty. Pleased to make your acquaintance."

"How come you're not attacking me?" I wanted to know.

"The rules say there's got to be a brawl but no one is forced to fight. I usually sit most of it out. Always a couple trouble makers like Onard who like to test newcomers. Don't worry anyone is going to blame you for starting one. The regulars here are always hoping for a quester so they can settle old scores in a good natured way," Monty said.

---

[7] As long as Keran didn't run and Jak didn't accidentally hurt her instead. On second thought, maybe she should be concerned.

"The two trolls in the back did seem rather eager to go after each other," I remarked.

"Oh yeah, Tozene and Kayo sometimes have a go at each other even when there isn't a brawl on," the elf told me.

"It occurs to me the patronage of this Inn is uncommonly diverse, especially considering where we are," I commented as an octopus like creature rolled past with a ghoul wrapped up in its tentacles.

"Where did you come in from?" Monty asked. "Tiriaq hosed you down so there must be a swamp nearby? Evil Empire?"

"You mean to tell me we can use this place to get to another part of the Eigen States?" I demanded.

"Normally you could but..." Monty trailed off as what appeared to be an animated tree stalked over to us. "That's Gotor. She and I have an ongoing feud. You'll have to excuse me."

As the elf walked off to confront his archenemy, the brawl itself began to wind down. Which didn't mean we'd be left alone. The dragon who sat in the back knocked out his friend and came in my direction. I thought he looked a bit familiar but I didn't realize I knew him until he stood in front of me. This was Kofi, the head of the branch of the International Gold Fund back home. The regional branch served seven nations and I only met him a couple times. But I'd never mistake his lapel pin anywhere.[8]

"I must say, this is unexpected," Kofi said as he peered at me. "You wouldn't be Malhun and Osman's daughter, would you?"

"Who else would have the ill luck to get herself stuck on a quest?" I asked in turn.

"Ah yes, I remember you had a quick wit," Kofi said.

"Can't be her you remembered," Jak said as he stepped up next to me.

As the brawl hadn't wound down yet, I leaned over and swept his legs out from under him. Jak toppled backward and fell against a lamassu who helped him stand up. "Watch it there,"

---

[8] Mostly because it had a diameter the size of his head. I really don't know how any of his clothes stayed on with that much weight pulling on them.

she said before trotting off.

"And a temper," Kofi said with a laugh. "You and your friends must let me buy you a round of port. It's legendary. Tell me how your quest is going and I'll send your parents a message when I get back to the office."

It wasn't every day a banker offered to spend money on you so of course I agreed. At this point, the brawl was drawing to a close and I looked down at the bar stool still in my hand. "I understand I'm supposed to smash this."

"Please, allow me," Kofi said. He took the stool, dashed it against the ground and stomped on it. There was something incongruous about seeing a dragon, especially one as prim and proper as Kofi, whose tunic fit tightly around his broad shoulders, smashing a bar stool with such enthusiasm. I barely caught my laugh before it burst out.

I did an impressive job crushing my amusement until Kofi finally left us, called away by his friend Donna, the adlet. About the same time, Monty came over and I pointed at the bandage around his shoulder. "What happened to you?"

"Gotor got a bit carried away and stuck me with a splinter. She's more upset about it than I am. She tried convincing me to tear one of her limbs off," Monty said as he rolled his eyes.

"That hardly seems proportional," Jak said.

"It's not so horrible as it sounds. She can grow it back within minutes. Doesn't mean I want to do it. Silly arboreal," Monty said. Once he got done shaking his head, he introduced himself to everyone else in the group. "Now, where were we when Gotor interrupted us?"

"You told me there's no way to skip the rest of the Evil Empire by taking advantage of Rosen's Bridge," I answered.

"Aye and I'm sorry for it too. You'll forgive me for saying something so obvious but the Evil Empire is not a nice place. I had to travel through it myself once, though not on a quest. I think I still have a map somewhere. Hold on a minute." Monty departed briefly and came back with an Atlas. I immediately felt jealous. Why couldn't my parents have sent us off with one of those instead of our stupid map?[9]

Monty set his Atlas on the bar and pressed his thumb into the flat portion at the top representing the Floating Isles. A small knob popped out of the stone figure's chest. Monty carefully turned the knob and squinted. Finally, he made a noise of discovery and pushed the knob back into the figure's chest. A rolled up map sprang out the top of the Atlas and expanded to its original size.

I tried not to stare as Monty put his Atlas back into his pocket. I recalled the room full of maps back home and imagined how much easier our lives would be if I could take them along without fear of ruining them in the course of the trip.

While I pined, Monty spread the map out on the table and everyone gathered around to take a look. I recognized the basic shape of the Evil Empire, a sort of twisted half circle fatter at one end than the other. The larger map in my own pocket showed that as well as the matching half circle of Fairyland. Smaller details missing from my map were filled in here.

Monty tapped a finger on a spot labeled Rosen's Bridge. It sat not far past the border between the Evil Empire and Fairyland. "This road winding east is your best bet if you want to get out as soon as possible. Thing is it winds past two trouble spots. The first you'll pass in a couple days. You'll be tempted to stop for the night but don't. The town is a rat's nest of assassins and thieves. Avoid it by taking the smaller road here. It's the second spot you really want to stay away from." Here he moved his finger over something drawn to resemble a circular burn mark.

---

[9] Monty had a nice one too, the small figurine made out of stone instead of the usual wood. Otherwise, it looked like every other Atlas. It stood about two inches tall and featured a muscular man holding up a flat disc, a very rough representation of the Floating Isles. A very old myth involved the story of some god holding up the world on his shoulders. Nowadays, everyone except for the goofballs over at the Round World Society knew that a series of thick metal wires kept us floating in water. Plenty of people traveled to the edges of the world to confirm it. Anyone who said different was just delusional. In any case, people were stuck on tradition so everyone pretended not to know how wrong the figurines were.

"This, my friends, is the stronghold of the Evil Overlord."

"Definitely want to avoid," Jak agreed.

"Give it a wide berth," Monty said. "I don't know what the place looks like firsthand and I hope never to find out. Dangerous place, to say the least."

"How about selling us your map?" I asked.

"Can't do it," Monty answered. "But I can make you a crude copy. Should be enough to carry you the rest of the way." He got up and went to ask Tiriaq for a piece of parchment. As he drew, we went to see Tiriaq ourselves to arrange for the night's lodgings.[10]

By the time we settled everything, Monty already finished the map. It was nowhere near as detailed as the original but then, he drafted it in about ten minutes flat. Besides, we'd probably drop it into a swamp or two before the end of the week so it hardly needed to be a work of art.

We thanked him wholeheartedly but Monty waved us off. Then he told us he needed to depart. "Gotor insists on taking me to her house so she can patch me back up. None of my protests are working so I'll go to make her happy. Let me know if you're ever in Relaut."

"Nice guy," Keran commented. "I almost forgot not all elves are murderous racists."

"Oh no, are we in the lesson learning stage of the quest already?" I wanted to know. "Surely that should come after all the heroic deeds are complete."

"It's disputed," Jak said after some consideration. "Some think it comes after the heroic deeds. Others say the lessons run concurrent with the deeds. Of course, there are those who say the lesson learning process spans the whole course of the quest but I doubt you want to hear that."

"You're right," I agreed. "Let's drop the topic before we learn any more lessons."

Knowing we'd be pretty safe against marauders in the Inn, we

---

[10] He said we pumped some life into the Inn and gave us our rooms for free. The dragons would be horrified by his business model but I certainly didn't mind.

all slept well. Tiriaq sent us off in the morning with a hearty breakfast and well wishes for the completion of our quest. Kofi too, saw us off and promised to give my parents a highly embellished account of our adventures thus far.[11]

The landscape looked no different when we walked out the door. The trees were still as dead, vegetation still as uninviting and the sky just as grey. Nonetheless, I felt better.

We stayed on the road all day and the next. Just like that, we were halfway through the Evil Empire. We saw plenty of people and soon got the hang of how greetings worked. First of all, you had to strut, not walk, with confidence. That wasn't a problem for me. And when you met someone else on the road, you didn't wave. Rather, you raced to be first to holler curses. If you came up with a good one, people saluted as you walked past.[12]

All in all, I had a blast. Jak commented this would be my sort of place. Jazmin, of course, was too busy being horrified at the sort of curses and foul words coming out of my mouth to join in. Luckily, the haughty look that served as her best approximation for a leer passed muster.

The second night out from the Inn though, things started to go south. As darkness descended, we came up to the wall of a town named Den.

As soon as I saw the sign, I ground to a halt and pointed at it. "Is that what I think it is?"

Keran looked up and nodded curtly. "Yes, says Den alright."

"As in of the assassins and thieves Monty warned us not to get close to? Jak, you navigated today?" I asked.

"Yes," Jak answered slowly as he stared at the sign in astonishment. He took the map out, preparing to point out the road. "Look, I took us down the left fork this morning. I swear it should have taken us around Den!"

"Well something is not right here," Naga commented.

I had a nasty feeling I knew what happened. The burst of

---

[11] I thought seriously of asking him to carry back lies about the horrible condition we had been reduced to but finally decided I didn't have it in me to be so cruel.

[12] In case anyone wondered, I came up with good ones.

warmth from the map in my pocket only confirmed it. I took it out but I already knew it would be the third inviolable rule glowing.[13]

I traded my map to Jak for the one Monty drew us. As soon as Jak handed it over, I rolled it up and shook it a few times, utterly confusing everyone but Jak. When I unrolled it, I sighed. The map went back to normal, once again reflecting reality. The left fork in the road shifted back to its rightful spot, leading to the front gates of Den.

"I don't understand," Jazmin said. "Did the map rearrange itself?"

"It did," I said. "Just another delightful consequence of our questing status. It's a map disruption. You ever get the feeling something is just off with a map? Well that's because of this effect. Most of the time it's confined to small affairs. A river changing course slightly, a town moved an eighth of a mile to the west. It's more dangerous at sea than on land. A change of this magnitude is nearly impossible. Which is where the third inviolable rule comes into play. I suppose it's past time for it to come along and bite us," I said. "You and I are both royals. Jak is at least half."

"And me," Keran said with a sigh.

"What?" I demanded.

"I'm the heir to my mother's position as leader of the pack," Keran said.

"So you're a wolf prince?" Jazmin asked. "I wonder if it would make my parents happy to know a prince rescued me. Although you did very little of the rescuing."

"Putting that aside, you didn't think to share this information?" I asked Keran. "And don't give me any drivel about how you didn't expect it to matter. You know every royal adds to our improbability resistance." When Keran couldn't give me a straight answer, I nodded in understanding. "You thought it might be dangerous to bandy your identity about."

"It's not I didn't trust you. Well, that's exactly it," Keran finished lamely.

---

[13] The one about how probability didn't apply normally to heirs and such.

"Don't worry. It wouldn't have changed much. We'll have to keep on the lookout for more things like this." I waved away Keran's attempt at starting an apology and continued on.

"We're not uhh, staying here for the night, are we?" Jazmin asked.

"It's too late for us to backtrack to the fork. The longer we stay in the Evil Empire, the worse it'll be," I said.

"Everyone stay vigilant," Jak said. "Keep your hands on your valuables and your eyes peeled for assassins."

"We are all going to die," Keran muttered.

"Probably," Naga agreed.

CHAPTER SIXTEEN

We followed the usual procedure when entering dangerous situations. I took point, keeping one hand near my sword and another clenched around the hilt of a dagger stuffed up my sleeve. The front gates stood wide open and we saw no guards. Presumably few travelers ever arrived to be robbed or killed.

The town itself looked no different from any of the others we passed while in the Evil Empire. Everything seemed a bit run down though not terribly so. A very thin layer of soot from an unidentifiable source covered everything and shadows seemed to bend and move in impossible ways.[1]

We hadn't gone very far before a group of townsfolk hailed us. They walked over when we stopped. The woman at the head of the group smiled. "Say, we don't know you. On a quest?"

"That's right," I answered, looking her over from head to toe. She wore a loose fitting outfit of no particular distinction so I could tell nothing about her profession. And I really only got there in my examination before she walked close enough to slug me in the face. The ring on her middle finger scored a cut down

---

[1] The last might have been a result of the fading twilight and our paranoid imaginations. I didn't want to take chances so I watched everything carefully.

my cheek and I reeled back. "What the hell?"

"You're on a quest," the woman said, still cheerful despite her aggressive stance and actions. "I need to put you to the test."

When she lunged, I caught her arm as she swung at my face and used her own momentum to throw her to the ground. I pulled the dagger out of my wrist sheath, wrapped my arm around her neck as soon as she rose to her knees and shoved the point against her throat.

As soon as the metal touched her neck, the woman held her hands up and started to laugh. Since she didn't seem inclined to continue fighting, I let go of her and took a few steps back. The woman rose, turned to look at me and nodded in recognition of my victory. "I didn't expect such speed. You're a bit skinny for a fighter so I made what could have been a fatal mistake. I don't get the chance to be humble often."

"No, I can't imagine you do," I agreed as I looked at the blood on my hand after I touched my cheek. "It isn't often someone gets the jump on me."

"Probably the best compliment I'll get all year," the woman said. "My name's Rosa. I'll pass word around to my guild you're not to be touched. You won't have to worry about any harassment from us during your stay. I make no promises about the nasty thieves floating about. If you go down the road five blocks you'll come to a three-story building with a shop in the front selling garrotes. It's one of our guild houses. You give the shopkeeper my name and he'll put you up for the night, free of charge, as an apology for bloodying up your face. He's got a salve for the cut too."

"Fair enough," I told her. "No hard feelings." I think I surprised myself by believing it.[2]

Rosa and her group of assassins moved away, leaving us alone in the street. Jak came over to look at the cut and said, "It's shallow. Let's get to the guild house so we can get it cleaned up."

"Yes, let's," I agreed as I dabbed at my face with the wet cloth

---

[2] Honestly, I think it's because the whole thing was crazy. Shock erased all the anger I might otherwise have felt.

Jak offered me.[3] "I've had enough of this town already."

"Wait, why did she attack you? Was she an assassin?" Jazmin asked.

"Yes indeed," Keran told her. "A leader among them too if I don't miss my guess."

"The ring looked like a signet so you're probably right," I said.

Jazmin frowned at the receding backs of the assassins. "How can she be an assassin? She looks so normal."[4]

"This isn't Fairyland anymore," Jak pointed out.

"If assassins don't look like assassins, how do you know they mean to kill you?" Jazmin asked with some hesitation as if fearing we'd think her foolish. I forced myself to recognize she lived her entire life in Fairyland. The workings of life in other states would be as alien to her as the strange laws of Fairyland were to me.

"The point is to make it so no one can tell you're an assassin," I told her. "Or else it'd be a lot harder. No one is obligated to telegraph their intentions. The Storybook has no power here."

"I'm going to have to unlearn a lot," Jazmin said.

"It will probably be harder than learning how to use your magic. How's it going by the way? I don't understand what most of Jak is talking about when he gives you those lessons," I said.

"I don't either," Jazmin admitted.

"You could have let me know," Jak told her.

"It's hard to get a word in edgewise when you start off on your lectures," Keran said.

"No, it's fine," Jazmin assured Jak. "I've learned more in the past few days with your help than I have in all the time I spent experimenting on my own. In fact, I might be able to heal the cut for you."

"Don't worry about it. I don't want you to waste magic on

---

[3] Don't know where he produced it from. You couldn't count on him to be much help in a fight but he always did have my back on practical matters like this.

[4] For what it was worth, Jazmin was right. Average height and build, tan skin and brown eyes. Perhaps that's why I didn't expect her to slug me in the face. Guess some of Fairyland's foolishness rubbed off on me after all.

something this minor.[5] We may need you to be in tip top shape later on tonight so don't tire yourself out," I said.

"Jak mentioned a limit to the amount of magic you can do before collapsing in exhaustion and it confused me. That doesn't happen back home," Jazmin said.

"You mean magic is limitless? You can do anything you want as long as you can come up with a proper spell?" I asked.

"That's the way it's supposed to be," Jazmin said.

"There's no way," Jak declared after a pause. "There has to be a cost to magic. If not, mages would run rampant. If there are no consequences to what they do, mages from Fairyland would have taken over everywhere by now."

"We're going to stay on the safe side and have you preserve your magic," I told Jazmin to resolve the issue. "Unless this salve is not all it's cracked up to be."

Rosa was true to her word. The shopkeeper who sold garrotes let us into the back as soon as I mentioned her name and brought out a tub of the salve for me. As I applied it, I glanced toward the door leading back into the shop.

When Rosa mentioned the shop, I imagined they kept a few in stock. In fact, this shop only sold strangling devices. The sheer variety astonished me, even from the brief look I caught as we passed through. Some were made of wire, others of rope. I even saw a couple constructed out of harpsichord strings. Some included handles. Others possessed no grips for greater ease of concealment.

All of us knew this town was full to the bursting of assassins but I wondered how many there must be to sustain this shop. Or perhaps this place, being a guild house, served as less of a shop and more of an armory. It seemed the assassins in this town did little to hide their activities. Monty didn't tell us much about it since we weren't even supposed to end up here. I thought he meant assassins and thieves had a large presence here, not that they ran the place.

At this point, I hoped the assassins' guild really was in charge

---

[5] Also I figured enough people messed with my face today. I wasn't vain but even I feared the prospect of an extra nose or the loss of an ear.

for then we might get out of this town without being bothered again.[6] I'd consider it worth taking a punch. Unfortunately, I knew we would not be so lucky.

After the shopkeeper led us to our rooms, I pulled Jak aside and he nodded in agreement before I said a thing. "I heard what Rosa said too," Jak confirmed. "Given we only ended up here through a titanic stroke of bad luck, I have no doubt the streak will continue."

"It's settled then. Now we just have to figure out which room is the largest," I said, proceeding down the hallway.

All the rooms turned out to be approximately the same size, a size insufficient to comfortably accommodate all of us. I put Jak by the door so he could at least block it with his bulk if thieves came to bother us. Keran got to sleep by the window. I stuffed the gold underneath the mattress, which I rather thoughtfully ceded to Jazmin instead of seizing for myself. She didn't appreciate it as much as I thought she should, having the gall to complain about being unable to sleep. Rather than argue with her about the physical impossibility of feeling the coins through a mattress so thick, I tossed the blankets to the floor for her and flopped onto the bed.

Given that we were in a town full of assassins and thieves, I fell asleep surprisingly fast. I woke refreshed when Jak passed the watch to me. I sat in a chair next to the door, letting Jak sleep on the bed for the last couple hours before dawn. Not long into my watch, I got out of the seat and went to go take a look through the window.

The door squeaked open just as two darkly dressed figures came in through the window. I caught a glance of the lightening sky behind them as they swung into the room. Trusting Keran to control the situation by the window, I turned to face the door with both my sword and a dagger in hand. I lunged, taking the man who stepped into the room by surprise. Before he could blink, I had him pressed against the wall with my sword at his chest. I heard a vicious growl behind me and some thumps and

---

[6] Which is probably not the best reason to hope for assassins having run of a town. I can imagine it might be a bother for the ordinary citizen.

curses as the two other thieves realized we had been prepared.[7]

Jak and Jazmin also woke and looked around the room at the standoff. I put a bit more pressure on my sword and nodded at my prisoner. "What are you doing here?"

"Who are you?" the man asked.

"Look, I don't think you understand how this works," I said. "I have the sword so I'm asking the questions."

"We're from the thieves' guild," the man finally said. The door burst open and more of his compatriots started to come into the room.

I brought them all to a halt by hollering for them to hold it. Seizing the man by the neck, I pulled him away from the wall and along with me as I retreated to the other side of the room. "Keran, let those two join their fellows."

Keran snapped his jaws at the man and woman pressed up against the back wall one last time and walked away. They waited until Jak motioned for them to get moving before stumbling toward the door. When they joined the rest of the thieves, they made an even half dozen.

"You're not assassins, are you?" my hostage asked.

"Not that we know of," Jak said.

"Then what are you doing in one of their guild houses?" demanded the woman Keran cornered earlier.

"Until you lot burst in, we were trying to get a decent night's sleep," I told them. "What do you want?"

"If you're not with the assassin's guild, we have no quarrel with you," my hostage said. "We heard reports of a group coming into this guild house and thought you might be newly sworn in. I apologize for disturbing you but this isn't exactly neutral territory."

"What do you mean by neutral territory?" Jak asked. "You make it sound as if there's a war going on."

"You don't know?" one of the other thieves asked. "Say, we don't get many travelers. You wouldn't happen to be on a quest?"

"Rosa could tell at a glance earlier," Jak mused. "What makes

---

[7] Well, sort of prepared. They did still get in the room.

it so obvious?"

As soon as Jak said this, all the thieves released a noise of collective realization.

"So you encountered Rosa already. That's why you're here. It all makes sense now," the man still in my grip said.

Like the assassins earlier, they seemed to have relaxed so I let go of the man, slid my sword back into its sheath but kept my dagger out just in case. "I'm glad it makes sense to you but we'd appreciate some elaboration."

"Rosa always greets questing parties the same way. Most who run into her get kicked out of the city pretty quickly. You must have impressed her if she offered to let you stay here. We can tell you're on a quest because only people from faraway lands would be unaware of the war between our guilds. And really nobody comes to our land unless they're on a quest,"[8] my former hostage explained. He rubbed at his neck and took a few steps away.

"If they're liable to get attacked, I can understand why," I said.

"We really are sorry," one of thieves said. Then he addressed the man I caught earlier. "Darro, we should probably get back to the fight."

"Right, of course," Darro agreed. "If you stay here until dawn you should be alright. If anyone else comes to harass you, just give them my name." And with that, the thieves ran down the hallway and clattered down the steps.

"We're not going to wait until dawn, are we?" Jazmin asked.

"Definitely not," I answered. "I'm not sitting here and waiting for the next group to come barging in. It will be light soon enough. Jazmin, get your spells ready. Keran, buff your teeth or something. Jak, try not to kill any of us on accident."

To avoid misunderstandings, I kept my sword sheathed although I pushed the blade out enough it would be but a moment's work to slide it free. I kept my dagger in hand as I eased the door open and led us down the hallway. The stairs were dark so I proceeded carefully. I slowed my steps even more

---

[8] No one else unlucky enough, apparently. I believed it.

when I heard a rhythmic thump echoing up the stairwell.

CHAPTER SEVENTEEN

When we got to the bottom of the steps, I looked around the corner and saw the shopkeeper writhing on the ground, banging his legs against the side of the nearest counter in a bid to get out of the ropes binding his hands and feet together. I would have walked over to cut away his bonds if not for my shock that his assailants[1] left him almost completely naked.

Only Jazmin gasping at the impropriety shook me out of the surprise of coming upon this scene. "Diego, calm down, I'll get you free."

"I'll get him some clothes," Jak said as I walked over to free him.

"A great idea," Jazmin said, her voice muffled as she covered her face.

I cut through Diego's gag and he spit the rest out. "Thank goodness they didn't go after you. Rosa would have my hide."[2]

---

[1] No doubt the thieves we met moments ago.

[2] Perhaps literally? Monty relayed a rumor the assassins in Den liked to take less than sanitary keepsakes from their kills. I thought and Monty pretty much agreed it was all just rumor and nonsense but people in this town were turning out to be out of their minds.

"They did," I told him as I sawed through the ropes tying his hands together. "We convinced them to move along. I can be eloquent with a sword like you wouldn't believe."

"Also they figured we were neutral because we're from out of town," Keran remarked.

"That too," I admitted. Once I cut through the last of the bindings on his hands, Diego took the dagger from me and began working on his feet.

"Damn thieves stole the clothes right off my back and half my stock, no doubt!" Diego said.

Jak arrived and gave Diego a hand up. He also passed over some clothes and Diego clambered into them before bustling away to check on his shop.

"How is it?" I asked when he returned.

"Looks like you ran them off before they had time to get into the back room. Still a loss but not as bad as I feared. I'm in your debt for running those thieves off before they could take more," Diego said.

"Tell us how to get out of this town and your debt will be more than repaid," I told him.

"I fear you didn't come at an opportune time," Diego said by way of apology. "The feud between our guilds is ongoing but only rarely breaks out into such overt action. I'd say only a couple times a year.[3] This is serious provocation, breaking into a guild house and manhandling, shall we say, the keeper. I wouldn't be surprised if it breaks into all out war soon."

As if his words summoned it, the war he spoke of came in through the front. Really. Three dueling pairs crashed through the windows in the front of the shop and continued to fight even as the glass rained down around them.[4] I ducked instinctively when the crash sounded out though the glass didn't reach us near the back of the room. Diego shouted his thanks again before throwing himself into the fight, lending his muscle and my dagger to the battle. Good thing I didn't bring my favorite

---

[3] Oh yes, *very* rare.

[4] Raining down in a fine powder because that's exactly what happens when people crash through a pane of glass.

141

dagger along because I had no intention of wading in to get the weapon from him.

"It's time to get out of here," Naga chimed in.

"Thanks for the reminder," I told her as I pulled another dagger from my belt.

Jak made a gesture indicating the side of the room and I nodded, agreeing this would enable us to stay out of the thick of it. I motioned for everyone to go, saying, "I'll bring up the rear. Hurry up."

Keran didn't need any more urging. He darted to the nearest wall and followed it until he got to the front of the shop, upon which he took a flying leap out the hole that had once been a display window. Jak followed closely while Jazmin proceeded more hesitantly. She went so slow I had to prod her to move every so often. She took occasional glances at the brawl in the middle of the room and each seemed to freeze her where she stood as if the raised fists and vicious kicks were aimed at her.

Finally though, she got to the window and Jak gave her a hand out. As I waited for her to move out of the way, one of the combatants backed into me and lashed out with a fist on reflex. I caught his wrist before he could clonk me on the head and kicked out at his ankle. He tipped over and fell on top of the woman he'd been grappling with before he made the poor choice to involve me in their fight. I left them to their struggle and let Jak haul me out of the shop.

The noise of the fighting inside the shop masked the sound of the chaos out in the streets. Here too, members of the assassins' guild and the thieves' guild clashed with each other. Only they attacked each other in larger numbers, engaging in miniature charges and hollering at the top of their lungs as if laying siege to a fortress. I knew there were two sides fighting in the mess but I couldn't tell the difference between them once the two groups collided with each other.[5]

For our purposes though, it didn't matter. It was probably best to stay out of everyone's way. As we tried to avoid the worst of

---

[5] They didn't do anything helpful, such as wearing uniforms or all dying their hair a certain color so I had no idea who was who.

the fighting, I noticed out here the same thing I noted earlier inside Diego's shop. Sure, everyone fought viciously and shouted as if they wanted to kill but for all that, no one sought to. Most of the combatants clenched knives or daggers in their hands but few actually used them to take swipes at each other.

Even so, plenty of people got hurt. As I watched, someone broke her nose against the ground and a man took a punch to the head that knocked him clean out. Still, it seemed plain this wasn't a fight to the death. Which made sense if such brawls happened every few months.[6]

Despite our best efforts to stay out of the way of the conflict, it inevitably came to us. A large group of fighters spiraled into us, pushing us away from each other. I ducked and wove through the crowd to collect my companions, first yanking Jak from between two women so focused on charging at each other they did not notice him in the middle. Then I pulled Jazmin away from the side of a building she retreated against to get away from the fighting.

"Where is Keran?" I demanded.

"I last saw him making decent headway down the street," Jak said. "He moves pretty fast when he wants to."

"He'll wait for us up ahead," I said. "The two of you stick close to me."

"I saw a woman kick another in the knee and then pull her back to her feet. They were both laughing. Laughing!" Jazmin exclaimed.

We soon saw proof of this as we encountered another group of combatants who all stopped fighting to laugh at a young man when he tripped over his own foot and ran headlong into the side of a building. As he tottered around after picking himself up, the older woman he'd been fighting caught him and pressed him back down to the ground. "Take a rest over here. We'll finish our fight next time around."

"Is this feud of theirs for fun?" Jak asked as we continued on.

I glanced back to see the older woman throw herself back into

---

[6] I'd think it a problem for the regular residents of the town if not for the fact that I was beginning to suspect everyone here belonged to one of the guilds.

143

the fight and shook my head. "No, this feud is serious but I think it's been going on so long they've reached an equilibrium. The tension builds for a while and they release it in a massive brawl. The longer they fight, the less hostility and more respect they develop for each other until they're all doing it almost for show. It's meant to be cathartic I think. Then, the next day they go right back to hating each other as they nurse their bruises and set their broken noses."

"These people are out of their minds," Naga said.

"Truer words have never been spoken," I told her.

By the time we got close to the other side of town, it became difficult to find any empty space in the main thoroughfares. And still, people burst out of buildings[7] and out into the street, crowding against each other, throwing punches and hitting people they didn't intend to truly strike.

"Is everyone in this town either an assassin or a thief?" Jazmin asked after I shouldered a path through a particularly concentrated group of struggling bodies.

"It looks that way," Jak said. "I don't understand how it's sustainable. How do this many assassins make a living if there's no one around to pay them to go on jobs? And who the hell do these thieves steal from?"

"If this place made any sense to us, we'd belong here," I told him.

"Thank goodness it doesn't then," Jazmin said. "This is horrible."

I certainly had no love for the town but didn't quite agree with the censure in her voice. I might well rather live here than in Fairyland.[8]

Many bruises later, we arrived at the border of the town and pulled ourselves free of the worst fighting. Only a dozen

---

[7] Through windows as well. Whoever sold glass in this town must be making a fortune. They could just open their door on a night like this and listen to all the money make itself.

[8] True, the factions here nursed a hatred as irrational as the hatred of those in Fairyland for their neighbors. But at least the people here made no secret of it and could laugh with their enemies. Which is not to say they hated each other any less, only that they realized there needed to be balance.

assassins and thieves fought in the space we needed to cross to be free of this place. In the middle of it all, Rosa and Darro circled each other, moving warily. Everyone else gave them a wide berth and paid them little attention, as if it was a common thing for the two of them to pair off like this. During our approach, neither made a single move. They paced around each other, eyes never deviating to anyone else as if they were engaged in an elaborate and dangerous dance.

They noticed us at the same time and exchanged a glance. Rosa nodded, stuck her dagger into its sheath and relaxed. Darro did the same and turned to face us. "You're making your way out, I see."

"We thought we'd get an early start today," I said.[9]

"No worries," Rosa told me. "We understand. I didn't give you the warmest welcome."

"And then I brought a group bursting into their room to disturb their sleep," Darro added.

"What, did you think I'd put new recruits in an unguarded guild house?" Rosa asked.

"Unlikely, but there's always a chance you could be slipping. I only planned on sneaking in and neutralizing them but they got the drop on us," Darro said.

"I can't remember the last time anyone got the best of both of us in one day," Rosa told me with a grin. "I'd say you have a good chance of completing your quest, whatever it is." She took a few steps back and indicated we could leave if we wanted.

Reminded by this, Darro also stepped back and bowed at us. "Happy travels. One word of warning though. Further down this road lies the fortress of the Evil Overlord. I'd avoid it."

We thanked him for his warning and Rosa for giving us a place to stay.[10] And with that, we left Den behind for good. As soon as we passed them, Rosa and Darro went right back to their fight.

Once out of earshot of the fighting and clashes, Jak sighed. "If

---

[9] I think the overflowing enthusiasm in my voice really went a long way to convincing them I liked to rise before the sun.
[10] A grudging expression of gratitude from me at least.

not for the madness they're involved in, they would almost be normal."

"Yeah and the fact both attacked us unprovoked," Keran said as he came padding out of the shadows and loped along next to us as if he'd never been absent at all.

"It's hard to believe they're evil," Jazmin mused.

"They're assassins and thieves. Maybe they're not good people. Evil though? I don't think so," I said.

"But evil wins out here. They have an Evil Overlord as a tyrant," Jazmin said. "Their *motto* is Evil Never Loses."

"Mottos are not hard and fast rules are they? It's certainly not the case in Fairyland. I saw a lot of selfishness, ignorance and bigotry driving people to push others around. Plenty of the people doing the pushing talk about justice but I didn't see them practicing it. Maybe once upon a time the magic of the land ensured those who were good won out. Even that I doubt. What I do know is that it's no longer the case. Those kings and queens in their high castles decided they were good because they won. And so it doesn't matter anymore if what they *do* is good," I said.

"Something tells me you're right but everything I've ever been taught wars against it," Jazmin said.

"Of course I'm right," I said with a laugh. "I'm a downright philosopher, couldn't you tell?"

"Must have missed all the clues," Jazmin said after a pause.

"I'll think you'll be alright," I told her. "I really do."

Because we started so early in the day, we covered more ground than we planned. Enough so if we got up with the sun the next couple of days, we might make it out of the Evil Empire quicker than anticipated. Everyone greeted this prediction with exclamations of delight, almost as much delight as we felt halfway through the day when Jak proclaimed we successfully made it past the Evil Overlord's fortress. If stumbling upon Den was really the worst thing to happen to us in this segment of the trip, I'd be fully satisfied.[11]

---

[11] Worth a blow to the face. Told you I wasn't vain.

CHAPTER EIGHTEEN

About an hour after passing the Evil Overlord's fortress, we rounded a corner[1] to see five youths pushing, shoving and hollering abuse at each other.[2]

Now, the mere sight of people fighting caused us no alarm. Just this morning we saw a couple of giant lizards clawing and snapping their jaws at each other in the swamp. And then we stumbled upon two groups of travelers who seemed to have run each other off the road. We tried to mediate but only managed to unite them in fury so we moved on as quickly as possible. In fact, we encountered ongoing battles so often you could practically count off half hours with them. The last few days gave us a chance to observe just about every pairing imaginable.

---

[1] Come to think of it, rounded is probably the wrong term here. It was one of those sharp corners, the ones you can't see around until you've already made the turn yourself. The roads here seemed to have a lot of these. The better to set ambushes for unsuspecting travelers.

[2] Curiously, another effect of these sharp corners is it's impossible to hear around them. If an elephant sat around it and trumpeted her heart out, you wouldn't be blown off your feet by the sound waves until you made the turn. Someone should study that particular acoustic phenomenon. Could definitely be exploited.

So what made these young men and women unique was not that they fought but that they fought so horribly.[3] If we'd not been inured to strange sights, perhaps we would have paid more attention and avoided the following misfortunes.

I didn't notice the problem until we came right in front of the five. One of the girls wore a circlet around her head. Another a headdress. One of the young men boasted a full on crown far too big for his head and a shield every bit as clunky and useless as Jak's first sword. The last two also wore various royalty signifying garments.[4]

The map in my pocket pulsed frantically but I didn't need it to know we were in serious trouble. "We need to get away. This instant. Move!" I shouted as I pushed them back up the road in the direction we came.

"What are you doing?" Keran asked as he retreated sideways.

"They're all royalty. And so are we. Do you have any idea of the sheer amount of improbability resistance collected here right now?" I asked.

The others understood the extent of the problem too late. We hardly started our retreat when a gust of wind came out of the blue and knocked us over. I fell to the ground so quickly I didn't even have time to put a hand out to break my fall. Needless to say, I felt a bit dizzy as I looked around to try and figure out what was befalling us now.

Our surroundings became a blur, obscured by a cyclone of deadened leaves the wind whipped up as it wound around us and took us in its grasp. The wan light of the sun flickered in and out. The world continued to spin and finally, I gave up trying to understand. I let my head fall to the ground and closed my eyes

---

[3] Seriously, these were some impressively ungifted warriors. They fought like oversized toddlers at the age when they could barely keep their own balance, much less muster enough coordination to attack anyone else.

[4] Where did all these princes and princesses come from? How could it be just about every other person we met stood to inherit a kingdom? Even given that we were on a quest and counting at least three and half royals amongst on our own party, it still seemed statistically dubious. Were there even enough realms for all of them to rule?

as the wind continued to howl with such force and volume none of us even tried to communicate. Why bother when your words would be plucked away and sent into the void before you finished forming them?

What seemed like ages later, the wind finally faded to a breeze. The sun reestablished itself, shining with more vigor than before. In fact, the warmth of the sun beating down on my face woke me from the half conscious state all the noise and fury drove me into. I sprang immediately to my feet, inviting a headache so bad I spent some time muttering dire curses down on the heads of everyone who had a hand in getting me here. The others got up more slowly, thus avoiding the pain I brought upon myself.

That none of them said a thing even though I could hear them get up told me we were in trouble. So I knew, even before I looked, where the force left us. And sure enough, as soon as I caught sight of the fortress to our south, the map started to pulse out a rapid beat, as if I didn't know we were in terrible danger of having our heads separated from our bodies. Then again, perhaps the Evil Overlord who called this place home had more creative methods of dealing out death.

The fortress was a strange piece of architecture. Constructed out of pale stone, it was topped by a couple of decorative and ill-positioned minarets as well a lopsided dome probably knocked together when it became obvious the fortress lacked refinement.

The walls themselves were the best thing about the structure for even from a distance I could tell they were thick and solid. It might be a stylistic mess but at least it looked very defensible. If competently commanded, a fortress like this could hold out almost indefinitely.

In short, it seemed the sort of place a lesser lord might live. It didn't at all look like the stronghold of an Evil Overlord, except for a dark tower of unidentifiable material stabbing at the sky from the middle of the fortress. As far as I could tell, it didn't have windows, the walls of the tower being unbroken and smooth. The material glittered under the sun, which shown brighter here than anywhere else in the Evil Empire. The effect jarred the eye. You sort of expected the epicenter of evil to be a dark, sunless place, crouching in the shadows.[5]

"Well, this is not good," Naga said.

I turned my attention away from the fortress and toward our surroundings instead. For one thing, we were alone. Perhaps the other group ended up somewhere else. Perhaps the force that picked us up let them alone. Then again, perhaps they already sat in the Evil Overlord's dungeon.

"I think it's time for us to get going," Keran said.

The force dropped us off in the middle of a narrow road leading up to the fortress. Unsurprisingly, the path did not seem well tread. All of us trooped off the road and into the trees. Unlike most of the ones we'd seen since we came to the Evil Empire, these were very much alive. So too was the undergrowth so we proceeded a good distance into the forest before hiding behind a row of particularly tall ferns.

"We can complain after we get out of this. Given our luck today, we should expect the worst. This Evil Overlord probably has a lot of patrols," I said.

"So we sneak through the undergrowth as quietly as possible?" Jak asked.

"Unless Jazmin can do anything to hide us better?" I asked.

"I haven't taught her those spells yet. They require more finesse than the brute force methods she's been using," Jak said.

"I'll lead the way," Keran offered. "What do you think his patrolmen smell like?"

"I don't think anything as helpful as the Reek of Wrongness exists here," Jak said.

"Too much to hope for," Keran said.

"If you just help us avoid anyone and everyone, that would be great," I said.

As it turned out, these forests absolutely crawled with life. Keran kept his nose high in the air searching for scents. He found a new one every few minutes so we had to backtrack and

---

[5] But actually, it made sense. Were I the Evil Overlord in a land that never saw the sun, I'd sure as hell make sure I got a few clear days. What use being a tyrant with absolute power if you couldn't even get some good weather? And besides, the ruler of the empire didn't need to hide.

follow astonishingly complex routes in our bid to get out of the forest and back onto the road we'd been following before this fiasco.

For a while, I thought we might make it out without disaster. Then we heard shouts and screams of fear coming from behind us. "We were so close!" I shouted in frustration even as we stumbled through the forest in the direction of the shouts. Under normal circumstances, we might have proceeded with more caution but it seemed safe to assume these people were in mortal danger. Still, we should have taken more precautions. For our headlong sprint brought us into a clearing before we even realized it. The five royal youths from before stood in the middle of at least twenty men and women at arms.

I'll say one thing for the Evil Overlord, her or his minions certainly looked sharp. They dressed in dark clothes, not precisely identical but with thematic echoes involving red stripes. Their weapons had been painted to match their clothes and even the metal of the blades made black.

All in all, we faced a very bad situation. If the way they'd been pushing at each other earlier indicated anything, these five would be no help whatsoever in a fight. Jak would be only slightly better than useless. Keran could hold off a few but that left me responsible for fending off approximately two dozen minions. My improbable skill didn't extend *that* far.

As if those odds didn't already look bad enough, what sounded like an army of horses came stampeding toward us from behind, driving us into the middle of the clearing along with the people we came here to save.[6]

When the horses thundered into the clearing,[7] they raised a cloud of soot that hit us right in the face. It billowed up from the ground in increasingly thick waves, enough to blot out the sky. Only later would I realize it had been a spell. No way anything short of a herd of wildebeest could raise a dust cloud so thick. In the moment, I was too busy considering whether to try and

---

[6] Or, looking more likely by the minute, accompany into the grave.
[7] Incidentally, why were they riding horses through the forest at top speed? Seemed like a good way to kill the horse and yourself to boot.

make a run for it while still hidden from sight.

Unfortunately, I never got to communicate this excellent plan to anyone else. The dramatic arrival of the riders and dust obscuring the sky was all a distraction for an ambush. The soldiers standing around the edge of the clearing appeared next to us and seized us by the arms. The others were taken without much resistance and I only put up a token one, not seeing the use in sneaking off on my own. I struggled enough to make it believable and in the process shoved the smaller knife in my left shoe further down. I also managed to slide the knife on my arm up. That probably wouldn't survive a search but one could hope.

In the meantime, the dust settled with unnatural rapidity, revealing a group of riders as well turned out as their steed-less fellows. In the middle sat the man who could be no other than the Evil Overlord himself.[8] As the last of the dust vacated the air, slamming into the ground as if suddenly magnetized back onto it, he gave his cape a toss so it snapped once. For a split second before the cloth succumbed once again to gravity, he struck an imposing figure.

It almost, but not quite, made you overlook how the part ill-suited him. He was not physically imposing in any way, being average in every direction. He had mid tone skin not so different from my own and features that made it easier to imagine him being jovial than diabolical. In fact, the expression he wore now seemed more like a grimace than a sneer, as if he needed to concentrate on looking fierce.

The sneer vanished temporarily as the Evil Overlord waved a hand at the soldiers, an unnecessarily flourish as who else could he be directing? "Take them back to the fortress."

All in all, it seemed a very dramatic affair, more suited to a stage than anything else. And oh, how I wanted to comment on it. Jak shook his head at me. "Rahni, don't you dare. Don't do it."

But of course, I couldn't help it. I grimaced at him in a sort of apology before turning my attention back toward the Evil

---

[8] I could tell because his cape near about reached the ground even though he sat on horseback. You had to wonder if the horse ever feared tripping on it.

Overlord. "I should have guessed you'd be another failed actor. Some nemesis getting all the plum parts set you over the edge, did it? What doomed you? Nose too pinched? Eyes bulge out too much? Or maybe you just couldn't cut it when asked to create even the slightest jot of dramatic tension. That's it I bet. You can barely order your own minions around with authority. What does it say about your thespian ability?"

Even I didn't expect the man's violent reaction. He looked at me in anger for a couple of seconds before his mask of fury broke. He grabbed the collar of the cape and ripped it from his neck, attempting to dash it against the ground.[9]

"You're right!" sobbed the man I suddenly doubted could be the real Evil Overlord. "I *am* just a failed actor. They were all right. I could never get a starring role. I always got bit parts, playing a footman here, a servant there. They wouldn't even cast me as a henchman. I always had to be some disgustingly noble steward so boneheaded as to be willing to die for the master exploiting him for labor. I didn't have the face for it, they said. I thought taking this job would make a difference. They would all see my potential. But those lies I tell myself are falling apart right in front of my eyes. I can't do it anymore. If only I could act, if only I could command a stage with as much skill as I can lie to myself."

"You know, if you channeled your frustration, it might go better for you," Keran said from under the crush of bodies keeping him on the ground. "You just gave a pretty moving performance. Lots of pathos. I give it a nine out of ten."

No one paid any attention to him, us because we were surprised at this latest turn of events and the minions because the henchpeople were busy engaging in a collective eye roll.[10]

One of the women holding onto my arms shook her head. "Now you've gone and done it. This must be his worst meltdown yet."

---

[9] I say attempt because it ended up getting tangled on his sleeve and then, finally, sort of fluttering down.

[10] Ridiculous things must happen around them with regular frequency because it was remarkably synchronized.

Her partner, the one holding onto my other arm, snorted in response to this statement. "You only say so because you weren't present for the one after the Day of the Dreadful Groundhog Incident."

"Only time I've ever been thankful for a stomach flu," the first woman said. "I hear everyone got an earful from the boss."

"I escaped the talk thank evil. Patrol duty," her partner explained.

I followed the rest of their gossip only tangentially. I paid more attention to the alleged Evil Overlord, who bent over the saddle horn and sobbed directly into the mane of his horse. The riders to either side of him sidled over and tried to comfort him though his weeping only increased in volume when they patted him on the back.

As the conversation between the two women who had me in their grasp hinted, this must happen often because his ostensible henchwomen and henchmen took charge very quickly. One rider swung off her horse and came over to speak to us.

"I'm sorry you're seeing this," she said.

"I've seen worse," I commented. "Mostly when reluctantly passing close to the pens where we keep the most troublesome of my toddler age relatives[11] but still."

"No, I mean sorry because now we're going to have to kill you," the woman told us.

"We could forget we saw it," Jazmin suggested.

"That's not how it works. I'm sure you understand we have a reputation to uphold or else the entire system falls apart. Just because we're evil doesn't mean we can toss the rulebook[12] out the window! Law and order still matters. Or else it'll be chaos and we can't have that. Makes it much harder to enforce evil.

---

[11] Toddlers are an annoying species as a general rule. Toddlers with any relation to a royal family only more so. You wouldn't believe some of the antics the smarter ones get up to. In one memorable case, one ran an incredibly elaborate and successful candy pyramid scheme. I let it go on because I found it incredibly amusing but finally exposed the little rascal when the crying of her fellows began to bother me.

[12] I really hoped she meant this as a figure of speech. I'd really hate for there to be an evil version of the Storybook we'd been violating this entire time.

Today, it happens to be bad luck for you. I don't suppose it's helpful to know now but we planned on letting everyone we caught today escape. We do it every so often so people can spread stories about us," the woman said.

"What are we going to do?" one of my captors wanted to know. "There's the group still in the dungeons. We could let them escape."

"It's up to the boss," said the woman who told us of our impending demise. "She might not want to release people who've seen the new dungeons. I think she's happy with the latest renovations and wants to keep them for a while. She'll be in a foul mood so she may doom them all."

"Wait," one of the princes said. "So he's just a front man?"

"That's right. The boss doesn't have time to run around doing PR[13] stunts to maintain her image. Her time is valuable. And now she's going to have to deal with this. She'll have to prop up Ferdinand's ego, yet again, and she really hates it. I imagine she'll come up with a particularly painful death for all of you. Wouldn't want to be in your shoes, that's for sure," one of the henchwomen said. "Let's all get moving. The faster we get back, the faster she's finished grilling us for letting things go so belly up. Move people, move!"

"All you had to do was keep your mouth shut for once and let me try to talk us out!" Jak shouted as they hauled us away. "Once in your entire life!" The poor boy went apoplectic with rage and I don't think my shrug in response really helped matters.

"I think the real shame here is I didn't even come up with any good taunts. So cliché of me to make fun of his appearance. I fell right into that old trap. A regrettable slip," I commented.

My reaction being so typical, Jak could do nothing but calm down. He got frustrated at me so often, I understood it to be his resting state and it didn't affect our relationship. He could be furious at me for pissing off a visiting foreign dignitary but

---

[13] No idea what this meant. Proof of Repulsiveness? Public Rampaging?

laugh along as I repeated the joke to Ila later in the day.[14] By the time a henchwoman stripped away our swords and drove our two groups into separate carriages for transport to the fortress, Jak was almost complacent.

As soon as they slammed the door shut and turned the key, Jak looked to me. "So how are we busting out?"

"First we assess available resources. I still have two daggers on my person as well as Naga, who I assume can do useful things such as retrieve keys if properly bribed." At this, Naga poked her head out of my pocket to nod. "Jazmin has her magic, as yet undetected. Keran has his ability to swallow coals so we can volunteer him for the task should it turn out to be the death this boss woman ordains for us. Jak, I guess you have a few inches of height on the rest of us, right?"

"Not to mention an astonishing tolerance for the foolishness of others," Jak said.

"Oh, add slowly sharpening wit to your list," I told him.

"Let's focus on the task at hand please," Keran said. "I have no intention of dying here, thank you very much for asking."

"I can break us out of this cart," Jazmin said. "Gosh, I taught myself to bust past locks first thing. Idiots who designed my prison not only locked the door at the base leading outside but also the door to my bedroom. I couldn't even get to the non-perishable food items they stockpiled for me. I lived for three days on the snacks my little brother hid underneath the bed because he felt so bad about the whole thing. He said he'd break me out as soon as he could. I had vague plans of pretending to still be trapped when he did come around."

"Sounds like your brother is a decent kid," Jak said.

"Wonder if your parents will train it out of him," Keran said.

"This is not the time for one of your morale boosts," I told him.

"It's a legitimate avenue of inquiry," Keran said.

"I think so too," Jazmin said with a sigh. "He's spirited but

---

[14] In one case few years ago, I tricked a traveling mage to cast a spell on every single statue in the castle so they would shout curses at the King of Hitten when he came to visit. May very well be my finest moment.

then so was I a few years ago. I still let them trick me into the top of a locked tower."

"People, we are in the back of a locked cart. Yes, I had a hand in getting us into this situation but now I'm trying to get us out. The time for introspection and concern for relatives is later, when we are safely away from the clutches of whoever has us in her clutches," I said.

"I'm ready to go whenever the rest of you are," Keran told me.

"Except I don't think we should make our escape yet," I said.

"Come on," Keran groaned.

"Of course," Naga echoed.[15]

"The prisoners already in her dungeon?" Jak asked.

"We can escape and probably take our friends in the other cart along but whoever's sitting in her dungeon will get it worse because of us. I'm not willing to have that on my conscience," I said.

"I'm pretty willing," Keran said. "I don't see why there should be anything on our conscience. This boss they keep talking about is the morally culpable one, not us."

"In principle, I agree with your cynicism but I'm not standing by while murders are committed. If you don't want to come along, which trust me, I understand, I'm sure we can fix it so you escape first. Maybe our pretend Evil Overlord can even take some tips from our performance," I said.

"I don't like it but of course I'm sticking with you. You think I'd abandon you in a moment of crisis?" Keran wanted to know.

We all paused to look at him. "I hate to point this out," Jak said, "but isn't that precisely what you've done throughout this trip?"

"Technicality," Keran said, waving a paw at him. "You were never in any real danger before."

Mentally, I ticked off all the times we'd been in mortal danger and briefly considered listing them. In the end, I decided against

---

[15] I swear she actually sighed and lowered her head in frustration. I would need to talk to someone about her when we got back. Surely this wasn't normal behavior.

it.[16] "If it's settled, everyone prepare themselves to almost die."

"Almost?" Jak wanted to know. "This makes me a little nervous. Who knows how many minions are inside the fortress?"

"We have nothing to worry about. You heard them. The boss is going to make the usual mistake of dealing with us personally. We neutralize her and we're home free. Plus, the good thing about being on a quest is you almost certainly cannot die before you get to the final test. We're not even through with our heroic deeds yet," I said.

"You're bending the maxim a little bit," Jak pointed out. "*You* can't die before the final test. The rest of us though, are perfectly eligible to become Random Fodder at any time."

"For one thing, all of you are mentioned in the prophecy so you must be a little more important than that. Also, I can't imagine this woman's planning skills are anything to write home about. She sends out a neurotic failed actor in her place. Any fool could tell you that's a bad idea," I said.

"True enough," Keran agreed.

Jak shrugged. "I'm with you on this. Just wanted to point out it's not exactly a jaunt in the park. You always make it seem as if nearly impossible things are easy. It doesn't help you end up being right most of the time."

"I've said it before and I'll say it again. Everything works out better for princesses. Should be an inviolable rule," I said.

"Good to know," Jazmin commented.

When the sound of the wheels clattering against the road changed to a more rhythmic thump as we passed over the drawbridge,[17] we all prepared ourselves to react.

We continued past the drawbridge for some time before stopping. I thought for sure they would throw the back of the cart open and drag us out. Instead, they kept us waiting until we all twiddled our thumbs in boredom. Each of us pressed our ears to the wood in case the minions said anything useful but we got

[16] At least in part because I feared it would take too long to detail them all.
[17] We noticed the drawbridge earlier and it seemed they built it only for show. The fort didn't have a moat around it. Or even a dirt ditch.

nothing aside from the usual useless gossip.[18]

Finally, after what seemed like an age and a half, the cart began to move again. At first, it rolled forward slowly. Then, it swung around so fast, we knocked against each other. The whole cart tipped over, sending us sliding toward the back. Just before we hit it, the back of the cart flipped open so we spilled out onto a stone floor.

---

[18] Someone named Constance adopted a lemming and planned to raise an army of them. Evidently no one had the heart to tell her it was male and would be useless for producing an army on his own. Besides, lemmings were not exactly fierce creatures.

CHAPTER NINETEEN

I rolled across the ground and nearly went over an edge into a vast pit of ice. I jerked back in surprise. A glance around showed me the cart dumped us onto an outcrop jutting above the pit. The outcrop gave the slightest of jolts underneath us. The wall of stone blocking us off from the rest of the room made the purpose of the outcrop clear. It would recede little by little until we fell into the pit below.

Almost directly across the pit, the other cart tipped over and dumped the five young men and women we meant to rescue out onto an outcrop just like ours.[1] As they looked about in confusion, I turned my attention to the task of getting us to safety. I nudged everyone aside to examine the join between the wall and the outcrop and determined it would be the work of a moment to ram a dagger into the space and stop it from sweeping us into the pit.

Before I took out my dagger, Jak tapped me on the shoulder and pointed to the door on the other side of the room. A middle aged woman with spiked hair walked through and glared at us.

---

[1] They released a lot more wrenching screams, of course. You'd think the torture already began or something.

160

Unlike the would be Evil Overlord we met earlier, there wasn't a jot of drama in the way she carried herself. If not for the fact that she aimed to kill us, I'd almost be tempted to like her.

She commanded the room without resort to the sort of histrionics her stand in used. She needed no cape, no rearing horse, no flourishes to call attention to her. Just an abundance of confidence.

"These are the fools who broke Ferdinand?" she asked her people.

Before anyone could respond, I stepped away from the others and raised my hand. "Actually, just me."

The woman completely ignored me and waited for someone to clarify the situation. The henchman who got volunteered for this task finished by saying, "We dumped them over the pit for you."

"Good job," she said. "Don't think this means you're off the hook. But that will come later. First, it will be my pleasure to watch these troublemakers die."

I looked over the edge and down into the pit. It was not as deep as I first thought. In fact, we probably wouldn't even break our legs if we tumbled over the edge of our outcrop, especially with the piles of snow softening the jagged edges of the ice.

"It's going to take a while for us to die," I pointed out. "You might croak before we do at this rate."

"Did you just call her old?" Jak whispered to me. "Is that what we've come to?"

"Just an opening salvo," I hissed. "Probing her for weaknesses."

"Alright," Jak said, patently unconvinced.

The boss spared the other five prisoners only a cursory glance. They were busy cowering and pushing against the wall with their backs.

"You lot are more spirited than the usual groups," the woman said as she reached the edge of the pit. She kicked a lever by her foot and a section of the floor extended out over the pit. As she strode out onto it, I judged the distance between our outcrop and hers. Keran and I could make the jump when we made our break for freedom. First though, I wanted to get as much information out of this woman as possible. If we were going to break into her dungeon and free her prisoners, it'd be nice to have an idea what obstacles awaited us.

"That's because we're not from the Eigen States at all," I told her.

"I don't give a rat's arse where you're from," the woman[2] told me. "I need only know this. You upset Ferdinand and now I have to spend valuable time reassuring him he makes a good villain even though I'm appalled by his penchant for overlong capes.[3] Do you have any idea how hard it is for me to lie to his face?"

"Excuse me," Jazmin interrupted. "Aren't you the source of all evil? How can it be hard for you to lie?"

"Is she from Fairyland?" the woman asked me and nodded in understanding when I confirmed it. "Figures. Everyone in the place is delusional, down to every toddler and old biddy. Always crying out about the victory of good over evil and what not. And yet you don't even realize telling the truth is often the worst thing of all."

Jazmin might have to cock her head and give this statement a ponder but I knew she was right. Don't get me wrong. The woman was off her rocker but that didn't mean she couldn't also be right.

"This is all beside the point," the woman said. "Don't think you'll be able to distract me with your half formed questions. I have an empire to oppress. I'm a busy woman."

"You can feel free to leave the room and attend to your business. I mean, where are we going to go? I'm sure you've seen plenty of people fall to their deaths. Why would you need to watch us go to our doom?" Jak asked.

"Do you take me for a Storybook villain?" the Evil Overlady[4] questioned in turn, "So cocksure even fools may defeat me? Why turn my back on you when I have their example before

---

[2] Who I assume should be called the Evil Overlady? Why isn't there a proper term, come to think of it?
[3] A mark in her favor if you asked me, murderous tendencies aside.
[4] For lack of a better term.

me?"

"Why shouldn't you be sure of victory?" I wanted to know. "I thought Evil Never Loses. Or perhaps you don't think you're evil enough to win?"

"Please," the woman said, nearly scoffing at the thought. "It has nothing to do with being adequately evil. I've heard enough cautionary tales about underestimating a group of questers. Strange things always seem to happen around your kind. I plan on sticking around to make sure everything goes according to plan today."

"Speaking of which, what exactly is the plan?" I wanted to know. "You do realize this is a pit filled with snow and ice? Wouldn't you do better with a pit filled with fire or lava?"

"Where am I going to get on my hands on lava, much less something that will get and keep it liquid?" the woman asked. "And to think, however briefly, I thought you might have some sense. As for the fire, well, we tried it. Smoke does no wonders in enclosed spaces. I had a half dozen henchwomen and men faint from the smoke before I decided to look around for new options. We're giving ice a shot first. Shark infested waters have been suggested but I'll have to send away for those and that's a titanic bother."

"Have you thought about investing in flesh eating plants?" I asked. "They're relatively easy to maintain. They can't move so they can't be turned against you unless you're foolish enough to get pushed in. Just chuck them a troublemaker or two every once in a while and they'll maintain themselves."

"Glenda, remember that. I like it. Thank you for the suggestion. We'll try it out next. Don't think this means I've changed my mind about having you killed," she told me.

"Oh, I wouldn't imagine you changing your mind about anything," I remarked. "Which is why it's such a surprise to hear you'll be releasing the group already sitting in your dungeon."

"You're not going to get me to reveal anything with a few ill placed taunts," the Evil Overlady said.

And because I believed this and pretty much despaired of

getting anything useful out of her,[5] I said, "That's a shame. Jazmin, are you ready?"

By way of an answer, Jazmin shouted, "Get down."

Jak and Keran dropped to the ground and covered their heads but I had something else in mind. As I spoke with our captor, I backed up until I stood close to the wall keeping us on the outcrop. As soon as Jazmin raised a hand with a spell to knock it down, I dashed forward and took a leap.

I heard the wall crack and split behind me as Jazmin's spell blasted into it. My feet hit the edge of Her Vileness'[6] outcrop and threw myself forward so as not to flip off. I caught her by the arm and swung her into the open air above the pit as I lunged away from the edge.

She hadn't expected anything so sudden and didn't have time to react. Her Vileness hit a pile of snow and seemed no worse for the wear though I could practically feel the force of her rage as she struggled free of the snow and demanded someone run me through.

I sidestepped as the closest henchwoman tried to do that with a halberd. A well timed sweep with my right foot sent her sailing into the pit to join her boss. I managed to snag her weapon before she fell. The next man laid a hand on the lever controlling the panel under my feet, with a mind to dump me into the pit so I threw the halberd and cut the lever off right at the base.[7]

The man fell back and I ran to engage the other minions rushing in my direction. I knocked two into the pit on my way around to help the princes and princesses out of their dilemma. Meanwhile, Jazmin already broke through the wall and began firing spells every which way with surprising accuracy. Keran

---

[5] Other than a good idea of how to hold myself if ever I decided to go the evil tyrant route.
[6] Evil Overlady didn't really do it for me. Sounded almost derogatory. She should be locked up but didn't deserve being made fun of, as if she weren't a good villain. I'm all about giving credit where it's due. As long as it suits me.
[7] Sounds a little bit ridiculous, I grant you. I had to throw the halberd with enough strength and accuracy to cut through the lever while hoping it didn't bounce off. I refer you to the third inviolable rule.

made himself useful by making feints and lunges at anyone who tried to get close to her. Figuring they could handle themselves for the moment, I turned my attention to the lever controlling the royals' panel.

I looked at it uncertainly, not quite sure which direction to push it.[8] After fighting off another one of Her Vileness' soldiers, I grabbed the lever and pushed it to the right. Immediately, the outcrop began to retract faster and they all started to shout abuse at me. "Sorry!" I called back as I yanked the lever the other way.

The wall disappeared into the ground and all of the royals spilled onto the floor, panting in relief. I left them there and headed back around the outside of the pit so I could help my companions. I encountered several challengers on the way. Three charged me at the same time. All wielded spears so I beat a quick retreat. As I dropped to the ground to avoid another coordinated strike, I muttered a wish to have my sword back.

A noise very much like an explosion came from somewhere deep in the fortress but I didn't connect it with my offhand wish until an object blasted a hole through the nearest wall. Blocks of stones went flying across the room and one actually broke the heads off the two spears coming toward me. I held up one of my daggers to fend off the last spear but then, my returning sword pulled my hand to its hilt and the momentum ripped me about two feet into the air. It surprised me but I didn't miss a beat. With the sword still holding me in the air, I swung myself back and then forward to deliver a powerful kick to the jaw of my closest attacker.

The sword nearly pulled my arm out of its socket but I was happy to have it back in my hand where it belonged. When the magic that brought the sword back to me[9] finally wore off, I dropped to the ground and dove into the fight with particular vigor.

With sword in hand, it didn't take me long to make it back to the others. They had their backs together and did a decent job

---

[8] I should have paid more attention to what Her Vileness did. In my defense, there were a lot of things going on.

[9] Through goodness knows how many solid walls, no less.

165

fending off all comers, mostly, I think, because most of the henchpeople came after me. Even if they couldn't tell who posed the biggest threat, they had their boss shouting at them to get the ugly one with the braid first. That she resorted to such low grade insults pleased me to no end.

"Jazmin, can you surround all of us with a shield?" I wanted to know as I approached them.

Jazmin lobbed the clump of purple goo already sitting in her hands before turning her efforts to do what I asked. A short time later, she said, "It's done."

Given nothing changed, I hesitated to congratulate her immediately. Apparently Keran felt the same way because he asked, "Where is the glowing dome?"

"Mage shields are invisible, of course," Jak told him, so utterly exasperated I was glad I didn't voice my own doubts. "Why bother wasting energy to make your shield produce light? Not to mention it would show your enemies exactly where your shield ended."

While Jak explained, two people ran full tilt into the shield and fell on their backs, giving me a good idea of its extent.[10] "Less blabbing please. We need to go grab the princes and princesses and find the dungeon. Everyone stick close together so no one ends up outside the shield. Jazmin, how much abuse can this shield take?"

"I have no idea," Jazmin responded.

"Great," I said. "That's the sort of certainty I like." I started off at a jog and the others followed, even if Jak first released a heartfelt sigh. Everywhere we went, assailants bounced off the shield, ejected in all different directions. It amused me to see their looks of astonishment as what seemed to be a solid wall of air lifted them off their feet and tossed them halfway across the room. All the henchwomen and men had no choice but to peel away in front of us.

Unfortunately, no one gave much thought to what the shield would do to the royals. When we got close, the shield pushed at

---

[10] About seven feet in diameter, just big enough to more or less comfortably hold all of us.

them as well, sending the whole group sliding across the floor in a heap of tangled limbs. They slid for an impressive distance, knocking over quite a few of Her Vileness's henchpeople in the process.

"Ohh," I said with a wince. "Ten points for style though. Jazmin, Jak, options?"

"We can disable the shield and recast the spell once we get them," Jak said.

"No guarantee we'll all fit. Here, I'll leave the shield and corral them. You guys use it to ram a path clear to the door." I darted out from under the shield and headed over to our fellow former[11] prisoners. I dragged one prince to his feet with such force his crown fell off his head, rolled across the floor and dropped into the pit. It must have hit someone in the head for there was a yelp of protest in response.

"My crown," the young man said, making as if to lunge after it.

"Forget it," I said, yanking him back. "Get another one made when you get back. Don't give me crap about how it's a family heirloom. You want to live long enough to have children to pass heirlooms to, you do what I say."

"Who are you again?" the prince wanted to know.

"This is not the time for introductions," I told him, grabbing one of the princesses by the shoulder to haul her up. Confused, frightened and impressionable, the royals were easily coerced to start running for the door. They didn't question me when I said we'd be heading toward the dungeon, in too much shock at their repeated reversals in fortune to push back. I thought about leaving them here and picking them up on the way after we visited the dungeons but figured we best not risk it. I wouldn't put it past Her Vileness to have them put to the sword to assuage her wrath. She might sometimes seem coolly competent but the woman was also plum out of her mind, especially since I stoked her into a fury.[12]

---

[11] And perhaps future as well, depending on how this rescue mission went. We were herding ourselves to the dungeon after all.
[12] Strangely enough, I often had that effect on people.

We made it to the door without losing anyone to the
henchpeople who continued to come after us with fervor. Once
in the hallways, it became easier to keep them at bay. In the
front, the shield did its job, repelling all who thought to attack
us. In the back, we had something almost as efficient—me with
a sword and an abundance of annoyance. I let Jak, Jazmin and
Keran lead the way and served contently as the rear guard until I
noticed us rushing down the same hallway for a second time.
"What are you guys doing up there?" I demanded. "We've been
here before."

"We know," Jazmin shouted back. "We can't figure out
where the dungeon is."

"Keran, what do we keep you around for?" I demanded.

"There are a lot of scents in this fortress," Keran complained.
"I'm doing my best. I've never been there before."

"I doubt it's that hard to find. Wet stone, rotten straw and so
forth right? Like any other dungeon," I said, kicking an attacker
in the gut hard enough to make him retch.

"If you think it's so easy, you sniff it out," Keran told me.

Unfortunately for his dignity, I spotted a stairwell almost
immediately and led everyone down while Keran complained
he'd been on the right track.

When we finally did get to the dungeon, I understood why
Keran couldn't find it by searching for conventional smells for it
did not look anything like a conventional dungeon.[13] For one
thing, so many torches and lanterns hung on the walls we
needed to squint against the light. For another, the walls were
not slick with water and other unidentifiable liquids. In fact,
paintings tastefully decorated the walls and all in all, it looked
more like the upper floor of a rich merchant's mansion than the
dungeon of the tyrant of the Evil Empire.

"Is this right?" Jazmin asked when she came out of the
stairwell.

"We'll find out," I answered as I pushed forward. After a few
more hallways, all of which looked similarly benign, I cupped
my hands over my mouth and shouted, "Will any prisoners

---

[13] Not that I planned to admit he had a point.

please release some bloodcurdling screams?"

The answering screams came almost immediately, echoing through the halls and assaulting our eardrums. Then a scream came from our left, so loud we all reached for our ears.

CHAPTER TWENTY

"Calm down," I shouted in response. "We're going to get you out. Jazmin, would you?"

Jazmin unlocked the door by slapping a small handful of bluish goo on top of the lock.[1] One of the princesses made herself useful by grabbing the door despite the layer of goo and pulling it open. The room, like the dungeons as a whole, did not look anything like what you might expect. The furnishings were, dare I judge, tasteful in their simplicity, making the rooms neither too ornate nor too bare of decoration.

The girl who stepped out of the room was plainly a princess of some sort. If the way she held herself didn't clue me in, her enthusiasm in greeting one of the princes tagging along on the rescue mission would have made it obvious. I broke up their embrace by pushing them further down the hallway. "Make out later. Matters of life and death now." Both were scandalized by my comment but it made them move so I couldn't care less.

"How many people has she locked up down there?" Jak asked

---

[1] I got the impression magic involved quite a lot of goo. Messy business. Perhaps that's why mages often wore such appalling outfits. No big loss if subsequently ruined.

the princess we freed as we continued on.

"I don't know," said the princess, who the princes' shout of recognition identified as Cala. "They captured me with three companions and I've heard their screams."

"Have they been torturing you?" I asked. "You look fine."

"Oh it's been absolutely horrid," Cala said. "Don't make me repeat what I've seen."

"You've gone and made her upset," Basir said, patting her on the shoulder.

The girl did seem rather upset and if she truly did face torture here, I didn't want to dig up any bad memories so I let it lie. "Stick close to us and we'll get everyone out. As long as no one freaks out or charges off in a panic, we should all leave this fortress alive. Sound like a plan?"

"I like it," one of the princesses said.

"Good. What's your name?" When she replied I could call her Mina, I nodded at her firmly. "You help me keep your companions in check, alright?"

Mina smiled wryly, plainly aware of my censure. "Of course, my captain." I was too pleased to discover at least one of the people we rescued had half a brain to mind the sarcasm.[2]

Before we proceeded far enough to free anyone else, a short man with tightly curled dark hair burst out of a hallway to stop us. He bore no weapons but he planted himself directly in front of us with such determination I stopped short instead of booting him through a door.

"You can't go any further!" the man declared. "You'll ruin everything if you come in with your weapons and your righteous fury."

"Who are you?" I asked.

The man shook his head at me vigorously and refused to give me a straight answer, repeating only, "I won't let you pass."

"He's the interior decorator," Cala said.

Everyone turned to look at her.

"You've got to be kidding me," Keran said.

Evidently Cala didn't know her way around the wide end of a

---

[2] I rarely really minded sarcasm, even if not my own.

sarcastic comment because she shook her head. "No, I'm serious. He's the one responsible for making these dungeons so livable. Nice guy."

"I find that hard to believe given his choice of employer," Jak remarked.

"No, no," Cala said. "Thing is, only she would employ him. Turns out there's not much use for interior designers in the Evil Empire. Gamil turned up on the fortress doorstep one day hungry and she put him to work. A horrid woman to be sure but he's done good work for her dungeons."

"They were a crying shame when I arrived," Gamil said. "Dank and dark like you wouldn't believe. You can't have the source of all evil looking like a pigsty. It's unseemly. What will the other evil tyrants think? That's why I can't let you pass. You'll ruin everything I've built, I just know it."

I looked at the earnest expression on Gamil's face and weighed our options. I could knock him out easily enough but I saw no need to hurt such a harmless man. In fact, he had a shocking lack of malice about him, just like the actor I reduced to near tears earlier today.[3]

"Look, Gamil, is it? We don't want to mess up any of your hard work. Thing is, we've got a job to do. We have to rescue all the prisoners your boss locked away. You lead us to them and we can get in and out fast. There won't be any damage."

Gamil looked at me skeptically. "That doesn't sound like a good idea. She'll tan my hide. Or worse, throw me in the pit of fire."

"It's made of ice now," one of the princes told him.

"Beside the point," I said, waving for him to shut his mouth and let me do the talking. "There are a lot of us and only one of you. I don't think it will take a stretch of the imagination to assume you were coerced. Speaking of that pit though, I booted

---

[3] There seemed to be a bit of a trend here with our favorite villain and the downtrodden. It was a bit hard to square with her generally unfavorable disposition. I tried to imagine her being patient with a man like Gamil and couldn't. But it was hardly the time to puzzle over the mysteries of her personality and purpose. Right now, we needed to use Gamil.

your boss into it. And if I can do that to her..."

Gamil might be careless with his life in the defense of his precious work but he wasn't stupid. He got the hint and motioned for us to follow. "The boss has four more prisoners down here."

"My companions?" Cala asked.

"They're here," Gamil confirmed. "Tonlaq and Simah are in the same cell. Zosen is a bit further down."

"Are they all right?" Cala wanted to know.

"Their spirits were low last time I talked with them but they remain unharmed," Gamil told her.

We reached the Tonlaq and Simah's cell first and heard them both moaning with pain. "They don't sound fine," I commented.

"It's okay, we're here to rescue you!" Cala called to them as she ran to the door.[4] Her friends acknowledged her but continued to groan and shout in horror.

"What is happening to them?" Jak demanded. "Are they strapped onto a torture machine?"

"Oh no," Gamil said. "What kind of people do you take us for? The boss might be evil personified but she's not *that* cruel. It's their turn today to play host to the Vulture. Foul creature."

"Solid pun," Naga commented before I pushed her back into my pocket. We didn't need her right now.

I would have asked Gamil to explain how a bird caused them so much pain, but Jazmin already unlocked the door. When we yanked the door open, the vulture Gamil mentioned was nowhere near Cala's friends. It sat on a perch in one corner of the room while Tonlaq and Simah writhed with agony in their bonds on the opposite side.

I halted in my confusion, not sure exactly what to do given that I didn't know what caused them such pain. Then, the vulture noticed us. It turned its fleshy head and fixed its eyes at one of the princes. "Haider of the Aging Sands,[5] the woman you

---

[4] I nearly rolled my eyes when I saw her tugging at it. Of course her efforts did nothing given the lock and she got in our way, only delaying our ability to free her friends.

[5] Want to know where that is and how it got its name? Beats me.

call your mother stole you from the cradle." His eyes practically bulged out in surprise and he keeled over in a faint, hitting the ground with a smack because no one reacted fast enough to catch him.

The vulture turned his attention away and fixed his gaze on a princess, "Nihhad of the Aswat, your betrothed has always been a serial womanizer. It is delusion to believe he would change after your marriage." Nihhad's dark skin all but turned ashen at these words.

And just like this, the vulture went around the room, dealing blow after verbal blow. Some collapsed like the first prince did. Others shouted as if to drown out the words. All of us though, were transfixed, unable to move. Even I couldn't force myself to lift a finger to stop the damn bird from saying another word. And believe me, I tried my hardest when it looked Jak straight in the eye and said, "Jak Pai of the High Castle,[6] you will never be able to take back your home. You are weak, hiding behind your protectors and pretending you offer your fair share though you can but offer questionable advice."

Oh, I growled in anger but some force held me still so I couldn't even reach over and reassure Jak when he stumbled back a half step in response to these words.

Keran came under scrutiny next and the wolfhound cringed even before the vulture said, "Keran Silverback of the Coolsen Pack, you fear you caused the disappearance of your people. You are right."

Satisfied with the devastating effect it had on Keran, the vulture looked at Jazmin. "Jazmin Isa of Sivas, you were right in thinking your parents preferred the giantess kill you rather than letting you shame them with your powers. You are a problem they proved only too happy to lock away. And your brother? He will soon forget you existed. The effect you imagine you've had

---

[6] The basic story here is Jak's parents used to control a very small plot of land not too far from my own nation. Both of them and most of the others who lived there were mages, powerful enough working together to raise, get this, a structure called High Castle. Upon the death of his parents, Jak got kicked out by one of their more power hungry students. And that's how he ended up at our door.

on him is but illusion and dust." Jazmin exhibited more strength than I expected by glaring at the vulture defiantly even while tears leaked down her face.

Last of all, the vulture looked at me. I tilted my chin, daring it to do its worse. "Rahni Gazi of Savay, you disdain those who put up a front for the world but you are the worst charlatan of them all. You are no rebel. The independent streak you believe so central to your character is but a flimsy façade to hide your weakness. You think you'd strike out your own path no matter where life put you but the truth is you only have such luxury because you were born to royalty. In any other life, you'd fold and accept what you were told more readily than anyone else here. You believe you are in control and make that a point of pride. But it is false, that conceit, built on top of a lie. For the truth is, you control nothing at all, least of all yourself or your fate."

I couldn't deny its words would haunt me but I resisted the urge to think about them. I gripped the hilt of my sword as the vulture's hold over me vanished. While everyone else picked themselves up and tried to shake off the melancholy brought on by having terrible truths slapped into their faces, I charged over and grabbed the vulture by the neck. The bird's eyes widened and it made to open its mouth again.

Before it could say anything else, I clamped my other hand over its beak and held it closed. The vulture panicked, giving me scratches until I squeezed its neck hard enough for it to realize I meant business. The vulture went limp in my hands and I soon trussed it up like a bird about to go into the oven. Only when I finally dropped the vulture into the hay did I allow myself to wince over the wounds all over my arm and neck from the vulture's claws.[7]

I saw Gamil make for the door and caught him before he could slink away. He looked up at me sheepishly and stopped struggling immediately, no doubt recalling my efficient motions in sorting out the vulture.

---

[7] At this rate, I would have scars over half my body by the time we returned home.

"Jak, get over here and keep a hold on our friend," I ordered. "Jazmin, free Cala's friends. The rest of you snap out of it. Slap the unconscious awake, pick your jaws up from the ground. Move!" At the last word, I slammed the end of the vulture's stand against the wall. The stand bent in two from the impact and the wall sustained a gash that caused Gamil to nearly faint in abject horror.

Only then did I remember my promise not to do any damage. I might have apologized if not for the fact Gamil didn't see fit to warn us what awaited on the other side of the door. I went over to him and gestured at the vulture. "What is that thing?"

"It's a Vulture of Veracity," Gamil said, wasting no time being evasive, exactly the sort of behavior I applauded. "As you might have guessed, it has the feature, shall we say, of being able to see precisely those truths we try to deny."

"Aye, well I'd like to deny them a bit longer if it's all the same to you. Are there any more of them?" I wanted to know.

"Not in the dungeons," Gamil said. "Her Vileness keeps one in her own rooms."

"That paralysis, another delightful feature?" Jak asked.

"It usually only happens the first couple of times. I'm afflicted every time though," Gamil said with a sigh. "Or else I'd be free and away."

"Don't sound so wistful," I told him. "If you ran off, I'd personally drag your sorry behind back and lock you in a room alone with it."[8]

After I had Gamil cowed, it didn't take long for everyone to pile out of the room. He practically jogged to the next room, not so far away. As Jazmin and the only half recovered royals took care of bursting inside and freeing Cala's remaining friend, Jak and I took up positions in the hallway, facing the way we came. Consciously and purposefully, we avoided the topic of the vulture's words. There was plenty to say, too much to talk about

---

[8] I wouldn't actually do anything of the sort of course. Having been forced to stand there and listen to each of the cruel things the vulture said, I wouldn't subject anyone else to it if I could help it. Gamil didn't have to know and he cowered satisfactorily when I glared at him.

now.

"I don't understand why it's taken so long for her soldiers to come attack us," Jak said.

"They know precisely where we are," I said. "So they know we've added members to our party. If I had to guess, I'd say it took time to haul Her Vileness out of the pit and then some more time for her to organize everyone to come and yank our heads off. She knows we're not going anywhere soon."

"Great," Jak said.

"This is not even to touch on the fact we are adding more royals to our group as we speak. I don't even want to know what our improbability resistance is like. I'm sure we're causing famines halfway across the Eigen States,"[9] I said.

We lapsed into silence and when Jak opened his mouth, I could tell he meant to broach the dreaded topic hanging over us. I shook my head at him. "Later, if we make it out of this alive. There will be plenty of time to pick it apart on the road. It's going to be a straight run for the border, I think. She is not going to be happy about our escape."

"Fine but I think we will need to discuss it," Jak said.

"Yeah, yeah, I know. Every quest needs its moment of earnest soul searching," I told him. Half to make sure this conversation didn't proceed in precisely the direction I hoped to avoid and half out of genuine confusion, I demanded, "What is taking them so long?"

I turned to look and saw the door to the cell standing wide open. Cala and her companions embraced and stood in a circle talking enthusiastically about how much they missed each other. Or at least, that's what I imagined. I confess I made no effort to figure out what passed between them. I pushed through them to get to Gamil. "Why aren't you leading us to the fourth prisoner?"

He tapped his fingers together and looked away. "Did I say four? I meant three, truly. Always very bad at math. That's why I went into the arts and became such a big disappointment to my accountant parents. They used to do number based logic games

---

[9] Might sound farfetched but it had been known to happen before.

177

at the dinner table to encourage me to learn. It never worked."

"Sorry, no good," I told him. "We're not buying it."

Gamil blew out a long breath in his frustration. "You don't want to free the last prisoner. Just take everyone and go. It will be better this way."

"Better for everyone but the last prisoner," I pointed out. Since I made it clear I had no intention to budge on this point, Gamil released a sigh of long suffering and nodded at me. "I warn you're not going to like what happens."

Knowing better than to ignore a comment like this, I caught his arm as he turned away. "What do you mean? What's going to happen if we release the last prisoner?"

And with so much improbability resistance, it should be no surprise Her Vileness and her henchpeople showed up then. Gamil started and prepared to run to his boss but I grabbed him by the shoulder and shoved him at Mina. I handed her a dagger and told her, "Threaten him with this until he agrees to lead us to the last prisoner. Jazmin, Jak, Keran, you're all with me."

I struggled through the crowd of royals with the three in tow even as Mina got Gamil to lead us further into the depths of the dungeon. I planted myself in the middle of the hallway and watched as Her Vileness' people assembled so they blocked the entire hallway. They looked more apprehensive than fierce, holding up their spears and swords with something approaching hesitation.[10] They moved forward in pace with us as we retreated down the hallway.

"Jazmin, another shield would be nice," I suggested.

"Working on it," Jazmin reported back. She stopped halfway through the spell and looked about in confusion before tipping over and flopping to the ground in a heap.

---

[10] Now, one might wonder why they didn't think to bring weapons as useful as bows and crossbows. You'd think those would be very effective in such closed conditions and you'd be right. To that I say, the odds are already stacked enough against us, why would you want to make it harder for us to get out of this alive?

CHAPTER TWENTY ONE

Keran came forward to sniff at her face and confirmed she was just unconscious.

"Fatigue from the magic," Jak told me as he picked her up and put her over his shoulder.

"She did a lot of spells in quick succession," I agreed as I turned my attention back toward Her Vileness' people. "This could be a problem. I counted on her as our ticket out of here. You go back and cajole Gamil into moving faster so we can collect our last prisoner and try to find a different way out. Keran and I will hold them off here."

"Will I?" Keran wanted to know as Jak left.

"There isn't anywhere to run," I pointed out.

"True," Keran conceded. "I warn you though, I'm going to be very mad if I die."

"Don't worry. I'll be mad too," I said. "Where am I going to find someone to fill in for you in our questing group?"

Keran chuckled and shook his shoulders to loosen his muscles in preparation for the fight. I twirled my sword around a few times less out of habit than out of a desire to be doing something to strike fear into the hearts of the henchpeople.

When Her Vileness marched up to the head of her soldiers, she looked a lot calmer than I imagined she'd be, especially after the way she hollered during our performance back in the room with the pit. She appraised us with a cold anger as we retreated step by step and urged her followers forward slowly.

"I'll admit I underestimated you. It doesn't happen often," she said.

"I can't imagine that's true," I said. "The way you bandy confidence about, you'd think every other group you pick up would be able to turn it against you." From behind me, I heard a rhythmic clanging and didn't have to turn around to guess it came from Jak banging the hilt of the dagger I handed to Mina against the lock on the last door.

Her Vileness perked up at the noise and craned her neck to try and get a count of our numbers. Unfortunately for her, most of our heavily enlarged group stood beyond sight around the corner. I was just wondering whether she might ask what we intended when Gamil went ahead and answered the question, shouting, "Watch out boss, they're trying to fre—" The last couple of words became a muffled shout of protest and a thump as someone tackled him.

It was a surprisingly competent move but I cursed the unknown party who did it for while Her Vileness knew precisely what he meant to say, it left me in the dark. And I had a feeling what Gamil wanted to tell us was important. Given he seemed to fear freeing the prisoner, I guessed it would be good for us. But there was always a chance whatever Her Vileness locked up would do us as much harm as her. She might be a tyrant and harbor far too much enthusiasm for killing strangers but it didn't take much of an imagination to conjure up something worse. Her Vileness didn't waste any breath trying to talk us out of it even though I wanted very much for her to talk to me and give me a good reason why we shouldn't do this.

The narrow hallways made it easier than it would have been otherwise to face so many opponents. Improbably good[1] at this fighting business though I might be, no one could take down a

---

[1] Another function of the fact that Everything is Better for Princesses.

castle full of henchmen and women with only such an unwilling partner as Keran. We faced death, or worse, if that vulture from earlier came back and Keran could barely muster up the will to snap his jaws at the spears when they came close to me.

I grabbed one by the shaft and yanked it out of the hands of the man who tried stabbing me in the face with it, no doubt giving him horrific splinters. Deservedly so, if I could be permitted to judge. Once I had the spear, I handed it off to the nearest prince who wandered close to the edge of the battle as if eager to get in on the action. "Get this to Jak," I ordered and he snapped to it. The speed with which he moved made me feel pretty good about myself, especially given our dire situation and the events of the past couple of hours. Reprehensible to the extreme but after all, there was a reason so many people aspired to be and turned into tyrants.

The spears turned out to be less than optimal offensive weapons in close quarters and more of Her Vileness' henchmen got hurt hitting themselves in the eye with the blunt end of their weapons than by my kicks and blows. The ones I did fell served as good roadblocks, lying squarely in the way of comrades trying to come forward to take a crack at me.

When the process of subduing me took too long, Her Vileness yanked a spear from the hands of the woman next to her and stalked in my direction. Her people gave her a wide berth and without her needing to say a thing, focused on cornering Keran so she could come at me without hindrance from outside parties.

To be quite honest, that suited me perfectly fine. I wasn't worried, even though I could see the muscles on her arms born of years of practice.[2] I had full confidence in my ability to wipe

---

[2] I on the other hand, remained remarkably slender and physically unimposing, no matter how much exercising I did. People were often surprised by my speed and strength, which didn't insult me as much you might expect. After all, sometimes I looked in the mirror and couldn't quite believe I once took out a whole squadron of Flying Tresses (It's a long story, trust me. Suffice to say it was not my fault they attacked in the first place though it may have been my fault they tried to strangle half the palace guard.)

the floor with her though I knew better than to drop my guard. One of us already made the mistake of underestimating the other. I saw no need to round it out. To that end, I let her take the first couple of blows so I could get an idea of her skill.

As I expected, she fought well, moving her spear with precise motions unmarred by excessive showmanship. I matched her blows with parries cautiously at first, testing her strength without revealing too much of my own abilities though after what happened earlier, she knew I had to be stronger and more agile than I looked.

I heard the door to the cell of the last prisoner give with a crash behind me, followed closely by a whimper of protest from Gamil, who sounded as if someone heavy sat on his chest. Her Vileness noted the development too and gritted her teeth in frustration. She didn't let the anger showing on her face bleed into her movements. We continued to exchange blows and I pressed forward instead of maintaining a defense. I took control of the fight, getting enough hard blows in amongst the back and forth to determine the direction we took.

I could have ended the fight but I wanted to give the others enough time to free the last prisoner. Now I had vague plans of seizing Her Vileness and using her as a hostage so her followers would let us leave the dungeon.[3]

All of a sudden though, a spear came from over my head and clashed with Her Vileness' weapon. I ducked in surprise and flung myself to the side in case the other party meant me harm too. When I looked over, I saw a woman a few years older than Her Vileness engaging in battle with her. The way they looked at each other made it clear I had no place in this fight so I backed off. Jak, who still had Jazmin slung over his shoulder, came to meet me and answered my question before I voiced it. "No idea who she is. She grabbed the spear from me the moment we struck off her chains and started running in the direction of the fight. Everyone got out of the way quick."

"No one gave a thought to whether she might be out for me, I

---

[3] Hardly a plan that ever worked but I figured, you know, it might for supposed heroines.

see," I remarked as I watched the battle. The women seemed evenly matched even though the former prisoner had been in chains for a while. As I thought this, she pressed forward with a sudden lunge, forcing Her Vileness to take a few hurried steps back.

The prisoner we rescued didn't rush to press her advantage, biding her time. It occurred to me, watching them fight, how their styles echoed each other. I turned my attention away from their fighting and toward their faces.

"Jak, you notice anything about the two of them?" I asked.

Her Vileness rushed forward in an ill advised attempt to break out of the corner her opponent pushed her into. It was the first time she did anything remotely driven by impulse[4] rather than cold calculation, which only reinforced my impression these two had a long history even if no shared blood. Only that, I think, could make her lose her cool in a situation like this, with so much at stake.

From my position, I thought I caught the ghost of a smile on the face of the woman we freed as she caught Her Vileness in the stomach with the pole portion of the spear. The blow sent Her Vileness stumbling back until she landed on her back right front of me. I waved down at her as I placed the point of my blade against the hollow of her throat.

Acting rather authoritative for someone we just freed, the victor of the battle nodded at me to acknowledge this and then turned to face the bulk of the henchpeople. She stared at them for some time before making a dismissive gesture. "Out, all of you."

At first with hesitation and then with a bit more speed, they lowered their weapons and shouted at each other to retreat, the end result being the whole lot moving away from us, looking rather dejected. The woman smiled with satisfaction and called out, "Gamil, leave with them."

I heard a shuffle behind me but didn't look away from Her Vileness for fear she might try something. Gamil shuffled past us, keeping to the wall, perhaps in fear. I thought it might be my

---

[4] Well, in this fight at least.

fault since I threatened him until he took a few furtive glances at the older woman. Only when he went a distance down the hall did he call out and address Her Vileness. "Boss, I'm really sorry I led them to her. I didn't want to."

"It's alright," she told him. "Just go."

Given permission to run, Gamil wasted no time, hurtling down the hallway faster than I expected. The former prisoner watched him go and asked, "What did you tell him? He seemed afraid to look at me."

"I told him your escape would threaten his position, which is true, after all," Her Vileness said.

"Hold up. Are you two sisters?" I asked, looking from one to the other.

"Cousins," Her Vileness said. "Not friendly."

"I never would have guessed," I said as I took a few steps back and put away my sword.

"Probably should've introduced myself," her cousin said. "I'm Yara, the rightful ruler of this land. You can call her Ann."

"Give me a break," Ann[5] said. "You forfeited that claim when you decided to change course."

I preempted Yara's retort by holding up a hand. "Look, I'm sure your family drama is very interesting but frankly, I don't care. I just want to get out of here. So Yara, if you want help locking her into a cell, I'm all for it. But then we're going."

"You mean you don't want to stick around to watch Yara take a bludgeon to the sanctity of the Evil Empire?" Ann asked. She was no less sullen when we tossed her into a cell and slammed the door shut after her.

"Look, I know I might not be the brightest flame in the room[6] but won't her people come back here and free her?" one of the princes asked.

"Don't worry about them. They belong to me now," Yara said.

---

[5] It seemed a very short and innocuous name for someone who terrorized an entire nation but whatever.
[6] At least he knew. There's something to be said for self awareness of this sort.

She seemed pretty confident on this point so I didn't question but Cala and her companions exchanged a few glances in disbelief. As far as I could tell, this boded well for their chances of survival upon leaving the fortress. We let Yara lead the way out of the dungeons and up the stairs, figuring if anyone would be stuck full of spears, it would be her and not us.

At the top of the staircase though, we saw Ann's henchmen and women all assembled in a line with their heads bowed in obedience. Yara didn't give them so much as a second glance, leading us through the fortress with the natural ease of someone who knew its twists and turns. She brought us to the front gates of the fortress and had them thrown open.

Most of the group spilled out into the bright sunshine and started down the road immediately, calling back their thanks or their goodbyes as they sauntered away.

"I guess they've forgotten about the vulture," Jak said.

"A mercy, I think," Keran said.

"I didn't know you cared so much about their wellbeing," Jak said.

"I don't. I'm talking about it being a mercy for us," Keran clarified. "Can you imagine having to listen to their groans?"

"That sounds more like the friendly wolfhound I know," I told him.

"You're a questing party I assume?" Yara asked.

"Unfortunately yes," I said. "Even more unfortunately, it's mine."

"I figured," Yara said. "Before you continue on your quest, I have some advice for you."

"You've missed the boat," I told her. "The mentor phase of this quest came and went a long time ago. We're no longer accepting any more bids for older mentors with dubious wisdom to share."

"I'm no mentor. I have no prophecies for you. I'm just a temporary ally if you must place me somewhere. You need only listen to me for a few minutes and I'll be out of your quest for good," Yara said.

It wasn't worth fighting her over it and she did give us a

hand[7] so I nodded for her to begin. "Make it quick please."

"I'll do my best," Yara said with a smile I couldn't begin to read. "You've been wondering, I'm sure, why your parents sent you on this quest against your will." At this, I looked at her suspiciously, wondering how she knew this.

"And just as I started to think not enough weird things were happening to us," Keran remarked.

"Your parents gave you a reason and it's true in its own way. But it's not the only reason. Truth is, you had to come on this quest because you needed to end up here," Yara said.

"Come again," I said. "Are you trying to tell me my parents sent me on this quest to break you out of your own dungeon?"

"No, it has nothing specifically to do with you or me or anyone else who will be swept into the whole mess. There are forces beyond our control at work here. We are all of us caught in the middle of a Realignment, the shifting of the balance between good and evil," Yara said.

"I'm beginning to think Gamil told us the truth after all," Jak whispered to me.

"And I'm beginning to think Jak is right. You might want to get to the point before I decide we should back away slowly or let your cousin loose. Because I'm telling you, there were times when she seemed more lucid than you sound right now," I told Yara.

She looked at us and apparently decided to try a different tact. "Have you ever wondered why in all the Eigen States, only Fairyland and the Evil Empire are constant? They shift, they grow and they shrink but are always present and balanced. Strange, no?"

"Migraine inducing," I admitted. "But then again, so is almost everything about the Eigen States."[8]

"I'll grant you there is very little about the Eigen States anyone can be sure of, especially someone who lives here. Still, your parents have a hint of the reason for the strangeness of

---

[7] Actually, we gave her a hand but I saw no reason to belabor the point.
[8] Sometimes literally for there were states filled exclusively with bright flashing lights and ear piercing sounds.

these two states and so do all the others reviving the old traditions back home," Yara said.

I admit I still thought she had a few corkscrews loose in her noggin but the last comment made me look at her with more suspicion than ever. How could she know this? "You mean to tell me there's a reason beyond the dying gasp of reactionary old farts who can't keep up with the times?"[9]

"Much more," Yara agreed. "You see, the Evil Empire and Fairyland are not simply individual states. They are touchstones by which good and evil are judged."

"Okay, I was with you, sort of, until the last bit, when you made it seem as if good and evil are absolutes," I told her.

"You're not wrong to be skeptical. Still, whether you like it or not, there is something unique about these two states. The changes you've seen in them are a sign that the balance between good and evil has been tipping, now in one direction, now in another. That's because of Realignment. History has a way of repeating itself if you widen the scope of time. It is only a recent innovation to say time travels in a straight line, you know. The older myths are closer to the truth. Time goes in a circle. Everything repeats itself, one way or the other. Every four hundred seventeen and a half years, the definitions of good and evil reset themselves," Yara said.

"Seems like an odd number," Keran remarked after a pause.

"No odder than any other number," Yara pointed out. "Why should the cycle occur according to what you perceive as a round number?"

"Just because you've got a point there does not mean we're buying the rest of what you have to sell," I told her.

"That's fine. Keep listening. Now, I said the two states serve as a touchstone but perhaps it's more appropriate to say they act as a record for who won and who lost the last battle to determine the paths of good and evil. Each time the cycle completes itself,

---

[9] I didn't mean this as a joke. There really had been a push for revival of tradition back home but I thought it was the old guard trying their darnedest to push back against the inevitable march of time. Holding onto power by their fingertips and all.

the opportunity arises anew to redefine them."

"Why, that's ridiculous," Jak said. "You're saying what, the winners get to call themselves good, the losers get labeled evil and each holds sway in one of the two static states?"

"Precisely," Yara agreed.

"Hmm, actually makes a lot of sense," I admitted.[10]

"Don't tell me you're taking this seriously," Jak said.

I made a noise that could have meant anything and gestured for Yara to continue explaining.

"At the beginning of the cycle, Fairyland and the Evil Empire are held in stasis by powerful magic. The rest of the Eigen States and the rest of the Floating Isles are free to evolve and change as they will. At first, nothing does. The sort of victory coming at an end of a cycle is absolute and the power of those at the top is not easily broken. But people are difficult. They are foolish and brilliant by turns and in the grind of everyday life, morals change and the pillars of society shift. Eventually, the forces that won such a resounding victory begin to break down. You've seen this of course. Out in the rest of the Floating Isles, people have stopped accepting the divine right of rulers to their positions.[11] It isn't only humans who occupy the upper echelons of society. And thank goodness, even when humans are in charge, it's a more diverse group. As these changes occur, the magic over our two states begins to weaken so they too can be molded," Yara said.

I noticed the way Yara looked at us and thought I knew where she wanted to take this.

"You know what I'm about to say," Yara remarked. "I'm sure your parents don't know much about Realignment. Few do towards the end of a cycle. They only know there is change in the air. And they know there's something critical in the ways

---

[10] And it did, in a way. I always thought the standards of good and evil peddled in the twin states seemed outdated by a few hundred years. Which was not to say the standards outside the Eigen States were so much better. The irrationality was just better concealed. And the rhetoric more convincing, which only made sense if people had been honing it for so long.
[11] Though they didn't question enough, if you ask me. Or else surely the Kings of Hitten would have been booted out of their country a long time ago.

quests work that enables you to have an outsize impact on how things fall into place. In freeing me, you've dealt the opening salvo, acted as the catalyst in the struggle against the status quo for I will aim to be very different from the traditional tyrant. In fact, everything you do here in the Eigen States will have an impact on what wins out and loses in the end."

"I don't want that responsibility!" I exclaimed.

"This is the time we were born into. Two hundred years ago perhaps, we might have been born into different lives and never questioned them. But I did. That's how I ended up deposed by my own cousin and locked in a cell. And you did too or else you wouldn't already have shifted the balance. You've chosen a different path and unless I miss my guess, will continue to do so. Hard as it is, I think it's better to have the ability to make these decisions than to be denied them," Yara said.

"Me too. The thing is I'm not choosing for myself but for generations. I have no right," I said.

"Of course you don't. It's a good sign you think so. Which does not mean I'm comfortable leaving the course of the future to you," Yara said.

"Shows good sense," Jak remarked. "This girl is my best friend and I hardly trust her with greeting the head of another state unsupervised,[12] not to mention the fate of good and evil."

"You are not the only ones on a quest," Yara reminded us. "The responsibility lies with all of us, whether we will it or not. And if we have no choice about this, perhaps we can make it so everyone else does in the future."

She looked earnest and I could tell she meant it but I couldn't bring myself to accept she might be right. For if so, this quest meant much more than simply checking the boxes to get out from under a curse. There were days when I dreaded the responsibility of running a small, inconsequential nation and took it less seriously than I should. How much more horrifying to me was the prospect of having a hand in the lives of so many

---

[12] Also stemming from the unfortunate visit by the King of Hitten. I really didn't like him and let's just say I made no secret of it. Even aside from the statues spelled to curse him.

people in a way no one could hold me accountable for?

"You don't have to believe me," Yara told us.

"Good because I don't," Keran said.

"But you will keep it in mind for the rest of your quest?" Yara asked.

"I think we can manage it," I agreed.

"That's all I can ask. It's a lot to take in, I'm sure," Yara said.

"You bet," Keran said.

"Have a good journey," Yara told us, waving us off.

"Wait, what about the weapons your cousin confiscated from us? We want those back," I said.

So we fetched them and went on our way. As soon as we left the fortress, I set a rapid pace, wanting to get as far away from it as possible. Yara seemed confident in her ability to control her new minions. Still, they were loyal to Ann too when she wore the title. As we saw, things could change in an instant. If someone decided to free Ann and she took control, I didn't doubt she'd come after us with a vengeance. I planned to be out of the Evil Empire when and if that happened.

I turned over what Yara told us and still didn't know what to make of it. The longer we traveled, the more surreal the whole thing became and the less and less I could believe she meant it seriously.

Because we traveled at such a pace, none of us[13] could comment on what really hung on our minds. Perhaps subconsciously, I set such a punishing pace on purpose to avoid addressing the words the vulture unloaded upon us.

---

[13] Jak in particular.

CHAPTER TWENTY TWO

That night though, when I reluctantly allowed us to make camp, there was nothing to do but stare at the fire and think. Jazmin woke up around the time we made camp, groggy and suffering from a mild headache, more from bouncing around on Jak's shoulder than from casting her spells. We updated her on what happened after she passed out and Jazmin echoed our own skepticism on what Yara said.

Once we clued her in on Yara's strange story however, there was little to keep us from giving voice to our thoughts. Jazmin actually broached the topic first. She passed out not long after we trussed up the vulture so it made sense it would be foremost on her mind. "Gamil said the vulture spoke the truth. Does that mean it can see the future?"

"If I know one thing about prophecies, it's that they're not as static and set in stone as they're made out to be. If you catch a prophet or a seer in a candid moment,[1] they'll admit nothing really is," Jak told her.

---

[1] This is very rare of course. Candidness is not the natural state for anyone who spends their life peddling a mixture of lies and truth through games of confidence. They were also very hard to trick, being masters at it themselves.

191

"I don't know your brother," I admitted. "But if he's anything like you, I think he'll turn out different than your parents expect."

"I feel helpless," Jazmin said. "This might be half the reason my parents sent me away but I tried my best to impart some things to him. I didn't want him to grow up like them and our grandparents before."

"If one thing rings true in what Yara said, it's that times are changing. And if so, your brother has a good chance of breaking the cycle. If he does, it'll be because of you. But only in part. In the end, what he decides to do is beyond you. It's his choice," Jak remarked.

"Is it though, given what Yara said?" Naga wanted to know.

No one really had an answer to this so I finally interrupted. "Look, we'll all drive ourselves crazy if we start thinking seriously about what Yara told us. If she's right, then these are forces big enough to be beyond our control. The best we can do is act as if they do not exist. And if they don't exist, then we are as much responsible for our own actions as anyone else and as much absolved of guilt for the actions of others as before. Jazmin, it won't be your fault however your brother turns out but you aren't powerless either. Far from it."

Since this wasn't a Storybook quest, my words didn't fill Jazmin with the confidence she needed.[2] Even so, she recognized elements of truth in what I said and did her best to swallow it despite the roar of her own self doubt. I had a feeling before the night ended, we'd all know the feeling too well.

As Jazmin already opened up the can of worms, we went around and reflected on what the vulture said. Mostly because I wanted to avoid it as long as possible, I made myself go next.[3] "What the vulture said about me is probably true but the bald head doesn't get any points for originality because it's not anything I haven't thought of myself. You know, so what? Just because I might have done the same in their position doesn't

---

[2] Though for once in my life, I wished they could.
[3] Perhaps that was a sort of cowardice too. I bet that stupid vulture would have something to say.

make my condemnation of idiots any less true. And hell, what if my flaw *is* in thinking I'm always in control? Surely there are worse." Truth be told, most of this came from bravado but pretending as if I believed it went a long way toward making it sink in. Any fool could spout the psychology of it. Perhaps if I said this out loud, I'd really believe it.

I must have sounded appropriately defiant because Jazmin smiled at me before turning to Keran. "Well, do you care to repudiate what the terrible creature said about you?"

"I'm not sure I can," Keran said with a grimace.[4] "Do you remember the man in the broom closet in your palace, Rahni? It all started with him."

"You said you had history," I agreed.

"That's the crux of it," Keran said. "I always thought it might be my brush with him that started off the latest round of persecutions. And before you say it's not technically my fault, of course I know. But there's a point where technicalities are little comfort, especially with the knowledge my actions, rightly or wrongly, led to the exile or worse of my people."

"Well, I have nothing to add," I said. For this comment Jak punched me in the shoulder and I didn't protest. What Keran needed wasn't a verbal challenge like Jazmin or silent affirmation like me but comfort and no one would ever accuse me of being good at such a thing. Truth be told, I usually messed it up so I kept quiet. Jak took over and though Keran looked no happier by the time he finished, at least he listened and had some positive thoughts to balance out the negative.

Then I kicked Jak in the shin and said, "It's just you now. Tell me what sappy things I should say and I'll do it."

"Don't worry," Jak said. "I never thought I had a good chance. I've gotten this far on denial and persistence. Might as well persevere."

"Upbeat as always," I said with a laugh more glum than

---

[4] It looked precisely as threatening as what you might imagine a wolfhound's grimace. Lips peeled back, eyes scrunched up, fur raised in tufts, the whole thing. Not that I would say anything about it, of course. Not at a time like this. Even I have some sensitivity.

cathartic. As we sat there, I had a thought and suddenly started fumbling through my pockets. I patted all of them down and couldn't find what I was looking for.

"The map?" Jak asked as he took it out of his own pocket. "I snagged it while you strapped all of your knives and daggers back into place."[5]

"Did you check it since we left the fortress?" I wanted to know.

Jak started as he realized what I meant. He nearly tossed the map down and spread it open on the ground. He pumped a fist in excitement as we all saw on the map what I expected: an X.

"Why an X?" Keran asked.

"The eXit?" I suggested.

"EliXir?" Jak proposed instead.

"Oh, who cares, we're one step closer," I said.

"Guess it's a good thing after all we got sucked back to the fortress," Jazmin commented.

"Too soon to tell," Naga said and I agreed.

"Overthrowing Her Vileness actually counts as our last heroic deed?" Keran asked.

"Makes sense. I can't imagine many things more impressive than taking down an evil villain. In which case, where is our reward? I feel it's worth a few horses," Jak said.

"We've been tricked," I decided at last. When the others looked at me in confusion, I chuckled. "You're not going to like this but the vulture dealt us the reward."

"Seems a pretty strange reward," Naga commented.

"Yeah well, this is the Evil Empire isn't it? Of course their rewards are screwed up and have an edge," I said.

"Which part was the reward?" Keran wanted to know.

"I think where we bond over our problems. Or, and please try to contain your groans, the truths were their own reward," I said.

"I can't believe I'm going to say this but I preferred

---

[5] He was almost certainly trying to point out my lack of attention to important matters but I ignored it. Besides, my weapons were important. What good would the map do if I could not defend us from enemies?

Fairyland's version," Jak said. We looked at each other and started to laugh because what else could we do?

When we finally reached it a couple of days later, the border between the Evil Empire and whatever land lay beyond was as abrupt as the one between it and Fairyland. Only this time, the landscape past the barrier changed continuously, in time with the changes on our map.

We stood there for a very long time, watching snowfields melt into green meadows, boil up into massive lakes and dry back into deserts. Windy chaparral replaced lush forests and mountains ground down into rolling hills.

"Standing here isn't going to help," I finally said. "We might as well jump in."

"Let's try to time it for a warmer climate please," Jazmin said. "I'm not dressed for a blizzard."

"We'll need to link hands," Jak said, "lest we get separated."

"Easy for you to say," Keran muttered.

"Oh don't be so sore. Jak, pick him up, will you?" I asked.

Jak wrapped an arm around Keran's midsection and heaved up so he hung with his legs trailing on the ground, muttering about the indignity of it.

Paying his complaints no attention, I grabbed Jak's other hand as well as Jazmin's. We walked up to the barrier and I waited for something promising.

"It's too bad we don't have anything like a Storybook to throw. Would be a good gesture against this place," Jak mused.

"Be quiet and wait for the signal," I told him even though I sympathized greatly.

I let a couple of acceptable looking places[6] flash by without moving so much as a toe to get a good feel for the timing. When fully prepared, I signaled for the others to make ready and shouted for them to jump when the time came. It all happened very quickly. One second we all had our feet planted solidly on the soil and the next we threw ourselves through the barrier as one. For a moment, we seemed to stick in midair as if the Evil Empire didn't want to let us go. But then we burst forward,

---

[6] Really anything without immediate dangers, at this point.

popping through the barrier and tumbling out the other side.

Not wanting to lose the others, I didn't let go even as we started to fall, the result being we all did face plants into the ground. Fortunately, I picked a good land to fling ourselves into. Instead of hitting ice or rock, we hit a patch of soft grass. I let the others go and tumbled enough down the slope to get back to my feet using my momentum. Everyone else fell in a heap and pushed themselves upright as I brushed myself down.

A quick look around confirmed that none of us looked worse for the wear and that we made it into the land I chose. We ended up a temperate climate, in a land with gentle hills rolling off in all directions. Grass so green it hurt my eyes blanketed every surface but for a dirt track following the curves of the hills.[7]

"Oh, good job," Jazmin told me. "It's beautiful."

"I chose it because it didn't look deadly but that's a good bonus," I told her. I kept scanning our surroundings, waiting for something to go wrong.

Jak caught me at it and laughed. "I don't think it's impossible for us to catch a break now and then."

"You'd be surprised," I said though I saw no monsters on the horizon come to devour us.[8]

I took out the map to confirm the two states we'd been mired in for so long were jumping around the landscape around our island of calm. And as the twin realms jumped from location to location, expanding and shrinking, I caught the momentary imbalances between them I thought I imagined so long ago. This made me think of Yara talking of cycles in history and the

---

[7] Almost too convenient, that. I didn't like it but I knew we'd follow it. Hopefully it didn't lead us to the doors of any more assassins or thieves and who knows what else.

[8] I almost wished, if it had to happen, for an attack now. At least we had the option of retreating and finding a different land. Although, come to think of it, we couldn't be certain escaping through the barrier would help us. Since we left The Evil Empire, it would be hopping around the Eigen States like any other realm. A glance back at the barrier confirmed this as it was no longer the dead trees and tangled vines of the Evil Empire but a changing landscape.

chance to reshape the nature of good and evil.

It was still too much to take in so I pushed it aside for a time, focusing my attention on the land we found ourselves in. On this scale, I could tell very little but that we were drawing closer to our target in the east. This realm seemed small, so small this map held few details. In fact, I imagined we might be finished with it by the next day.

Once everyone adjusted whatever our wild leap jostled out of place, I led us onto the road and we continued on our quest, more content than we'd been since we left the fortress.

As we went, I went through a list of the steps needed to make up a proper quest. We completed all the heroic deeds so as far as I could tell, we would probably be left alone until the final approach. At which point, things would get bad very quickly. The guide I had no choice but to memorize mentioned something about death and rebirth, which I did not like. For now though, I preferred to simply enjoy the sensation of walking through a place that as yet, had not sent anything forth to kill us.

We managed, as a body, to forget all the issues we hashed out the night before and pretend we engaged in nothing but a stroll through a strangely lush countryside. At least for a while. It didn't take long for me to start to feel uneasy once more. The land was still beautiful but the longer we spent walking down the road, the more I started to nurse suspicions.[9]

For one thing, the grass and the other vegetation seemed too healthy. The colors, everything from the deepest green to the brightest red, blazed with vibrancy. It looked more like a painting than a true landscape. For another, no matter how hard I looked, I never saw anything larger than a mouse moving through the grass. Every once in a while, I caught a glimpse of something flitting past the corner of my eye. It looked like a bird but no matter how quickly I turned, I never saw anything. Even the skies above remained bare except for a few clouds scattered within a bluer dome than any I'd seen.

I didn't give my concerns voice because I had no real cause for uneasiness save a general paranoia. The feeling of disquiet grew

---

[9] Almost because it was so beautiful.

as we walked until I decided to hold my hand above my sword hilt just in case.[10]

The first break in the uniform character of our surroundings came in the form of a small stream cascading in a miniature waterfall down the side of a hill. Though hardly a formidable body of water, we nevertheless decided to avoid wading in unless absolutely necessary. So we followed it upstream, hoping it might become narrow or shallow enough to ford easily. When we crested the next hill however, we saw a small wooden bridge arching over the stream.

It fit into the landscape as someone painted it a blinding red to match the flowers poking through the grass. Yet it also looked out of place for it was the first sign of civilization we'd seen since entering this land. I didn't see why anyone would build a bridge here, away from any other sign of inhabitation.[11]

Whereas the others might have blithely walked across the bridge, I preferred we take a more cautious approach. I halted long enough at the base of the bridge for Jazmin to get impatient and ask me what we were looking for. When we finally did step on, I led the way with sword in hand and ignored Keran's mutterings.

Right before we reached the halfway point, a hand appeared on a railing to our left and a troll flipped himself over it. He landed on his feet with a solid thump and flashed us a winning smile. Rather than attack him, I actually put my sword back in its sheath. The troll bore no weapons and though he clearly meant to block our passage, I couldn't see him actually hindering us. Unlike the troll in Fairyland, he looked to be my height and almost as slender. He had nubs of bone sticking out of black curls and greenish skin the shade of grass.

"Good afternoon, travelers," the troll said with a stately bow. "My name is Krum and I'll be happy to extract a toll from you

---

[10] Goodness knows how many times just during this trip my paranoia came in handy. I felt no self- consciousness about it.

[11] Not to mention, it looked far too peaceful. I've said it before but I'll say it again. I distrust anything too beautiful or too tranquil. Bound to be hiding secrets underneath the veneer.

today."

"Trolls on bridges taking tolls?" Jak said. "I thought we were done with that sort of thing."

"Look, Krum, you're not getting anything from us so go on and shift out of the way," I told him.

Krum sighed, aware we would not be easy customers. "I don't want much you know. I just need to get a return on my investment. Wooden bridges like these are expensive, especially when you need a home installed underneath."

I went to the railing and bent over to see Krum spoke the truth in at least one matter. I could just see a bedroom and a kitchen nestled against the bottom of the bridge with a ladder leading to the top.

"You built a bridge to extract a toll?" I asked. "Seems like a colossal waste of money."

"No other choice," Krum told me. "The old stone bridge my foremothers used fell apart in the last floods."

"But why didn't you build a real house and start a farm or something?" Jak asked.

"And grow what?" Krum wanted to know. "Gold might grow on trees over in Eldin[12] but not here."

"I know I'm still feeling a bit addled from yesterday," Jazmin said. "So give it to me straight. Is he making sense?"

"I get it now. You're not from around here. Well let me say my rates are low, all things considered. A couple pieces of gold will do," Krum said.

"We haven't used much since we left," Jak whispered to me. "He seems a bit out of his mind. Maybe we're better off giving him what he wants. Unless you really want to fight him."

I held my hand out to Jak and he slapped a couple of coins into my hand. "This enough?" I asked Krum. When he nodded vigorously, I flipped them both over.

Krum slipped the larger of the two coins into his pocket and

---

[12] It really did. Consequently, gold was worthless there, which inspired a lot of people to try and devise ways of getting it. So far, no one succeeded. It always turned to dust when you crossed a border.

tossed the other into his month. Even as he chewed,[13] he nodded to us in thanks and swung over the railing to return to his quarters underneath the bridge.

For a while after he left, we stood around in confusion. "Did he actually eat the gold or am I seeing things?" Keran finally asked.

"No, he ate it," I said. "Better we don't know the details. I say we keep going."

"With you," Jak said so we pushed forward.

We passed the bridge without incident, Krum never popping his head up to further confuse us. The dirt road we followed disappeared, leaving us to trudge through the grass. It didn't take long to reach another stream. No one expressed surprise when we came upon yet another bridge, this time made of stone.

"Shall we risk it?" Jak wanted to know.

"Let's do it," I decided. "We've still got plenty of gold and we might get more answers out of this guardian."

"Wouldn't bet on it," Keran remarked but I already stepped onto the bridge.

The closer we got to the top, the slower I walked, waiting for a troll to flip over the side of the bridge. I was looking in the wrong direction. One of the blocks of stone underfoot suddenly jerked to the side, making all of us jump back in surprise.

A middle aged yaoguai[14] clambered out of the hole and smacked his hands free of dirt before turning to us. "Excellent, I've almost run out. The toll will be four gold coins please. I'll take all currencies, as long as it's gold."

"Four?!" I demanded. "The guy back there only asked for two."

"That scumbag has a rickety wooden bridge. This one right here has quality written all over it." The yaoguai walked to the side of the bridge and slapped one of the slabs of rock. "Look.

---

[13] It sounded about as horrific as you'd expect. Teeth grinding on metal. The sound will probably haunt me to my grave.

[14] They usually adopted the appearance of humans but this one appeared in his original form. He had a ring of small horns on the top of his head and his fourth arm might be a tentacle but otherwise still looked vaguely human.

These stones cost a fortune to dig up and transport. I'm up to my eyebrows in debt. Tell you what. You seem like nice folks. Three coins."

"Why borrow money to build a bridge?" Jak wanted to know.

"What else could I do?" the yaoguai asked in turn. "This stream is my inheritance. I'm entitled to my livelihood, aren't I? Especially one passed down through so many generations."

Further questions yielded no better information so we handed over the toll[15] and kept walking. Almost immediately after leaving the yaoguai behind, we crested a particularly tall hill and saw a good portion of the upcoming land splayed out in front of us. Streams flowed across the land at increasingly frequent intervals, each with bridges so close together they practically ran one into the next.

Some shone with brilliance, made out of white stone gleaming in the sun. Others leaned alarmingly to one side, wooden ruins for all intents and purposes. At least in the sizeable chunk of land we could see, there was little sign of anything but the bridges and the streams. No towns, no cities, no signs of life other than the solitary posts of these guardians ready to demand a toll from us for crossing their slipshod bridges.

"Strange," Naga commented.

"If we keep paying the tolls, we'll be paupers by the time we get out," Keran said.

"Some of those are barely streams at all. That one right there? Looks like Naga could leap over it by herself," I said.

From our vantage point, we picked out a route to avoid as many of the bridges as possible. We came first to one of the narrow streams I pointed out earlier. It spanned only a few feet and a running jump allowed me to clear it with plenty to spare. Keran leaped after me, hitting the ground with a squelch that sent some mud skyward though I backpedaled out of the way in

---

[15] I didn't want to but Jak cajoled me into it. The yaoguai acted like an entitled brat. Giving him money made me extremely unhappy. I preferred to give him a good talking to and a couple smacks in the face. Unfortunately, saner heads prevailed.

time.

Jak would've leaped next, if an ifrit[16] didn't suddenly shoot out the bottom of the nearest bridge and hurtle at him.

---

[16] They range in size and characteristics like any other race. In general, large, winged and nearly always covered with fire. As you might imagine, you don't generally want to see them swooping down at you from above.

CHAPTER TWENTY THREE

I had enough time to wonder why we ever thought we could do things the easy way before I ran back across the stream and tackled Jak to the ground. The ifrit swept over our heads, raking the air with her hooves. I left Jak lying in the grass, winded from the impact, as I scrambled to my feet. Sopping wet from crashing through the stream, I pulled out my sword to confront the ifrit.

She swooped again and I dropped to avoid a kick to the head.[1] I followed her passage through the air as she rose up to make another pass. When she came at me with her claws extended, I waited until she couldn't possibly change course. I spun to the side and grabbed hold of her leg. Her momentum ripped me off my feet but the sudden imbalance also sent her careening into the ground.[2]

Already prepared for impact, I landed well in the soft ground and rolled to my feet without any real delay. Still powered by rage, the ifrit threw herself free of the mud, while the flames

---

[1] Someone was not kidding around, clearly.
[2] Not to mention strained the muscles in my shoulder. Surely, I was getting too old for stunts like this.

203

that guttered and died as she hit the ground roared to life once more. I held my sword up to block a strike as the ifrit tried to tear my face off with her claws. I couldn't compete with her strength and I didn't try. Almost as soon as I blocked the blow, I spun away and extracted my blade. I whipped it around and struck her in the back with the flat of the sword before retreating to a safer distance.

Predictably, the ifrit didn't leave off. She leaped at me again and I dodged with ease. During the next exchange, I shouted, "What do you want?"

"You tried to cross my stream without paying," the ifrit shouted back as she sent a plume of flame at me. I dived out of the way and scrambled back up again when she tried to leap on top of me.

"We didn't use your damn bridge!" I countered as I slashed a cut on her arm, not deep enough to do real damage but deep enough to hurt. She didn't take the hint and continued to claw at me, directing most of her attacks at my face.[3]

Just as I resolved to fight back, if only to avoid having my head taken off, Jazmin jumped in to help. She hit the ifrit directly in the chest with a spell that tossed her into the mud. I waved at her in acknowledgement and stepped forward to take advantage of the ifrit's momentary immobility.

A young woman darted out and seized me by the arm. I turned as she grabbed me and flipped my sword so the blade rested against her throat. She let go slowly and held her hands up. "I mean you no harm. I just wanted to stop the fight."

I kept hold of the front of her shirt a couple seconds longer, to drive home the point about who was in control. Then I let her go for she didn't seem to be threatening us.

"Next time you try to stop a fight, it might not be a good idea to rush in and start grabbing the people with swords," Keran advised.

"I'm sorry. I can't let you hurt Malak though. She's not like

---

[3] Incidentally, what was it with people and my face recently? First Rosa back in the crazy town. Then, the stupid vulture. The rest of my body made a much better and bigger target.

204

this normally, trust me. She's fallen on some hard-" Before she could continue, Malak got up out of the mud and lunged again.

I pushed the girl who interrupted our fight into the mud and knelt down myself. At this point, I no longer cared about the mess. I already rolled around in the water and muck enough to be covered with it. Meanwhile, as Malak went over my head, I reached up and gave her a push so she plopped into the dirt.

Jak walked over to give me a hand while the girl pushed herself up. She rushed to Malak before the ifrit could muster up the effort for another attack and shouted for her to calm down. "Malak, I know you're under a lot of pressure. But this isn't you."

"Nani, you know I need the money," Malak said as she tried to sit up.

Nani pressed her back with a gentle push to the chest. "I know it's bad. We'll rustle it up, alright?"

"From where?" Malak demanded. "In case you haven't noticed, we aren't awash with travelers laden down by sacks of gold. And we have competition, if you've no eyes to see."

Though hardly in a mood to be understanding, the anguish in Malak's voice concerned me. I stuck my sword into the mud since I couldn't put it back into the sheath without a thorough cleaning. I did my best to wipe the mud from my face and slogged over. "What is it she owes money for? Her bridge, if I had to take a wild stab?"

"That's exactly right," Nani agreed. "Like the rest of us, Malak took out a loan from the Leviathan Company to pay for her bridge. They slapped her with a steep interest rate and she's having a hard time paying it off. If she doesn't make the next payment in five days, they'll take the bridge from her and she'll have no place to go."

"And what exactly are they going to do with it?" Keran wanted to know. "They're not going to make money from it. This stream simply doesn't need a bridge."

"Mine doesn't either," Nani said as she pointed it out. I looked in the direction she pointed and saw an even smaller creek. Nani's bridge seemed a rather pitiful thing, made not of carved hardwood but slabs of driftwood.[4]

"No offense but does anyone uhh, cross your bridge?" Jazmin asked.

"No one recently," Nani admitted. "It's alright for me because I go around making repairs for everyone else, putting in shelves and other things. I scrounge up enough to get by and make my payments."

"You must have known about the competition when you set up shop here," I said.

"Everyone knows but we haven't got any choice. No ancestral bridges to call our own. Not much in the way of clout so we get stuck with the leftovers," Nani said.

"But why build bridges in the first place?" Keran asked. "I think there are enough."

"'Market saturation' I think is the term Leviathan keeps bandying about but there really is nothing else here in our humble land. I can explain but it's complicated and I doubt you want to be covered with mud while you listen," Nani said.

"Perceptive, aren't you?" I commented. "Good thing there's so much water around. I'm going to need a lot of it to clear the mud out of my ears."

"Why don't you come to my bridge? You can stay for the night if you'd like. It's getting late. My stream isn't good for much but it's still water. And I've rigged up a system of pipes so it's probably the only one in the area with a shower," Nani said.

"I like the idea," Jazmin rushed to say. She grimaced when we all turned to look at her. "There's mud all over my shoes."

I pointed at the splattering on her boots and then at the mud all over my own body. "I think we know who's getting the shower first. Before we go, how much does Malak owe?"

When I gestured for Jak to hand over the money, Malak and Nani both stared in confusion.

"Are we sure about this?" Keran asked.

"She didn't attack you so you get no say," I told him as Jak

---

[4] I decided not to question where the driftwood came from since I saw no ocean or other large body of water in view. There were mysteries aplenty about this place not to go hunting for more.

handed her the money. Then I gestured for Malak to shut up as well. "You go pay your debts. I'm going to get clean."

I caught Jak trying a hide a smile as we walked away so I glared at him. "Don't even think it."

"Oh come on," Jak said. "She tried to kill you and then you handed over your money."

"I handed over *our* money," I said.

"Regardless," Jak said. He didn't add anything but then, he didn't need to. I got his point even if I thought he took it a little overboard.

Nani caught up to us before long. "Malak went off to pay her debts but I want to thank you on her behalf. Us downtrodden members of society stick together and she's helped me out many times before. I understand it might be hard for you to believe but she really is a gentle soul."

"Desperation does things to people," I agreed. "Don't worry about it. If you want, consider it payment for housing us tonight."

Nani's bridge looked as broken down up close as it seemed from a distance. She opened the door for us and let us into a dark but impeccably clean house that hung off the bottom of the bridge. The stream flowing underneath the bridge must never get very high because the bottom of Nani's hanging house hovered only a foot or so above the water.

I did my best to track as little mud across the floor as possible on my way to the other side of the house. The shower turned out to be little more than a spout of water pumped up from the stream. It did the job though. I managed to get rid of the mud caked over my body and scrub my clothes approximately clean.[5]

When I emerged from the shower, I found everyone sitting around Nani's table digging into a feast made up of our supplies. Clearly, Nani didn't have much food of her own. She seemed sensible though so if anyone could tell us why all these people bothered building bridges to get money, she could. I broached the topic once we all ate.

"I think it's about time you tell us the story you promised," I

---

[5] It would have to do. Let's just say it's a good thing I preferred darker clothes.

said.

"I warn you now it's a bit strange," Nani said.

"We expect that given how illogical everything has been thus far," Jazmin pointed out.

To be fair to Nani, the story she told sounded a fair bit stranger than any of us anticipated. This land was not always an expanse of valleys and hills. In days long past, a vast lake, scattered with islands, filled this land. The original bridge builders, ancestors of those who talked so much about their inherited rights, constructed them so they would stretch between the largest of the islands. They charged no tolls, instead sustaining themselves, like everyone else, on the fish swimming in abundant shoals through the lake. For a long time, the realm remained prosperous. No one who could lower a line and hook into water need go hungry.

Then the Leviathan Corporation rolled into town.[6] They plied everyone with promises of greater profits if only they would allow the company to trim away the inefficiencies.[7] And for a time, the land exploded with wealth. Former paupers had enough money to build palaces. Those whose ancestors built and maintained bridges for the public benefit began to charge for it, making themselves the wealthiest of all.

For generations, this prosperity held until it seemed impossible it could ever fade. But then, slowly but surely, the waters began to recede, exposing more and more land. This by itself might not have been so bad if the slow disappearance of the water didn't also mean the disappearance of the fish on which the whole economy rested.

Panic ran through the community in short order. Some of the quick thinkers realized the bridge owners hadn't suffered. So they began to construct new bridges even as the falling water level revealed more land. These people couldn't build their bridges without buying materials from the Leviathan

---

[6] Or sailed rather, I suppose. Given the direction this story was going, I rather pictured them arriving amidst billowing fog.

[7] Poor saps. They should have known right then it would go poorly for them. Iron cage of rationalization rearing its ugly head.

Corporation.

Soon enough, everyone raised bridges and put themselves into massive debt. Meanwhile, all the fish disappeared so they had to pay Leviathan Corporation not only interest for money borrowed but also for food.[8]

All this was strange enough already but the oddest part followed. In the beginning, as more and more land lay exposed to the sun, of course people came up with the idea of planting seeds and reaping a harvest. Not a one of these harvests bore fruit for the lush green grass we saw covering every surface swept into the hills one day and suffocated all else. They consumed water and nutrients at such a ferocious rate little else could compete. And because they burned through so many nutrients, they also grew too fast to control.

"It's too perfect," Jak said after Nani finished telling her story. "As if a terrible plan came together."

"Oh it did. It's been the Leviathan Corporation from beginning to end. I can't tell you how. Everyone knows it but we can't do a thing. They've got us all by the throats, in ironclad contracts no one can break," Nani said.

"How about a revolt?" I wanted to know.

"People have tried but each year it gets harder. People get poorer, more desperate and grow to hate their competition. Sooner or later, it's all going to boil over. I don't know when and I don't know how but I can tell you it'll happen," Nani promised.

I thought it over and asked, "So where has this company set up shop? We didn't see anything conspicuously large and full of assholes on the way here."

"You wouldn't have," Nani said with a laugh. "Their base is to the east. You'll pass it on your way out tomorrow, I'm sure."

"Purely for curiosity's sake, what sort of defenses do they have?" I wanted to know.

---

[8] All except for the trolls of course. They apparently adapted to eating the gold, a fact to which Keran responded with a retch of disgust. I responded with disbelief. Unless trolls were tapped into some laws of nature the rest of us didn't have access to, I didn't see how they could adapt so quickly.

Nani looked at me for a while before shaking her head in a refusal to answer. "Are the rest of you aware she's out of her mind?"

"For some time," Jak said.[9]

"I'm just curious," I protested.

"Sure," Nani said. "Listen though, it's not a place a small group is going to crack even if being on a quest boosts your luck and even if, I don't miss my guess, you have a hearty helping of improbability resistance. If you tackle the Leviathan Corporation, you'll be killed in short order. It's not your fight. Leave it to us."

"I thought you said revolts were too hard," Keran said.

"I told you revolts were getting harder. Doesn't mean they're impossible. And because you're contemplating the absolutely insane, I'll tell you something I shouldn't. I'm organizing one. It might work. I won't give you details but this should prevent you from doing anything foolish," Nani said.

"Very few things in the world can prevent that," Jak remarked.

"All of you are being very insulting when I only asked a simple question," I complained without force for of course it was ridiculous to think we could take down an organization so powerful it kept an entire realm in their control. Thinking about it now horrified me. Defeating Ann gave me too much confidence in our abilities, made me think I could lend a hand in righting every single injustice.

Clearly, this quest did something to me despite my attempts to resist the most pernicious effects. Before we left, I would've known better than to try and stick my sword and neck into situations where I did not truly belong.[10]

We spent the night on Nani's floor. Not precisely comfortable but better by far than a night spent in the wet grass. As I lay thinking, Jak nudged me with his foot and said, "I already counted out the gold we can spare."

"What, this quest made you into a mind reader?" I asked.

---

[9] I would've resented this answer more, probably, if I didn't agree.
[10] Or at least enough sense to realize when I did.

"It doesn't take much to read your mind," Jak said.

"Apparently not," I agreed though I did feel pleased about not having to argue with Jak about it. He and I were usually on the same page but we would be taking a risk to give away so much of our gold. We were far from the end of our journey and might need it. In truth, Jak had a bigger stake than I. Unless I managed to get myself killed, I'd stumble to the finale of this quest no matter what detours I took along the way. Gold might smooth the way but it wouldn't make or break the success of my quest.

But his was a secondary quest and who knew, perhaps lack of gold might doom it. So that vulture could say what it wanted but Jak brought value to this quest.[11]

Nani sputtered when we presented her with a pouch of gold, the majority of our remaining stash. We did it before we left, after she handed us a crude map of the rest of the land and told us how to get to the border while encountering only those amongst the bridge guardians she counted as allies. She told us to mention her name and they would not challenge us.

Nani took the bag but gestured at Keran with it. "You seem sane so you'll accept this back."

"Not mine," Keran told her as he backed away. "You need it more than us."

When we refused to budge, Nani sighed and accepted the gold. "They will make my plans easier to carry out. I think they have a good chance of success already but so said every revolutionary on the eve of their attempt."

"I hope you do succeed, even if some of your followers might do well to stop attacking random people," Jazmin suggested.

"Don't worry," Nani said. "We're going to have a talk, especially as she's going to be a key piece of the plan."[12]

With Nani's map in hand, it didn't take us long to reach the border. At each bridge we crossed, the guardian nodded shortly at the mention of her name. They let us cross without question,

---

[11] Not in the least because every time I wondered whether the world might be spiraling into insanity, he made certain I knew our small corner of it need not follow it down. What were friends for, after all?

[12] It took almost a physical effort to stop myself from asking for details.

not even to ask how we knew her or where we intended to go. This held up so well from guardian to guardian I began to think there might be something to Nani's boast. I didn't know how she convinced so many people of different races and states of indebtedness to band together but it could only be a good sign. And of course, I couldn't help wonder whether I might to do half as well in her position. Or whether I might have accepted the status quo and done my best not to raise the ire of the Leviathan Corporation.

Times like this, I wished I did something a bit more violent to the vulture. But plucking his feathers would not get his words out of my head. I wasn't big on self-doubt. For one thing, it was terribly boring. Sure, no one could be sure of the truth and it's good to doubt everything. But sitting about and wondering if you were being truthful with yourself? I always saw it as weakness, an excuse to dither about as other people made decisions. Which was true, in a sense, but also wrong in the peculiar way of very true things.

So yeah, I didn't think much of the angst and finding yourself rut so many of my cousins fell into in their teenage years. Yet I couldn't deny the vulture's words made me question myself. It could be that my self-confidence acted as a shield for weakness and my desire to do sometimes insanely generous things for others came from cynical bids for affirmation of my worth.

In the end of course, it didn't matter. I learned long ago much of this was in how you saw it. And I chose to see this quibbling about my central motivations as inconsequential. What did it matter if there might be selfish roots to my actions if they benefitted others? The question should be posed to philosophers who sat around and thought all day,[13] not to me and not to the vast majority of people I knew. The rest of us philosophized with every decision we made in complicated world.

Perhaps fearing we might be tempted to indulge in foolishness,[14] Nani made sure, in drawing our path, to give the

---

[13] Disclaimer in case the guild gets down on me for this. All that thinking is great and probably necessary, just not for me. So calm down.
[14] Entirely my fault, I admit it.

headquarters of the Leviathan Corporation a wide berth. We saw it only from a distance and still found it worthy of its hyperbolic name.

The structure, as I had no word for a building so enormous, stretched across hills and valleys, filling the horizon. Had this been in the Evil Empire, we'd see birds of prey hovering overhead or broken windows aplenty. But no, here the building gleamed and shone.

We gazed at the building as we walked and so we didn't notice the barrier separating this land and the next until we came on top of it. As I prepared to ask what sort of land they preferred next, Keran broke into a run. He bolted toward the barrier without warning. There was a good chance we might lose him forever if he plunged through without us so I grabbed Jak's arm and he reached out for Jazmin.

Keran reached the barrier as it started to shimmer. Knowing the alternative might be never finding him again, I took a risk. Holding tight onto Jak's hand, I lunged. Here finally, our improbability resistance worked in our favor. As the tips of my finger brushed against Keran's tail, his nose hit the barrier. And in the instant of time before the land on the other side shifted away, it sucked us in.

CHAPTER TWENTY FOUR

Even before I hit the ground, I started to curse Keran and demanded to know what possessed him to do something so massively stupid. He didn't answer any of the charges I threw at him in the course of my abusive torrent. I didn't stop until Jak tackled me to get me to shut up.

Only then did I take a real look at our surroundings. This was a land of mist and fog where the moisture hung in banks, shifting and moving to undetectable currents. It wasn't the dense fog that suffocated everything it touched. But neither was it the cool fog lingering after a light rain. It clung to our bodies but didn't feel thick and heavy.

In particular, it didn't nothing to hide what made Jak tackle me. Not far away, a bird the size of a house gazed at us. Standing in complete silence, her[1] black eyes seemed to bore into us and I could only wonder what she thought. She did not look like a bird of prey, resembling a colorful sparrow more than a hawk. Feathers of all different colors made the bird stand out against the drab landscape.

---

[1] I couldn't determine the precise gender so you'll have to bear with me. Gender pronouns are a bit ridiculous anyway.

After an extended period of silent observation by both sides, the bird slowly lifted her wings and rose into the air. The slow and steady beat did nothing to shift the fog and the sloth with which she moved mesmerized us. Her tail was longer by far than the rest of her body and moved as if independent, floating back and forth in illusionary drafts. The bird gave us one last look before a sudden burst of untraceable speed sent her shooting up. She moved so fast through the layers of fog she might well have teleported away, as far as we could tell.

As soon as the bird disappeared, someone called out. "Move before she comes back!"

The voice surprised all of us but none more so than Keran who froze and stared in the direction from which it came. A female wolfhound slightly bigger than him stepped out from the fog and bared her teeth at us in frustration. "Move!"

So we obeyed, all except Keran, who had to be pulled and yanked. And a good thing we moved when we did for not long after, we heard a terrible screeching noise and turned to see the bird plunge to the ground precisely where we stood. Her feet sank into the dirt and she took large chunks of it with her when she shot into the air.

Seeing this over my shoulder gave me motivation to run and I bolted, dragging Jazmin along. Keran only kept running because the other wolfhound continued snapping at him. Jak soldiered along as usual, his long stride enabling him to keep up, at least in short bursts.

Immediately behind us, the bird crashed to the ground again, gouging the dirt once more. Unbelievably, we managed to run even faster though I couldn't see how to survive this. We'd never be able to maintain this pace for long.

Then a large boulder loomed out of the mist and we almost ran into it. The wolfhound darted around it and disappeared. I charged after her and saw her vanish down a hole at the base of the boulder. I pushed Jazmin in, figuring it would be better to ask questions after we escaped from the murderous bird. Jak and I worked together to toss Keran through. A mere look from me was sufficient to make sure Jak left me to take the rear. I jumped after him and the bird screeched again with cacophonic volume as I escaped its grasp.

The hole widened out dramatically and I ran along the slope to wind up in a sizeable room.[2] Only the dim light coming through the opening provided any illumination and it reflected off more than a dozen pairs of yellow eyes glowing in the middle of vague faces in the darkness. I wasn't as worried as I might have been because I had an inkling who these people were. Sure enough, Keran finally opened his mouth to say something, "Tilde, it really is you."

"A few months apart hasn't made you any quicker on your feet," Tilde said.

So now we had the answer to why Keran charged off and put us all in danger. If I hadn't seen everyone I loved in months and thought the chance to ever do so again might be vanishing before my eyes, hell, I'd run too. Which didn't mean I forgave him for almost killing us but I would let it slide.[3]

The eyes bobbed about as a new pair entered the room.[4] This wolfhound jostled to the front of the crowd and all but pounced on top of Keran. "We feared the worse when you didn't show up," she said.

"I ran into a spot of trouble," Keran said. "When I returned, you were all gone. I didn't even know you were thinking about leaving."

"We came to the decision under duress shall we say," the other wolfhound said. "We didn't have much time to leave a message. We thought you'd figure it out. We'd been talking about going back to another time for weeks."

"Was I supposed to know what that meant?" Keran asked.

"You're hopeless," said another wolfhound.

"As touching as this reunion is, none of us can see a damn thing. Is it alright if we get some light in here?" I wanted to know.

"You must excuse our manners. It is not every day our heir comes home to us," a gruff voice said.

---

[2] Or what I assumed to be a sizeable room given the way sound echoed.
[3] The difference between these I didn't even quite know.
[4] And probably the body they belonged to. I just couldn't see it.

"Who are these new companions of yours?" someone else asked.

"Mage lights are bright," I warned everyone as I asked Jazmin to go ahead.

All the wolves closed their eyes as Jazmin recited a spell and clapped her hands. A mage light blinked into existence and floated toward the ceiling to cast light on the whole room. The wolves raised their heads only slowly and took their time adjusting to the light.[5]

"It's been a long time since we've seen anything so bright," one of the wolfhounds commented, thereby confirming my own thought.

"This is a pretty drab place," I agreed. "With more deadly fowl than I generally like to see."

"No murderous elves though, as far as we've seen," one of the wolfhounds pointed out.

"There is that," Jak said.

The wolfhound who jumped on Keran took charge. She ordered everyone into one of the more comfortable[6] back rooms. From what I could see and what I could discern of wolfhound features, she looked similar enough to Keran to be a sister. In any case, we ended up sitting with a bunch of wolfhounds, nearly three dozen by my count, around us listening to an account of our adventures while Keran went off to talk with his family.

We were too far away to hear his discussion but this didn't stop us from speculating. Or at least, it didn't stop me. I posited all sorts of theories to Jak and Jazmin once we told our story and the wolfhounds drifted to the other side of the room to listen to the growing argument between Keran and his family.[7]

---

[5] A few of the wolfhounds looked at the light as if they hadn't seen anything like it in a while. Which I could believe, if the mist outside was as permanent as it appeared.

[6] This made me a little nervous because I wasn't sure what wolfhounds found comfortable.

[7] Perhaps unsurprisingly, neither Jak nor Jazmin had much to say in response to my proposals about what was going on. I tried, after a time, to read their lips, with no success.

Finally, we heard a few shouts of frustration from Keran and the crowd dispersed very quickly, all the wolfhounds scattering from the central room. I lost sight of Keran in the mix but he turned up soon enough.

"Didn't go well?" Naga asked.

"What happened?" Jak wanted to know.

"You'd think they'd be a little more enthusiastic about getting you back," I said.

"They're being as stubborn as ever," Keran said. "I don't even know why I wanted to find them so badly."

"We'd probably understand your frustration a bit more if you told us what happened. It sounded as if you had a temper tantrum," I said.

"It's justified," Keran grumbled. "I guess I should explain they didn't do what I always assumed they would. For weeks before they disappeared, my parents and my sister made vague comments about leaving. I thought they wanted to retreat to the otherworldly dimension our ancestors came from. But apparently that's not what they meant by going back in time. They meant it in a literal sense."

"Are we back in time now?" Naga asked as Jazmin opened her mouth, probably to do the same thing.

"In a way, we are," Keran told her. "It has to do with all the shifting and moving in the Eigen States. The barriers mark not only a difference in space but also in time. My family thought it would be a great idea to bring the whole pack back to truly pre-historic times, when all of the Floating Isles and particularly the Eigen States were wilderness."

"That explains the huge bird," Naga commented.

"Not to mention all manner of other fierce beasts that have it out for us. They've been reduced to a burrow. A burrow!" Keran shouted.

"I take it you're trying to convince them to go back home," Naga said.[8]

---

[8] I'll admit most of what she said were obvious questions falling under her domain. Still, it seemed strange to see her practically carrying on a conversation.

"You bet I am. What kind of life is this, running from everything that moves?" Keran wanted to know.

"You could tell them my parents and I plan to try our best to help. No guarantees since we tried to eradicate the Red Hoods and only succeeded after a hellish period but we are making an effort to round all the murderous elves up," I said.

"I already told them," Keran said. "The trouble is they don't want to fight. They think it's giving up a sure thing here for a risky attempt at staying one step ahead of our enemies back there."

"You mind going back to the part where you promised help I hadn't yet offered?" I asked. Keran ignored me so I let it go with only a sigh.[9]

"Everyone seems to have forgotten it's their home. I can't believe they're willing to leave it at the first sign of difficulty. As far as I'm concerned, it's cowardice," Keran said.

"You know very well that's not the case," his sister Vanna said as she padded over, glaring at Keran. "Our parents are a lot of things but they are not cowards."

"Then how do you explain hiding away in these dank underground tunnels?" Keran wanted to know. "I can't believe you supported this plan."

"Of course not. As I recall, I argued louder than you ever did for fighting back. I want to go home as much as you do. But that doesn't mean everyone who doesn't agree is a coward," Vanna said.

"She's got a point," Naga said.

"Oh what do you know? You barely even have sentience," Keran shot back.

Naga shrugged as best as any lizard could[10] and agreed, "True," before retreating into my pocket. I patted it a couple of times to reassure in case she did feel anything.

Then I spoke to Vanna, "You seem to be in a more stable state of mind than Keran. What convinced your parents to come

---

[9] I must be getting predictable or something. I must remember to do something about that.
[10] Not very well. Lizards barely had shoulders, after all.

219

here?"

"Our parents and the rest of the pack threw a lot of ideas around. They were all temporary solutions or stop-gap measures, designed to reduce the danger until this latest round of persecutions died down. But with this group rising so closely after the fall of the Red Hoods, a lot of people thought it might be a good idea to search for a more permanent solution," Vanna said.

"And this is what they came up with?" I wanted to know. "I can understand the impulse to leave but why come here? There are friendlier areas within the Floating Isles and there must be friendlier times and places in the Eigen States."

"There are plenty but this is part of the plan as well," Vanna said.

"It's part of the plan to be snatched up and pecked to death by massive colorful birds?" I asked.

Vanna proved hard to rattle for she only smiled wanly at the comment. "Not precisely. But you're right in a way. After much discussion, they agreed the only way to prevent our bloodthirsty enemies from coming in after us was to go to as undesirable and inhospitable a place as possible."

"I know this might be a little undiplomatic of me but what good is avoiding your enemies if you're all picked off one by one for your trouble?" Jak wanted to know.

"Not one of us has been hurt so far," Vanna said. "The elves who want us dead are intelligent and capable of setting sophisticated traps and ambushes. The creatures here are just dumb beasts. Good planning and constant vigilance keep us safe."

"But should you lose sight of it even for a moment, the results will be disastrous," Jazmin said. "It seems like a terrible existence, eking out a life here."

"Oh no, I'm not going to dispute that. We're all miserable," Vanna said.

"Then what's the use?" I demanded.

"It's undoubtedly safer," Vanna said. "My parents are right about that if precious little else. There are only two ways to stop these new Reds from slaughtering us all. Either we run far

enough and deep enough into some hellhole even their zeal isn't
sufficient to make them enter. Or we turn around and try to kill
them all in turn. Otherwise we will never be safe."

Keran struggled to answer this and practically growled.
"You've picked the first way out because you've got this idea
only these two options exist."

"I don't see what else there is. If I had my way, I'd want to
fight for what is ours instead of retreating and letting the enemy
think they've won. But I understand the opposing position.
We'd be fighting a war for our lives. None of us wants to kill.
Our enemies want us dead. We want to survive and be left
alone. I figure it'll be a losing war no matter how it ends,"
Vanna said.

A few weeks ago, my reaction to these words might have been
the same as Keran's, who uttered a simple scoff of disgust.
Mostly, I still agreed with him but I recognized there were notes
of complexity. To be sure, I thought Keran's parents were
wrong. It was one thing if an entire society set itself against you.
But almost everyone back home thought the Reds were off the
rails.

If they did not stand up in the face of the Reds' hatred, who
could say what the fanatics might do? They might disperse and
go back to the lives they had before they were gripped by this
desire to kill and maim people who had done nothing to wrong
them. Or, much more likely, they would move on to other
victims,[11] which while certainly not the responsibility of the
wolfhounds, should at least figure into their calculations,
especially as they held up preventing violence as the reason for
leaving.

"We should rest here and leave at night," Keran said. "Vanna
will show us how to get out."

"Us? You're coming? But why?" Jak asked.

"Your quest is over," Naga agreed.

"I can't stay here," Keran said. "I'll go out of my mind."

---

[11] I read through some of the propaganda they disseminated and boy, this
group of elves is nasty. They had something negative to say about nearly
everyone and really liked to lump people together.

"I can't believe I'm saying this but you really should pause and think. Don't do something rash because you're angry. You've come to the end of your quest. You found your family. Yeah, they're not jumping to do what you think they should but you can convince them," I said.

"I don't think my quest is finished," Keran said. "My aim was always to return them home. I won't be able to convince them if I stay here. I know them."

"The parents are not going to be happy about this," Vanna warned.

"Well they won't be the only ones," Keran said.

Jak and Jazmin looked as if they still wanted to argue with him but I shrugged. "You know I won't object if you really want to tag along for the rest of this horrible experience. Purely your choice. I don't want to hear any complaints later on when we're up to our shins in it."

"Not a single complaint," Keran agreed.[12]

"In that case, we better get some rest," Jak decided.

"Why at night?" Jazmin asked. "Wouldn't it be more dangerous?"

"Not here. Those birds can't see at night. And all the other predators are dianural," Keran said.

"So do their prey come out at night?" I asked. "Are they dangerous as well?"

"As far as I can tell, there isn't much in the way of prey," Vanna said. "Before you ask, no one has any idea how all of these predators sustain themselves without any prey."[13]

"Attack each other?" Jak suggested.

"Never seen it," Vanna said. "And I do a lot of patrols. Keran, come with me as I break the news. I don't think there will be any more shouting today as we've all reached our limit. But if there is, I want you to catch as much as me."

"Always so considerate," Keran said with a snort.

---

[12] We'd see about that. Sooner or later, we'd get to the Abyss portion of the quest, the part where things seemed their lowest.

[13] Of course there wouldn't be prey. All the deadly things had to keep busy trying to catch and eat us.

Once they left, Jak shook his head. "It's never easy is it?"

"If it were, none of us would be on this quest," I said and shifted to put my back against the rock. I watched Keran and Vanna go to their parents, who only nodded in resignation. They didn't bother to try and stop him. He was being foolish of course but I couldn't rightly say I'd do anything different. I understood his anger and I'd feel it too if I had to watch my family huddled here to hide from predators and bigots. I'd want to do whatever I could to put a stop to it, even if it meant continuing on a quest as ridiculous as ours.

CHAPTER TWENTY FIVE

Vanna, widely acknowledged as the best at evading predators of all types, did indeed volunteer to lead us out. The whole pack, which numbered in the hundreds, gathered in the room we first entered to say farewell to Keran. They packed into the room so tight they became a sea of teeth and eyes reflecting Jazmin's mage light.

Keran's parents asked us to take care of him and I agreed to do my best. Then Jak decided the rest of us should clamber out of the tunnels first to give Keran some privacy and a last chance to change his mind. I told Jak it wouldn't happen and of course Keran and Vanna climbed out onto solid ground not long after.

"We need to keep moving," Vanna said, "so as not to leave a scent behind. We'll need to move fast. No one get lost. On your own, you'll probably fall into a hole and die."[1]

"How comforting," I said.

---

[1] Good chance of falling into a hole even if we didn't get lost. Pits and holes of various sizes littered the ground, unexplainable and eerie. According to Vanna, enormous beasts the height of trees walked throughout the land and formed those holes. This seemed unlikely but then I remembered where we were.

The fog seemed thicker now so the pale moonlight barely filtered through the air. It was only enough for Jak, Jazmin and I to see each other though Keran and his sister had better sight. We moved as Vanna told us we needed to, sticking close to avoid losing each other.

To my surprise, we didn't come across anything that tried to kill us. I didn't know if this was because the land was less deadly than we first imagined or because Vanna knew it so well.

As Vanna explained before we left, she and the rest of the pack finally settled here in a very small square of land separated in space and time from everything else we knew. And so we came to the barrier only a few hours after leaving the wolfhounds' underground home.

"We made better time than I thought we would," Vanna commented as we came to a stop in front of the barrier.

"You have enough time to make it back before daylight?" I wanted to know.

"I'll move a lot faster without you dragging me down," Vanna told us. "Good luck on your quest. You'll need it if you have my brother along."

"You always were best at the heartfelt goodbyes," Keran commented.

"Just bring yourself back here after you finish this quest, alright?" Vanna asked. "Grandma has been pretty forlorn ever since we left you. I'm sure she'll fall right back into it after you leave."

"Are you trying to guilt me?" Keran asked.

"I'm only doing what's necessary to make sure you come back alive," Vanna said. She nodded at us and disappeared into the night.

"Your little sister is a hell of a lot more competent than you," I told Keran after a while.

"I know. She doesn't know it yet but I'm planning to give her my position once it passes to me. I know I'm not cut out for it. She's not either but she'll do a better job than I can," Keran said.

"I don't know anyone is cut out for leadership," Jak remarked.

"Knowing me for this long has convinced you, has it?" I asked.

"Amongst other observations," Jak said.

I laughed, though not too loud because who knew what might hear us, and gestured at the barrier. The dark made it hard to select a decent place for the next phase of our adventure. In any case, as we'd seen, appearance might not mean much. So I didn't take too long picking a likely place.[2] If we weren't happy with it, we could select a new one in the morning.

We found the ground a bit hard and the wind a bit sharp but no one saw any colorful birds the size of buildings so we bedded down for the night. A look at the map in the morning made it clear we entered the last leg of the quest, for better or worse. The letter X marking the spot of the elixir hovered within a range of mountains all the way at the eastern edge of the realm we arrived in the night before.

The land itself seemed incredibly flat and barren, an expanse of rock and dust as far as the eye could see. It sure became boring traveling through such terrain but after everything, I preferred boring. At least we could see trouble coming from afar.

For the next couple of weeks however, we encountered neither a break in the monotonous landscape nor another living thing meaning us harm. The wind whipping sand into our faces seemed vindictive and the sun beating down felt fierce. But nothing burst from the ground with the intent of devouring us. Nothing dropped from the sky with the intent of snatching us up and no other group on a quest came along to challenge us.

Keran remained quiet for the first couple of days and we left him alone. None of us, not even me, talked much.[3] For one thing, the heat stifled any attempts I might have made to crack jokes and try to make the trip more enjoyable for myself even if at the expense of my companions. For another, all the running about we'd done exhausted us and we had no energy to do

---

[2] So much did I worry about how one of those birds might swoop out of nowhere, I jumped at the first place that didn't have lava spewing out of the ground. This concern is actually more realistic than you'd think. Several of the lands that flashed by glowed red with molten rock. One time, a wave of lava splashed against the barrier, near about giving all of us heart attacks. I swear, this quest was shortening my life.

[3] Jazmin complained a lot but I'm not counting that.

anything but trudge forward and wish this quest might come to an end soon. Only with titanic effort could I even recall why we accepted this quest in the first place, despite the band on my arm tightening and loosening a little like a pulse every time I questioned the purpose of all this.[4]

We all knew what would happen. There would be a couple more trials to really test our mettle. We'd make it up the mountain holding the elixir and face a final test. If everything followed the formula, the attempt would nearly kill me but by some stroke of luck, we'd succeed anyway. Then we'd take the elixir and go back home. The stupid band of metal on my arm would finally let me go and I'd be free to saunter home at whatever speed I wished. Until then, I could march along without a word.

At one point, after a long day of travel, Jak did comment, "I hope for the sake of the listening public no one ever tries to make an epic of our journey. It would be verse after verse describing us walking. They'd run out of synonyms halfway through recounting our time in Fairyland."

"If anyone actually wanted to tell stories of our travels, it wouldn't be too hard to cut out all the boring bits. That's what they usually do," I said.

"I suppose you're right," Jak admitted. "If they cut out all the walking though, it's not a very accurate picture of our trip, is it?"

"I don't think accuracy will be high on their list of values." I said.

The first break in the monotony was a big one. It came in the form of a massive canyon, a gash in the red brown earth curving toward the horizon.

"Well, there won't be any getting around it," Naga said.

"We have to climb down?" Jazmin wanted to know.

"Hey, didn't Brendan's poem have something about barriers wide and deep?" Jak asked.

"I think so. I guess that answers Jazmin's question. This is

---

[4] At a certain point, I decided to make a game of it, forcing the band to squeeze and release every so often. Made me feel as if I had some control over it.

the part where we descend into the Abyss. No question about it," I said.

"Not much of an Abyss," Keran said. "Looks like a pretty innocuous canyon to me."

"For now," I pointed out. "I figure if there's anything we've learned on this quest, it's that, what's the appropriate cliché here, things are not what they seem."

"True enough," Naga said on Keran's behalf.

"I'm glad we settled that. Now we just have to figure out how to get down. I don't suppose any of you can fly," Keran said.

"I think you'd know by now," I told him as I leaned over the side of the canyon. From the edge I could see the drop to the bed of the canyon below was not quite as steep as I imagined. Still sheer enough to give me vertigo so I took a step back. Only when I regained my composure did I shuffle forward again. To give myself a greater sense of stability, I sat on the edge to scan our side of the canyon. A couple miles to the north, I thought I saw a likely collection of ledges and slopes we might be able to use.

I forced myself through the tedious process of following the whole passage down and thought it looked clear and as safe as anything like this could be. Still, we wouldn't know for sure until we reached a dead end or the bottom of the canyon. By then we might really have to learn how to fly if we wanted to get either down or up.

When I pointed out the path, everyone sat down on the edge as well and gazed at it. After a while, I urged them all back up to their feet and said, "We're going to give it a shot. Unless you all would rather sit here and bake in the sun?"

"Do you think it's cooler down there?" Jazmin wanted to know.

"There's shade," Naga remarked.

Jazmin lifted her thick hair away from her neck and set off ahead of us, quite determined to get to shade. She seemed a lot less enthusiastic once we arrived at the spot and she saw how steep the going would be in certain parts. As she looked over the edge, she had a sudden thought. "Wait. It's going to be as steep on the other side, isn't it? We'll never get out."

"We'll make it work," I told her. "If Jak and I have to climb first and haul the rest of you up, that's what we'll do."

"With what rope?" Jak whispered to me.

"We'll figure it out if it comes to it," I told him. "For now, play along."

Jak rolled his eyes at me but didn't give any other indication of his doubt. Meanwhile, I tightened all my belts and walked to the edge of the cliff. The closest ledge sat only two feet down so I jumped and landed lightly. The next step required a longer drop so I sat and lowered myself to the flat piece of rock. Then the going got a lot easier. The ground became relatively flat as I led us toward the floor of the canyon far below.

Going further and further down, we soon realized we had been very wrong thinking the temperature would become more bearable. In fact, the temperature climbed. Combined with the effort of hiking, I think I speak for everyone when I say we sweat so much it was a wonder the rocks didn't become slick with it. More problematically, we didn't do a very good job rationing our water.

By midday, when we still had half the height of the canyon to traverse, we nearly ran out. Jazmin begged for a halt so we rested for a time under the shadow of a large tree sitting precariously amongst the rocks.

Jak shook the last water pouch so its meager contents sloshed around the bottom. "This isn't looking good."[5]

"How long can we last without water?" Jazmin asked as she fanned herself with her hands.[6]

"In this heat, not very long at all," I told her. "We'll need to find water soon. I don't suppose you can do anything about it."

"Mages can't conjure up anything you want," Jazmin said.

"Just asking," I said.

"Sorry. I didn't mean to snap at you. Really, I'm just upset I can't," Jazmin said.

---

[5] This is the sort of thing Naga would usually chime in to say. I suppose the heat affected her as well. I thought lizards were supposed to be more active in the heat.

[6] I doubt it helped very much since she only moved hot air faster past her.

229

"In that case, we'll have to wait until we get to the bottom and hope the water is good enough to drink," I said.

"I know some purification spells," Jak said.

"There we go. We'll be fine as soon as we get to the bottom. No one is allowed to get heatstroke or faint before we get there. You especially," I said, pointing to Jazmin.

"I don't know," Jazmin responded. "I'll do my best."

About an hour later, Keran gave a shout of excitement and demanded everyone pay attention. He pointed out the direction with his paw[7] and we all turned to see a very small waterfall not far away.

Jak gestured at the open space separating the ground beneath our feet and the outcrop with the waterfall. "Can you make it?"

"We'll find out," I said. I unbuckled my sword so it wouldn't weigh me down and backed up as far as I could.

"This doesn't look very safe," Jazmin pointed out even as she rushed to get out of my way.

"Of course it's not safe," I agreed even as I took the last step back and prepared to charge. I measured the jump in my mind and figured I could make it. My feet left the ground and I hit the opposite ledge solidly. I pitched forward on instinct and caught myself before anything important smashed into the rock. I beckoned for Jak to throw me one of the water pouches.

It was terrible throw and I leaned out into the open air to snatch it before it dropped into the void. The arc when I tossed it back dropped it neatly into Jazmin's arms. I only laughed when Jak sent me a rude gesture and turned to get some of the water for myself as the others slaked their thirst from the pouch.

The water had a tang, a metallic taste[8] but also an odd sweetness. Really though, it didn't matter much to me. The water tasted more refreshing than anything else in the world.

Maybe because of the heat, no one bothered to question the

---

[7] It looked awkward, much as you'd expect. He had to sit down on his haunches and paw at the air to get our attention. I resisted the urge to tell him how much he looked like a begging dog and barely succeeded.
[8] Probably the high mineral content from being filtered through who knows how many layers of this reddish rock.

existence of this solitary waterfall or whether it might be a draw for people and creatures we didn't want to mess with. I certainly didn't question it until a large bulge of rock not far from my head burst outward. Instinct alone allowed me to drop to the ground in time and cover my head as chunks of rock hit every surface.[9]

When the shower ceased, I looked up to see what caused the explosion and stared up at an earthen beast soaring above our heads. It didn't look very aerodynamic, as you might expect of any creature with wings and body made of solid rock. I didn't see why it needed the wings at all. It couldn't be anything but magic keeping it in the air.

The creature opened a mouth filled with rows of curved fangs and released a bloodcurdling scream. Back on the trail, the others scrambled back against the rock face. Before I had a chance to ask what Jazmin could do, the beast dived straight at me.

As I didn't have anywhere to hide on this small outcrop and didn't even have my sword on me, I decided to run. With no time to back up and launch myself off the ground like before, I made do with a straight jump. I left the outcrop not a moment too soon because the creature smashed it into pieces.

My chest slammed into the rock on the other side of the gap and I barely caught the protruding edge of a rock to avoid tumbling to my death. Jak lunged forward, grabbed me by the hand and hauled me to solid ground.

Rather than take the time to thank him, I whirled around to watch the earthen creature extract itself from the hole its impact created. It examined the hole it made, perhaps searching for my crushed remains and screeched again in anger when my flesh and bones were nowhere to be found.

I took my sword back from Jak and we retreated. Unfortunately, we could not do this without making noise. We got an impressive distance away before Jak brushed his foot against some pebbles and sent them clattering down into the canyon. I didn't even wait for the creature to turn around before

---

[9] Every surface but my body in case you were wondering how this story continues without me narrating.

I shouted, "Run!"

Keran bolted as soon as I said the word, no longer sticking to the trail. He pulled far ahead of us, his low center of gravity making it easier to descend the slope. Jak and especially Jazmin had a much harder time though they also moved so fast I worried they might turn a foot and tumble to their deaths before the flying creature got to them. While they ran, I retreated a bit more slowly with sword in hand.

I thought I might have to shout to get the attention of the flying beast but it honed in on me without any prompting.[10] As it dived at me, I uttered a curse, turned around and vaulted over a boulder. I braced myself and again covered my head but the impact the beast made against the ground still tossed me aside. I rolled down a significant length of slope, knocking straight into Jak as he and Jazmin made their way down along a safer and more winding route.

Waving for the two of them to keep going, I got back on my feet and patted myself down, both to wipe off some of the dust and to make sure I didn't break anything.[11] Up above, the creature climbed slowly out of the hole he made and shook himself all over so the excess rock and stone fell away. He pumped his wings and went airborne again. I watched him circling us and glanced down at my sword.

I really didn't see how to fight off this creature. The sword in my hand could only take chips off the rock and stone. Who knew if it would even hurt him? At best, I could distract him[12] while the others made their mad dash toward the floor of the canyon. Very likely I'd be crushed sooner or later. In the old legends heroes could be smashed into the side of a cliff and then fall a couple thousand feet without injury. But hell, I could die here. Even if we all made it to the canyon floor, the beast might not let up on its attack. This wasn't one of the stories of old

---

[10] For once, I was thankful for it being my quest. Such attacks always came at me first. Saved me the trouble of having to throw myself in front of anyone.

[11] I didn't, as it happened. Another function of being the quest leader I'm sure since I smacked into quite a few boulders on the way down.

[12] I think I made our last enemy of unidentified gender female so I suppose I'm evening it out.

where such creatures were territorial and mysteriously left you alone once you ran far enough.

As these thoughts ran through my head, I wondered if I might be wrong. Most things in this quest followed pattern. Why not also this creature? I had little to lose by assuming so. I could hardly be crushed into pulp twice.

So while the beast continued to circle, I tried to follow the thought to its logical conclusion. What would someone do in one of those stories where the adventurers always won and went home without a single scar? I suppose I'd find the solution nearby and it would involve something silly and unrealistic like using the strength of my enemy against him.

I looked around in search for such a solution to my problem and my gaze caught on a big chunk of rock hanging over the path. Once the creature started to dive, I didn't have time to consider and figure out whether or not it would work. I ran as fast as possible to the base of the overhang and watched the beast come closer. I'd only have one shot at this.

I waited a little bit too long. By the time I darted out of the way, it was too late for me to get out of the impact zone. I could think of only one way to avoid being crushed under a landslide of stone. So, I did it. I jumped off the edge of the cliff and out into the open air. Behind me, the beast crashed into the rock, bringing the shelf down on his head.

Unfortunately, not everything went according to plan. I threw myself off the side of the canyon in the hopes of a ledge shortly below to catch me or even a shrub I could latch onto. In retrospect, I should have checked before I started with the whole crazy plan. For as it turned out, I saw nothing to catch me, nothing between me and the solid ground very far below but empty air. I know I'm supposed to say my life flashed before my eyes or something. Or maybe say I learned some lessons as I stared death in face. But none of that happened. So just pretend.[13] Before I could despair, a glowing net appeared in front of me and

_____

[13] Really, the thing I regretted most, moments from a messy and painful death, was not picking up the turkey leg and pegging it at Withercox. Missed a good chance there and if anyone deserved one to the face, it was him.

I slammed into it so hard my vision went black and I faded into unconsciousness.

When I woke, I saw stars splashed across the sky in a band of faded white, more stars in one place than I'd ever seen. Stunned by the pinpoints of brightness layered one on top of the other, I almost forgot what happened to lead to me being unconscious in the first place.

As soon as I did remember, I sat up. I tried to look around to see if the earthen beast had really been taken care of but didn't see much of anything before colors started exploding in my eyes. I moaned involuntarily and squeezed my eyes shut, willing the pain to go away. It didn't. I heard the scrabble of boots against the rock as the others came over and crowded around me.

"How are you feeling?" Jak wanted to know as soon as I looked up at him.

"Like a wild animal tore my brains out," I answered.

"I am so sorry," Jazmin said to me. "I did the first thing I thought of. If I made the net more pliable, you wouldn't have hit your head so hard."

"It's okay," I told her. "I'm grateful, at least until we find out whether I've sustained any long term brain damage. Still a lot better than falling to my death."

"This doesn't sound like her," Keran commented.

"Rahni, how do you feel about Margery?" Jak wanted to know.

"Don't mention her to me," I said. "I thought we agreed never to speak her name again."[14]

"How about Bey Cox?" Jak asked.

"Whatever passes for logic centers in his brain are always misfiring.[15] How do you think I feel about him?" I demanded.

"Sound more like herself?" Jak asked the others as he leaned back.

---

[14] Trust me, you don't want to hear the whole story. She's a nasty character with few scruples and even less street smarts. If you're going to be a jerk, at least do it well.

[15] This is a true story by the way. Man hasn't got a jot of common sense to trade for his life.

"Can't I even almost die in peace?" I asked.

"In all seriousness though, good job," Jak told me.

"I'm glad you're proud. I'll keep it in mind next time I decide to do something stupid. I assume it worked since we're all still alive."

Jazmin pointed behind me so I shifted to look. The light of all the stars above proved strong enough to outline the shape of the enormous pile of rock I brought down on the beast. Nothing could survive it, not even a creature made of stone and certainly not me. I gave an involuntary shudder and Jak noticed it.

"Hey, we're glad you made it. I don't think we could go on without you," Jak said.

"Of course not. It's my quest. If I kick the horse trough, no one is finishing the quest," I said.

"You know I don't mean it that way," Jak said with a laugh but dropped it when I waved for him to shut up.

"I see you didn't even bother to carry me further down the canyon," I said as I got up slowly, bracing against Jak's shoulder.

"Yeah, move you and risk making your injuries worse," Keran said.

I took stock as I went over to the fire, trying to see if any of the aches traveling up and down my body came from serious injuries. In the end, I decided I probably sustained a couple bruised ribs, a sprained right wrist and plenty of cuts. The wrist seemed the most serious out of all the injuries so I wrapped it up as the others told me what happened after I lost consciousness.

Apparently, Jazmin had been so afraid when I didn't move after hitting her net she almost dropped me. But Keran and Jak talked her through it as best they could and got me back onto solid ground. They continued down the side of the canyon until they realized the beast would not be extracting itself from the pile of rubble. In fact, it never moved at all. So they picked a shady spot and settled in to wait for me to wake up.

"So we lost hours of hiking," I complained. "We could be on the canyon floor by now."

"Well, do you want to start going now?" Jak wanted to know. "And have one of us break a foot on the way? Or worse?"

When the others started to yawn, I told them all to go to sleep as I'd take the first watch.

"You don't get a watch tonight," Jazmin protested.

"Nonsense. I've been asleep for hours. I couldn't sleep if I tried. Might as well do something with my energy." It took a fair amount of convincing[16] but everyone else finally agreed to let me be and went to sleep. Though I didn't lie when I said I wouldn't be able to fall asleep, that's not why I wanted to take the first watch. I took it because I wanted to be left alone to look at the stars and reflect on this quest.[17]

There was a lot of think about, most of it as jumbled in my head as it had been when I first found out I'd been cursed. I tried to keep my head down as we went, not get myself involved in the chaos. But I'd never been any good at this business of closing my eyes and pretending not to see, except perhaps when it came to myself.

And so we got ourselves dragged into one dilemma after another. Maybe if this had been a story, we would've picked up a moral or two for every dangerous encounter. But this, all this was the real world, messy even in the places where order ruled. Very often the order itself turned out to be no more than an illusion at best and a way to oppress at worst. What we learned from all of it I could not put into words. I could not even be sure it meant anything at all.

What were any of us to do in the face of so much bad in the guise of good and good for some coming as a consequence of evil? For it seemed clear Yara got something right even if all her talk of the balance and of Realignment was as much hogwash as it sounded. The same problem so galling to the rulers of the twin states we called Fairyland and the Evil Empire, that right and wrong would increasingly become muddled into a tangle, persisted throughout the Eigen States and certainly throughout the Floating Isles.

My philosophical pondering resulted in only the realization I had no answers and I'd doubt anyone who pretended to. So a

---

[16] And a fair bit of hollering incoherently to annoy the hell out of them.
[17] I hated having to do it, having to fall into the oh so customary moment of deep reflection. I needed it though, as would anyone after almost dying.

good night's work all around, if only because I accepted the inevitable, that sometimes our search for unambiguous answers could be the most dangerous thing of all.

CHAPTER TWENTY SIX

In the morning, my entire body hurt worse than when I lay down to go to sleep. So much so I found a tree and cut myself a good sized staff to lean on as we continued toward the canyon floor. I didn't even want to think about having to climb up the opposite slope, not to mention encountering another of those beasts.

With me slowing us down and the ever increasing heat dragging at all of us, it took the whole morning to make it to the bottom. The river responsible for carving this canyon looked almost pitiful up close, a mere shadow of its mighty former self. It ran surprisingly clear as it wound through the twists and turns.

Jazmin walked up to the water, pulled off her boots and stepped into the river. Since we needed to walk along the water to find a better spot to cross, we all followed her lead. Perhaps trailing our feet through the water slowed us but the heat was so bad we welcomed anything to help us cool down.

When we finally got to an area in the river narrow enough a well placed throw would get our packs over to the other side, I bundled all my weapons up before wading across, only swimming towards the very middle of the river.

As soon as I emerged from the water, I could feel myself drying off. I gestured for Jak to throw our packs over. Only he possessed the strength to hurtle them this far though all of us had serious doubts about his aim. As soon as he threw the pack, I splashed out of the water, dashed to my right and managed to snag it before it hit the rocks and smashed open.

"Good catch," Naga praised from my pocket even as she shook herself to get the river water off of her body. Given the praise, I thought it'd be a bit rude to complain about all the water she got in my face.

I put down the pack I caught and signaled for Jak to throw the next. After I piled together all our supplies, Jak jumped into the water and started to swim over.

Jazmin didn't move, just staring at the water so I shouted, "What is it?"

"I don't think I can swim," Jazmin finally said.

In the end, Keran had to ferry her over. I issued a stern warning for him not to get any ideas about dunking her in the middle of the river and they made it over without mishap. By the time everyone arrived on the opposite side of the river, my clothes were almost dry. I looked up at the rock face directly in front of us and shook my head, judging it too steep to attempt a climb[1] so we continued to follow the river.

We hadn't gone more than a dozen steps before the map in my pocket blazed with a sharp spike of warmth. I released a shout of alarm and ripped the map out of my pocket, but it continued to pulse so hot I could barely hold it.

I pinched the top of the map and gave it a shake to make it flip open. We were all treated to the confusing sight of two of the four rules pulsing in tandem. The first rule and the fourth both glowed and pulsed much brighter than ever before, warning us our lives were in danger and that the inviolable rules were not, in fact, inviolable.

"What does it mean?" Keran wanted to know.

---

[1] This may have been colored by the fact that even the thought of a climb in this heat made me want to lie down for half an eternity.

239

"I have no idea," I admitted as I looked around for signs of danger. "It's never been this bright."

"And the fourth rule has never glowed before," Jak added as he also cast his gaze about in a mixture of confusion and apprehension.

He and I exchanged a glance but neither of us could say what this meant. I figured we might need to fall back into violence though so I loosened my sword and beckoned for everyone to get closer. I was still looking around for a beast shaped rock when darkness descended.[2] It was a darkness so complete I thought I'd gone blind before everyone else started talking about not being able to see anything.

"Nobody move," I said.

"Not planning on it," Keran said.

I ignored him and squinted into the darkness, trying to make out anything that might tell me what was going on here. "Jak, ideas?"

"None whatsoever," he responded.

"Did you see that?" Jazmin asked.

I started to answer in the negative but then, all of a sudden, I did, a shred of faint light flitting through the darkness, too quick to see. It went past us and then overhead several times, which made me think of the flying beast from earlier. Only this time if it came for us, we wouldn't know where to run.

We never did find out what flew over our heads. But it wasn't one of those stone beasts for nothing burst from the sky to smash us apart. Instead, the air began to swirl with ever increasing violence, buffeting us into each other and then lifting us off the ground.

The darkness shattered and mixed with light as the wind threw us around as if we flew in a cyclone. I fought with the wind though it wasn't precisely an enemy I could hack at with a knife. So, as earlier, I forced myself to think in terms of the quest, to try and tease out what a supposed hero[3] would do in

---

[2] Only literally, not figuratively.
[3] And inevitably, it would've been a hero. Girls didn't belong at the head of quests, didn't you know?

such a situation.

I recognized this as the moment of crisis, when the darkness came closest to snuffing us out.[4] Everything before this had been but a joke, a shadow of this threat trying to engulf us now. All the lessons of the quest should come together. In one fell stroke, I'd have those morals I previously dismissed engrained in my psyche and learn something new about myself. Just thinking about the cheesiness made me want to roll my eyes.

But I could either think or continue to flail about ineffectually until we died of starvation. So I did it. I considered every hero's tale I ever heard and decided a heroine's greatest challenge could only be defeated by overcoming her greatest flaw. Which forced me to ask the obvious question. I did not like doing it, mostly because I already knew the answer.

As with most people, the worst thing about me was also the best. For all they peddle about virtues and vices, no one ever says it all depends on how you use them.

If I didn't miss my guess, I knew what I had to do. "Stop struggling," I shouted at the others. "Just relax!"

"What?!" Jak demanded, clearly having trouble believing what he heard, not only because of the content of the advice but because it came from me.

"Trust me," I told him before doing my best to follow the advice. It felt difficult of course, as any attempt to overcome your greatest flaw must be. Who'd need to go on a quest otherwise?

And my greatest flaw, you ask? Well, it's quite simple. The vulture already made it very clear it was the confidence that usually served me so well, my penchant for pretending control even and especially when I had none. So for once in my life, I needed to recognize I wasn't in control and let the wind carry us where it willed. Or so I thought. In truth, all this conjecture came from a theory, a tickling in the back of my head.

The trick back with the beast and the rocky outcrop felt ridiculous enough and stank of desperation. But this? I couldn't believe I was putting my trust in the magic of the quest to pull

---

[4] Again, literally.

us through. I'd be horrified if I weren't too busy counting on it to save our lives.

The wind tossed us around and around for an age, longer than I thought a cyclone like this could rage.[5] Every once in a while, one of the others would shout a comment or a question but I blocked it out. It would be a better ride for them if they relaxed and took a nap but their feelings didn't matter so much. At the end of the day, it was my quest.

No matter how fiercely the wind roared or how much I feared it would dash us against the rocks, I willed myself to remain calm and to accept things were out of my hands. I tried, tried really hard. But though I could force my body to relax and stop it from flailing against the wind, I couldn't stop my mind from issuing defiant thoughts. I suppressed a growl of frustration as I reflected this was a rigged game. If I needed to let go, forcing myself to that point wouldn't do the trick. Wasn't it just another form of control? As soon as I had the thought, something in the character of the winds changed. It wasn't a good sort of change though, as if it were planning to die down and let us settle softly to the ground.

If anything, the winds became more violent and we all slammed into each other. Jak reached his hands out and grabbed us. Jazmin cast a spell to bind us together with ropes of light and Jak let go. This resulted in an exceedingly uncomfortable jumble.[6]

"This is not good," Naga said.

"What did you do?" Jak wanted to know.

"Not a thing," I told him. "I thought I figured it out."

"Doesn't seem to be working," Keran said, his words muffled against Jak's chest.

"You think I can't tell?" I demanded. "I'm trying."

"More importantly, how can we help?" Jak wanted to know.

---

[5] Didn't mean to make it rhyme. Any chance becoming a poet will get me through the trial? Yeah, I didn't think so.

[6] I had the unique pleasure of feeling someone's knee knocking against my leg under every buffet of wind while my elbow choked Jak by pressing against the back of his neck.

"Jazmin? Anything?" I asked.

"I already tried," Jazmin said. "Nothing I can do."

An updraft hit us and sent us shooting up past the swirling darkness. We punched right through a bank of clouds and came out into the sunlight.

Two enormous figures sat to our right, floating atop their own personal clouds. One had the head of an elephant and the other looked like a human except for her extra set of arms and deep blue skin. The latter held a hand her forehead and released a groan that made the clouds around her scatter a bit as if in fear.

"The prayers getting to you?" the goddess with the face of an elephant asked.

"Are they ever," agreed the other goddess. "I grant there are times when only prayer will do. But the heavens have mercy, a stubbed toe is not an occasion for calling my wrath down upon an ill placed table. Neither is a rotten apple in a barrel occasion for asking me to deal death upon all merchants. And please, would they stop teaching their children to pray to all the gods to cover their bases? If I hear one more prayer about a child's fallen tooth, I may scream."

"I sympathize as a goddess so often mistaken as a patron of health. You know who's the worst though? Monks! Their chanting drives me out of my mind. And on holy days?"

"To tell you the truth, I knock back a few and sleep on those days. They can fend for themselves for a day here and there."

The elephant headed goddess stopped before replying and gestured at us as we reached the highest point of our arc. We simply hovered as the goddesses examined us.

"What do you make of them?" the one who stopped us asked.

"We're on a quest!" I shouted at her.

"Oh, that explains it," the blue goddess said. "Carry on." She flicked her fingers and we shot upwards once more, too fast for any of us to ask for help.[7]

We hit the next bank of clouds and emerged to see a trio of enormous female figures with leathery wings coming out of their shoulders. They stood together looking over their domain.

---

[7] Though, given their conversation, they might not be willing to.

Their level bustled with activity. Metallic boxes with arms sticking out of them at haphazard angles sat in rows in tandem with enormous spindles.

The arms sticking out of the metal boxes moved too fast for us to follow. From what I could make out, they seemed to be spinning string, measuring it out and snipping it at various lengths. Some were incredibly long, some incredibly short and there seemed no logic to it, no rhyme or reason.

One of the three female goddesses looked up as we passed and seemed to meet my gaze. She smiled and gestured at one of the boxes far to her left. When she spoke, the sound came from a spot right beside my ear even as we continued to speed away. "Your day too will come. But not today."

"What did she say?" Jazmin wanted to know.

"I think she told me we're not going to die today. Or at least I'm not," I said.

"Great," Keran muttered as we hit the bottom of another layer of clouds.

As before, I instinctively closed my eyes though these clouds were not damp. Passing through them left no mark on us and we might as well have passed through empty air. So I opened my eyes and looked around at the inside of the cloud. There wasn't much to see, just whiteness in every direction, so thick I could hardly see my feet when I craned my head and looked down. This cloud bank proved to be the thickest by far and Jazmin had time enough to play around with her spell to loosen the tight hold.

Finally, we burst free of the clouds. But when we looked down, the clouds were gone, replaced far, far below by a flat and virtually endless stretch of water. I knew we must be further up than I ever imagined for the sea lay completely still, smooth as a piece of blue cloth.

As we started to fall at an incredible pace, a dark shape appeared on the horizon. It grew larger and larger until it resolved itself into a beetle of colossal size. It moved its continent size body through the water, creating waves big enough to wipe out entire worlds. It came to a stop almost directly beneath us and scanned its surroundings.

244

Not seeing what it looked for, the beetle[8] dived into the water with surprising grace. It resurfaced gently, holding a mass of mud. The mud came apart and drifted outwards, forming the shape of the Floating Isles.

"I always wondered," Keran said.

"You think anyone will believe this story?" Jak wanted to know.

"Of course not. You want to try telling someone like Yutian the Floating Isles exist because some titanic beetle decided it wanted a perch. Not going to happen. He'll chew and swallow his own shirt before swallowing that," I said.

As we continued to plunge toward the surface of the water, enormous metal wires came down from the sky and grabbed ahold of the edges of the Floating Isles, keeping them on the surface of the water. I looked up to see where the wires came from but they extended too far up.

"It'd be nice if we could land home," I said. "If we ignore the part where we get smashed into smithereens against it and that this is probably long before we're supposed to be born."

"Cheerful thought," Jak commented. "What do you think is happening to us?"

No one had the slightest idea. We bandied about a few suggestions, none very convincing. You might not think it possible given we were falling toward our deaths, but we soon got bored. Enough so our attention soon turned to other matters. Jazmin in particular wanted to know what we were taught regarding the history of the Floating Isles. Of course, it differed entirely from her own understanding, enough to make me question what I thought I knew.

I never entertained the notion her version might be correct. They stuffed it far too full of doctrine and ideology to be any sort of real history, if any narrative of past events could ever be said to reflect reality. The point was that few back in Fairyland ever seriously questioned the narrative of a group of heroes

---

[8] Flat, round and mostly black. I have no idea what kind of beetle it is, especially since I didn't have much experience with world scale bugs before today.

seizing half the land from the mighty oppressors and building a paradise of independent and beautiful kingdoms.[9]

Nobody back home questioned our admittedly more realistic narrative, which featured an almost dizzying array of names, battles and edicts. Sure, there was evidence for much of it but it *could* all be hogwash. That no one ever considered this meant we were more open to being tricked and fooled than I wanted to believe.

After a time, I asked Jak, "Do you know any teleportation spells you can teach Jazmin?"

"You know teleportation simply isn't possible, not unless you want to get your brain and body parts scrambled into a giant mess.[10] Even if teleportation were possible, where would you want to teleport while traveling at these speeds? Smashing into anything save a mountain of down would kill us," Jak said.

"At least I'm trying to come up with ways to get us out of this situation," I shot back.

"What about a net?" Keran suggested.

"I'm not sure I can make one that doesn't do what the last one did to Rahni," Jazmin said.

"We'd be cut into blocks if forced up against one of those," I added, looking to Jak for confirmation.

"Sounds right," Jak agreed. "I really can't think of another way to slow us down though. Or, come to think of it, a way to get back to our own time."

"So we hope whatever magic brought us here brings us back?" Jazmin wanted to know.

"Looks that way," Naga said when none of us really wanted to agree and make it real.

It wasn't easy for any of us to admit helplessness. Then we started to fall with even greater speed. Already, the wind roared in our ears and pulled at our clothes. But we could still talk and keep our eyes open against the buffeting winds. Now, we

---

[9] Just thinking the words made me want to hurl. Yet a lot people bought this garbage. So many nobles, and not just in the Eigen States, truly thought they were doing the peasants a favor by oppressing them.

[10] We know this because plenty of people tried with let's say, mixed results.

weren't so much falling as being yanked down. We fell with such speed we began to lose consciousness. My vision, narrowed to a slit since I could only barely keep my eyes open, started to darken around the edges.

My thoughts moved sluggishly[11] as I faded in and out of consciousness. More disturbingly, even while conscious, I could not bring myself to feel much of anything. I knew this did not bode well for our chances of survival. I could not make this small portion of my consciousness care. So I floated on the edge of falling into the black as we continued to charge towards the water, the landmass and the beetle the size of a world.

Either way, it didn't seem so long before we hit the surface of the water. At these speeds, logic predicted no chance of survival. But logic had no place on this quest. It was only fitting it would continue to give us a wide berth. Indeed, the water flowed up to embrace us, defying all physical explanation. Which is when I blacked out for real.

---

[11] The deprivation of oxygen to my brain probably.

CHAPTER TWENTY SEVEN

This being the second time I fainted in recent memory, I knew not to start moving immediately when I regained consciousness. I felt the warmth on my face before I opened my eyes and even when I could see the sky above me, waited before pushing myself to a sitting position.

The others lay scattered around me, still breathing slowly. I left them alone to wake naturally and looked around. To our west lay the canyon where we met so many difficulties, cutting across the landscape like a great red wound.

We now stood at the base of the mountains we saw while on the far side of the canyon. I dug out the map and measured our position to find we were at the base of the very mountain we'd have to ascend. Somewhere up these slopes, green and vibrant with lush vegetation, lay the elixir we came here to fetch. I spent some time scanning the side of the mountain I could see, trying to find a hint of where the elixir might be.[1]

The mountain was only so big and I hoped we would find the elixir before long. I wanted to be done with this quest now more

---

[1] Don't know why I bothered. Of course it would be on the summit. They needed to make us climb as much as possible.

than ever. The sooner we could leave, the better. I was utterly sick of the repeated attempts to kill us off, even given all the beautiful and grand things I'd seen. This last episode, it really took the cake, the way they threw us for a loop.

But we'd done it, we passed through the ordeal and came out on the other side. Which gave us the right to seize our reward. For me, this meant not so much the elixir but the ability to leave all this behind and head home, where life at least made sense.

Even as I thought this, I understood it was a lie. Was my own land really less confusing? Didn't we have plenty of dilemmas as frustrating as anything we'd seen on this quest? Weren't they even more intractable? For while I might feel a certain responsibility for people who crossed our paths, it didn't come anywhere near the responsibility I felt for people nominally under my own care.

Jak cursed behind me and I went to help him sit up. He squinted at his surroundings and didn't even bother to ask how we ended up here. He simply shook his head.

"On the bright side, it's no longer broiling hot," I said.

"True," Jak agreed. I gave him a hand up. He stumbled, pacing back and forth a few times to get the feeling back into his legs. When he could finally move without wincing, he remarked, "At least I know we made it through alive. Or else surely my legs wouldn't be so cramped."

"Did you really think they were finished torturing us?" I asked. "There are a few more steps until this quest is over."

"I'm hoping we can avoid the whole bonus ordeal portion of the proceedings. We've already been attacked by a flying beast and chased by an angry mob. What else can they throw at us?"

"A foolish question if I've ever heard one. You know they can always do one better," I said as I turned to look up the side of the mountain.

Jak walked over to join me and followed the line of my gaze. "To the summit then?"

"I think so. They haven't made us climb anything yet so this will be it. Some sense of cosmic balance will be satisfied if we descend into the canyon and ascend to the top of a mountain for the final test."

"What about all the flying we did?" Jak asked. "Sure felt like an ascent to me."

That gave me some pause. Finally, I decided, "No, no, that's still part of the descent because we fell back down."

"You're making this up as you go along, aren't you?"

"Definitely."

"Aren't we all?"

It took Keran, Jazmin and Naga a bit longer to wake up and even longer to work themselves up to a state to travel. They tottered around unsteadily so we didn't make it very far up the mountain slope by the time we decided to call it a night. It became slow going for the mountain was all jagged angles and steep rock faces, not easy to navigate. It took us all the next day to come within sight of the summit but we made camp instead of pushing forth because the dying light would make it hard to see anything once we got up there.

And if a monster or guardian awaited, twilight hardly seemed the best time for a fight.[2] We felt a little foolish in the morning when we hauled ourselves up to the summit and found absolutely nothing there. We searched high and low, pacing over every piece of ground and found no elixir at all. Finally, we all sat down to take a breather and tried to figure out our next step.

"We know it's on this mountain, don't we? The only thing we can do is make our way back down in a spiral pattern," Jazmin said, making a motion with her finger to match.

"It won't be easy on this mountain but the general idea seems sound," Jak decided.

None of us were happy but Keran reacted worst of all. He sulked and didn't participate in the conversation. This confused me because he insisted on tagging along for the last portion of this quest. Then I understood. "You wanted the elixir, didn't you?" I asked him, interrupting Jak in the middle of a comment.[3]

Keran looked up and grimaced. "I wasn't planning to steal it

---

[2] Given we were in the midst of a quest, it was probably the worst time possible. That's the time of day people lost their heads and thought, for instance, hiding in a light shadow counted as a stroke of genius.

[3] I interrupted him a lot so Jak let me say my piece.

mind you. I figured if the elixir could save a nation from a great calamity, why wouldn't it do my people some good? Still, I'm sorry for lying about my intentions."

"As far as I'm concerned, you never did. Everyone on this quest has ulterior motives. It's my quest and even I'm not here because I want to be.[4] You are entirely welcome to the elixir. You heard my father. We have a collection of the things back home. I doubt this will make or break us. Sounds like it'll do you more good than me."

"I feel silly," Keran admitted.

"Good," I said. "Mission accomplished."

A flash of light sent us all ducking for cover. Not far away stood an elf holding a vial pulsing with light. I paid no attention to the elixir because I was distracted by the elf, who looked very familiar.

I felt the map in my pocket pulsing as Naga asked, "Monty?"

To answer everyone else's question, I held up the map, whose second rule lit up and extinguished itself to a steady beat. And indeed, the would be imposter's hair was a couple shades too dark.

"You're a little late," I told our new enemy. "I don't know what tales you grew up with but you're supposed to show up in the heroic deeds phase, when we're still questioning the reality of our circumstances. That way you can serve as a living metaphor for the shifting nature of reality."

"Who says I haven't been with you this whole time?" the sorcerer questioned. To prove this dubious point, he or she waved a hand to cast a spell. She changed to resemble Ann and then the yaoguai we met in the Land of Way Too Many Bridges[5]. I let the sorcerer continue this farce as I considered how best to get at the elixir. I knew this final showdown should involve lessons well learned but I felt more inclined to go the brute force route and ask questions later.

When she finished with her transformations, the sorcerer

---

[4] To say the least. I probably wanted to be here least of all, come to think of it.

[5] I don't think that's the real name but I'm going with it.

settled on the appearance of a human woman about a few years older than me. It wasn't anyone we'd seen before so maybe it was her true form.[6]

"Let's say we believe you," I said. "What do you mean by following us around? There are plenty of other questers. Why don't you stalk them?"

"What's to say they don't all have sorcerers tagging them?" she questioned in turn.

"Is there a point to this?" Jak wanted to know.

"The point is I'm not to let you get your hands on this elixir," the sorcerer said.

"Then why did you bring it here?" I wanted to know.

"We can't say you've failed if we don't even give you a chance," the sorcerer said. "It wouldn't be fair."

"Fairness. That's something I haven't heard about in a while," Keran remarked.

"We're wasting time here," Naga said.

I pulled out my sword and took a step toward the sorcerer, while signaling for Jazmin to get ready. "It's probably best you hand over the vial."

The sorcerer shuffled backwards and held up a hand to stall me. "Wait a minute. I'm not done saying my piece yet. We want you to know it's not anything personal, us messing with your quest."

"Seems awfully personal to me," Jak said.

"I'm telling you the truth. We can't let you win, especially now that the Realignment has begun," the sorcerer said.

I was prepared to use her distraction to my advantage but this last statement gave me pause. Everything about Realignment confused me so if she could shed some light on it, I was willing in turn to let her stay conscious for a little bit longer.[7] "Are you saying there really is some cosmic battle between good and evil?"

"It's not really a battle in the conventional sense. It's not as if

---

[6] I didn't really care of course. Whatever she looked like, we needed to smack her upside the head and get the elixir.

[7] Though not much longer if I had my way.

everyone gets out into a field and dukes it out, the winners getting to call themselves good and the losers relegated to lowly positions. It's not so straightforward. There's more manipulation than outright violence. It's political and power structures. So no hard feelings, I trust."

"Excuse me?" Keran said. "No hard feelings? It's not personal? That's what you're going with? You think it's all okay because you throw a few of those words around?" In a move none of us expected, he lunged forward.

The sorcerer didn't expect it either for she barely avoided Keran's jaws. She cast a spell, turned herself into a humanoid creature of rock and aimed a swipe at his head. I burst forward a beat after Keran and made it there in time to counter with a slash of my sword. The blade carved a groove down the side of the sorcerer's earthen arm and she stumbled back before she could further menace Keran.

I didn't let the advantage go to waste, chasing the sorcerer as she retreated. I landed two more shallow cuts on her arms before she could cast another spell. She turned into a fierce creature the size of a bear with serrated claws not at all suited to hunting. They were very suited to killing though as I reflected when they came within a hairsbreadth of my face. I saw the edges of the claws but pulled myself back to avoid being skewered.

It was hardly the first time I'd been threatened with physical harm on this trip so I didn't waste any time being incredulous or reviewing the many moments when it could have gone very wrong. I pushed forward, using the sorcerer's very strengths against her.[8] I converted the viciousness of her swipe into a benefit for I got behind her and hit the hand holding the elixir with a sharp blow.

The sorcerer dropped the elixir and tried to get her hand under it but I pushed her aside. I caught the vial and tossed it to Jazmin. When I turned my attention back to the sorcerer though, she was nowhere to be seen.

For a long time, I could not accept her sudden disappearance.

---

[8] Like I was meant to do. It really is hard to go through a quest without falling into the usual paths to victory.

We stood around holding our breath as we waited for her to pop out. Finally though, Jazmin walked over and handed the vial to me. As soon as I touched the vial again, the band of metal around my arm grew large enough to fall to my wrist. I shook it to the ground.

"You don't want to keep it?" Jazmin wanted to know.

I laughed and answered by taking a few steps back and kicking it off the mountain. The armband flew through the air in a thoroughly satisfying curve. Only when the armband disappeared from sight, lost amongst the rocks and stone did I affirm to myself this was it, the end of the quest.

But while I might be free, the rest of my party didn't fare so well. And in the end, it seemed my curse, even if it included a physical manifestation, was the least binding of all. Jak never saw any resolution to his desires. Jazmin remained a fugitive from her own land. Keran though, I could at least help.

Before I handed the vial to Keran though, it stopped glowing. I held it up to the light to see what made it so special. Not seeing anything, I plucked off the glass plug capping the slender vial and gave it a whiff. Then, before anyone could protest, I tipped the vial over, poured a drop onto my finger and stuck it in my mouth.

As the others looked on, horrified, I nodded, having confirmed my suspicions. "It's nothing more than lemon flavored water. If the ones back home are the same, future generations are going to get a nasty surprise."

Keran cursed and fell over sideways in a demonstration of his frustration.[9]

I replaced the top, walked over and knelt down next to him. "Sorry Keran. You can still take it back with you and pretend it's a talisman. Just don't let anyone actually drink it. Or pour it over anything that dissolves in weak acids."

"No, it's alright," Keran said as he got up again. "It was a foolish idea from the start. If my people are going to be convinced, it will not be through fakery. The elixir was never going to help me."

---

[9] Didn't even know wolfhounds could collapse like that.

"In that case, I think it's been a satisfactorily anticlimactic final showdown," I said.

"Is it really a good idea to say that?" Jak wanted to know.

"I'm doing it on purpose," I told him. "I figure if we can have our extra special surprise bonus ordeal here it'll be a smooth road home."

"You know it doesn't work that way," Jak said. "We need to be on the road back before they spring it on us."

"Thought it worth a try," I said.

"I don't understand. We have the elixir. I thought getting our hands on it was the last step. Isn't the quest over?" Jazmin asked.

"Not quite," I told her. "In an ideal world, quests would be over as soon as you put your hands on the reward. Unfortunately, we might have lessons to learn and a long and tortuous road back. Just because we've won doesn't mean we'll make it out unscathed. Isn't this fun?"

As if to emphasize my point, three clear notes rang out to announce the arrival of the worst enemy anyone could have. Instantly, I knew the sorcerer had not been the final trial after all. She was merely a distraction, as inconsequential as she seemed.

No, we had something much worse on our hands.

CHAPTER TWENTY EIGHT

"It's the Board," Naga announced.

"Not now," I told her, pushing her back into my pocket and turning to face the new threat. The Board was exactly what it sounded like, a giant sheet of wood. Featureless and flat, it floated in midair by no mechanism anyone could explain.

Names and records in all different languages filled its surface. They shifted around constantly, vanishing and appearing by turns. The Board was the stuff of myth and legend, a boogeyman to scare children and worry misbehaving teenagers. It held within itself a record of your entire life, an account of what would happen to you from the moment you emerged in the world of the living to the moment you left it behind.[1]

As I watched, all the names and words running across the surface of the board faded away, only to be replaced by four names written in larger script. The letters appeared one by one and I realized what I felt earlier within the dark whirlwind didn't approach this. I wasn't helpless the way we were now,

---

[1] If all this sounded like a load of crock, well then I sympathize. I barely believed in it myself but here it floated, the Board everyone spoke about in fearful tones.

waiting for our fate to be written.

This *would* be the true final villain, since the Board and all it represented was the antithesis of everything I believed in. If the Board determined our beliefs and our actions, we were helpless in a far deeper and disturbing way than when simply physically restrained. A decision to resist or to accept would be no decision at all.

So far, I didn't know any of this to be true. As soon as the Board started writing in Jazmin's name, I stirred myself up to say, "Hold on. What are you doing?"

The last letter of Jazmin's name stopped writing itself. Then all the words vanished and new ones began to scrawl into the wood. The Board had no mouth to speak but as these words appeared, a source-less voice read them out. "Making a record of today's events."

"A record," Naga echoed.

"You mean you don't make any decisions?" Jak wanted to know after exchanging a glance with me.

"Of course not," the Board said,[2] "even if it does make people feel better to think they don't have free will."

"What about the magic that controls Fairyland?" Jazmin wanted to know after a pause during which we tried to process what the Board told us.

"That magic has nothing to do with me. I'm a lowly scribe and let me tell you, I have it worse than you," the Board said. "I'm only here to make a record of your victory."

"Why?" I asked. "You don't make an appearance after every quest or else my parents would have known about you and not been so afraid of the consequences of not sticking to tradition."

"This is hardly an ordinary quest," the Board told me.

"Retrieving a useless elixir from a remote location? That's about the most ordinary quest I can think of," I said.

"You know that's not what I mean," the Board said. "Your quest is not unique for its goal and not even unique because of who you are. It is pure chance, like so much else, that you are

---

[2] This is probably the closest I'll ever get to fainting from relief. The world actually faded a little before I snapped myself out of it.

here to set off this chain of events."

"No chance of us getting inflated self-worth then," I remarked. "It'd be nice to know what exactly we've set off."

"Precisely what Yara told you," the Board said. "The frontlines of a great battle to determine good and evil have been drawn with your opening salvo. Your names and actions will be recorded and passed down as a part of what is to follow."

"Could you not?" I wanted to know. "Just the thought makes me uncomfortable. We're not special."

"You are not. But then again, you are. You're part of a new generation, the products of a new age. For better or for worse, the decision of what becomes of this world will lie with you. If you don't deserve a say more than anyone else, neither do you deserve less of one. Plus, I have no choice but to do my job. You think I want to float around being a glorified secretary? You think it's my cup of tea?" the Board asked.[3] Then it began to rock back and forth with such violence we all took a step back. A thin wind instrument made of reed dropped to the ground and rolled over to knock against my boot.

I bent to pick it up and raised an eyebrow at the Board. "What is this? Our reward for a job well done?"

Jak took it from me and turned it over a few times. "Looks like a duduk. I think I know what this is for."

The Board didn't bother to confirm or deny.[4] It flashed one more sentence across its surface before disappearing back to whichever dimension it came from. The Board read simply, "Realignment has begun."

"And I thought the sorcerer episode was anticlimactic," Keran said. "That Board is little more than a flying record book."

I couldn't completely agree because there was something to be said about the Board as the last enemy. I couldn't think of anything more existentially terrifying than evidence of not being free to make my own decisions. I shook off the chills still

---

[3] I mean, it was a board so I don't think it really had much experience with tea or any other food for that matter.
[4] In fact it seemed a little annoyed with us, as much as a flat piece of wood could convey this.

traveling up my spine and looked at Jak. "What's the instrument for then?"

"Might want to grab hold of me," Jak said as he pivoted to face west. One after another,[5] we put our hands on his shoulder. Jak raised the instrument to his lips and played a few somber notes. He played tunelessly but the small instrument produced echoing notes moving in a way perhaps none of us could have explained. So yes, the music was pleasant. But nothing happened.

After a minute or two, I lifted my hand from Jak's shoulder, removed Jazmin's and nudged Keran away as well. "Jak, I don't think it's working."

Jak seemed to come out of a trance as he stopped blowing and looked around as if he expected to no longer be standing on the summit of the mountain. When he realized we hadn't moved, he sighed. "I thought for sure it had to be a Traveling Flute. I figured it was our reward for completing the quest."

"What was it supposed to do?" Jazmin wanted to know.

"Ever hear a bard recount a hero's tale?" Jak asked in turn.

"My parents didn't believe in bards but I snuck out a few times to listen," Jazmin said.

"Then you know. There's a certain type of music they always play when the heroes are traveling across great distances and they want to speed things along. I thought I'd try to reproduce it. They're supposed to work how Seven League Boots do, only without all the complications of only being able to travel seven leagues[6] at every step," Jak said.

"I guess whoever distributes these rewards decided to be frugal today," I said as I took it from him. "I mean really? This is what we get for the last few weeks of labor?"

"That and the knowledge we've begun something," Jazmin pointed out.

"Let's not even talk about that," I grumbled. And really, I

---

[5] Each more hesitantly than the next, mostly because he didn't explain himself. I think we were all rather tired of going along with things we didn't understand.

[6] Not to mention the complication of not really knowing how long a league is.

didn't want to think about it. The idea disturbed me when Yara first mentioned it to us. It only bothered me more now that the Board confirmed it. I found myself thinking over our actions throughout the course of this trip to see what it might mean for those who came after. All in all, I didn't think we did a horrible job. We saved people I thought deserved saving and handed out some satisfying defeats.[7]

If the principles that guided my actions on this quest became some standard, I thought I could live with it. But it was one thing to say I accepted them and quite another to assent to them becoming law or even guidelines for everyone else.

The only thing that made it less horrible was the knowledge our quest was only the trigger. Presumably an event as large as the Realignment would not hinge upon us. Plenty of other people would have input. And rightfully so. I didn't trust myself or any other one person to be the standard of morality. As far as I knew, no one sane ever did.

"I got it!" Jak suddenly shouted. He grabbed my hand, slapped the duduk into it and shoved it at my face. "You play it."

"You think it's going to be like the sword in the ground?" I asked. "It's one thing for me to yank a blade out of the ground and quite another to ask me to play an instrument I've never even seen before."

"Just do it," Jak said.

"Alright," I agreed. "Everyone better prepare their ears." When I blew on the pipe, a strangled note came out the other end, so harsh I stopped almost immediately.

"Nothing happ-" Before Naga finished speaking, the world shifted under our feet. Some force tossed us a couple feet into the air and rather than pushing us over the land, grabbed hold of the ground and moved it underneath us.

Probably because I blew such a short note, the magic didn't take us very far, depositing us a few feet above the ground at the bottom of the mountain. Keran and I landed well, staggering

---

[7] Maybe with a little more irritability than strictly necessary but the world could deal with that.

only a little. Jak and Jazmin both spilled onto the ground and had to be hauled back up.

"I retract my previous statement," Naga said. "It worked."

"Odd," Jak said as he looked back up the mountain. "If it worked, why did it sound so horrific?"

"I think you're overestimating the amount of magic that can be packed into a simple instrument. It might be able to magically transport us across vast distances but turning my efforts into music? That's too much to ask," I told him.

"Is this how it's supposed to work?" Jazmin wanted to know as she rubbed her shoulder.

"In essence," Jak answered. "The ride should be a little smoother."

"I'd like to think so," Jazmin agreed. "Or else it's a wonder everyone doesn't die on the way back from a quest."

"Maybe it'll get better?" Jak suggested.

"I doubt it," I said at the same time Naga did. She darted back into my pocket when I glared at her. "We'll give it a try. Everyone hold on." They did, wincing so hard you'd think I already began torturing them with the duduk.

It's a good thing I didn't expect anything different or else I'd have been sorely disappointed. My attempts resulted in an even harsher series of notes but they did get us over and across the canyon. As before, the force accompanying the music tossed us into the air. The ground slid under us rapidly and vanished as it dropped into the edge of the canyon. I wanted to stop for the noise grated in my ears but I didn't know what might happen if I stopped playing[8] so far above the ground.

When we reached the other side of the canyon and I finally allowed myself to take a real breath, everyone stumbled away from me. They massaged their ears and tottered around. "I think you're all being a little dramatic," I told them even as I tugged on my own ear.

"No, we're not," Jazmin told me. "I think I'd rather walk the rest of the way."

We tried that for a while until we all got impatient. We had

---

[8] And I am using this word very loosely.

enough of it on the way here. Finally, Keran suggested we stick something in our ears to block out the noise. Which is when Jak remembered a rather unappealing spell. It involved the creation of Ear Slugs, which did precisely what you expect. Jak had to work pretty hard to convince us they wouldn't keep burrowing into our brains if we stuck them in our ears.

"How about I do it first?" Jak said after Jazmin did the spell like he asked.

"Oh, I insist," I said.

Jak held up one of the Slugs, tilted his head and dropped it into his ear. It squirmed in with a squelch and Jak gritted his teeth in a way that inspired very little confidence. Even so, he didn't hesitate before letting another Slug crawl into his other ear.

Once they were in place, Jak grinned and said, "This is great. I can't hear a single thing."

"In that case, let me say you look more and more like a toad every day," I tried. When he only nodded and smiled, I moved closer and shouted a few curses right in his ear.

"Nothing, nothing at all," Jak said. "Though I realize you're probably digging deep for the nastiest curses you know."

"I guess the Slugs haven't eaten his brain yet," I remarked. "Alright Jazmin. I'm ready to give it a try. Spell me up some slugs." The process of inserting the Slugs turned out to be even more unpleasant than Jak made it seem. Once finished though, none of us could hear a thing.

This lead to a rather comical sequence during which we attempted to communicate entirely through gestures.[9] When this failed miserably, I made a few violent motions for silence and forced everyone to gather around so we could continue our journey and later take the Slugs out to discuss.

With no need to listen to the harsh music, the next leg of our return journey went smoothly. I played slowly, letting each note die a long[10] death.

The longer I played, the faster the land sped past us until it

---

[9] I don't suppose we'll ever know what we tried to say.
[10] Not to mention very screechy.

262

became a blur. As we went, I gave some thought to whether we'd speed right through the border. I noticed a sort of blemish ahead of us. I stopped playing and we tumbled to the ground. As before, I stuck the landing best though the others began to also get the hang of it. Jak managed to land on his feet, even if he did stumble forward a few paces and fall almost directly across the nearest edge of a large, circular portal. The edges simmered much like the barriers between the states. The mist beyond the barrier looked familiar and I stared at it for a while before it clicked. This is where Keran's family secreted themselves away. Perhaps because of the duduk, perhaps because of the force propelling the quest itself or maybe a combination of the two, we'd been delivered right to the edge of the land into which Keran would need to return. In fact, I could see the very boulder marking out the entrance into his family's underground home.

I made a comment to that effect but of course no one responded. They couldn't hear me. I caught Jak's attention by grabbing his arm and gestured at my ears. He nodded his understanding and hit himself in the head. One of the Slugs popped out and hit the ground before dissolving into it. The other didn't come out quite as easily[11] but eventually also ended up vanishing into the ground.

The rest of us followed suit. My Ear Slugs knew what was good for them because they leapt free at the slightest pat to the side of my head. Jazmin's also popped free without complaint. We had to help Keran with his by bopping him forcefully on the top of his head.

Once we could all hear again, Naga said, "Looks like it's the end of the road for you, Keran."

"So it does," he agreed. "It's funny, I've spent the whole trip pining for this moment but I find I'm not quite ready. The end has come too fast."

"I don't identify with your sentiment at all," I told him. "I want to go home as soon as possible. Though I suppose your

---

[11] It meant Jak had to do a lot of tugging on his earlobe and hopping around, much as you'd imagine someone with water stuck in their ear might try to clear them.

reticence might have to do with the fact that your quest isn't truly over. You still have to convince your parents to move back home." At the expression on his face, I took pity on him. "Do you want us to go with you? I can try giving them my spiel about how I plan to force my parents to help."

"No, it's alright," Keran said. "This is my own quest." He said this with such force even Jak didn't have anything to say.

"I trust we don't have to tell you where to find us if you need help," I said.

"I might need it," Keran grumbled. He bumped each of us affectionately with his head in farewell before turning toward the portal. I thought he would plunge into it immediately but he paused with a paw in the air and turned around. "It occurs to me, Jak, you said you could do one spell. What is it?"

"It's weird. I thought for sure you'd have to pull out that ability at some point and we'd realize your magic is useful after all," I said.

"Oh yeah, a spell to make myself violently sick should really come in handy," Jak said.

"Even I get the point now about things mentioned at the beginning of a quest becoming useful before the end is nigh," Jazmin pointed out.

"We've got some road ahead of us yet," I said. "He might have to use it after Keran leaves."

"I certainly hope not," Jak said with a shudder.[12]

With this question settled, Keran made to leave before turning around with yet another question on his lips. I shot him a look and he sighed, agreeing to stop stalling. "You're right," Keran said. "Might as well get it over with. If I have it my way, I'll see you all soon enough anyway." He took off on a flying leap and slipped right through the barrier. Keran landed with surprising grace and darted quickly over to the boulder. Before he disappeared around it however, he looked back in a final

---

[12] All jokes aside, I didn't want him to have to suffer such a horrible fate. Not to mention I'd have to drag him the rest of the way home. As for how he found out about his ability to do only this particular spell, well, that was a long story.

gesture of farewell.

The instant he disappeared, the portal began to collapse in on itself, getting smaller and smaller until it imploded.

CHAPTER TWENTY NINE

"I'd like to walk for a while," Jazmin said once the portal closed up.

Jak and I both agreed so we started off across the land. Though still flat, dusty and lacking in vegetation, it looked ever so subtly different from the first time through. The feeling grew so strong I drew out the map once more and noticed a corridor of unmoving land cutting through the Eigen States.

When I showed it to the others, Jak laughed and said, "Nice of them to construct a land bridge for us."

I granted him a chuckle or two for the joke but Jazmin didn't make a sound, too preoccupied with her own thoughts to acknowledge us. I thought I knew what she was thinking so I left her alone as we continued to walk across the land, headed in a straight line toward the banks of the Zah River.

Sure enough, by midafternoon the next day, Jazmin got up the determination to turn to us and say, "I'm going back."

Neither of us needed her to clarify. She'd been acting shifty all day and no doubt seeing Keran go off to finish his own personal quest inspired her.

"My only question is whether you think you'll need our help," I told Jazmin.

"There will probably come a point when I wish I took it," Jazmin said, "if only for morale. But I don't think I'll need your sword. And you should probably finish your own quest before you get involved with someone else's."

"Have you met her?" Jak wanted to know.

"I guess you're right," Jazmin said with a laugh.

I glanced at the sky and enunciated, "I just don't know how you'll get home."

As if I called it down,[1] a portal fell out of the sky. It fell in the form of an enormous golden ring that melded with the ground. The shimmering barrier that marked every other border between the various Eigen States rose into the air, revealing the perfectly arranged landscape of Fairyland.

"Good job," Naga remarked.

"I know," I agreed as I looked upon the portal proudly. "Though it figures I'd only get the hang of it while we're on the way out."

"I'm glad," Jazmin said as she stepped forward to peer through the barrier. "This is excellent. This is close to home."

"In that case, I'll give you the same offer I gave Keran. Find us if you need us. She can cook up a spell for that right, Jak?" I asked.

"I think so," Jak said. I tuned out while he explained. The information would never do me any good,[2] after all. Instead, I plucked Naga out of my pocket and told her what I decided. Once Jak finished outlining the spell, I handed the lizard over to Jazmin.

"Bring some sanity back to Fairyland," I told her.

"Every good quest needs a companion to state the obvious," Jak said.

"Yeah, just like that," I commented.

"Well someone has to do it if Naga is leaving us," Jak remarked.

Jazmin thanked both us with hugs before letting Naga crawl into one of her pockets. Then she faced the barrier, took a deep

---

[1] Which of course, I did. Finally making these questing quirks work for me.
[2] Mostly because I planned to never go on a quest again.

ALDA YUAN

breath and stepped through. She paused like Keran earlier to wave goodbye to us. Then this portal collapsed like the last, cutting Jazmin off as she went to finish her own quest.

"Just us now," Jak remarked.

I gave him a look. "You don't need to take new your job this seriously, you know."

"I've got to find something to do. Apparently, it won't be taking back my lands."

I winced. "I'm sorry. Really, I am."

"Don't be. It's not meant to be, I suppose. And I don't know, this trip, it's got me thinking. Why do I want them back so badly? Do I really have a right to them?"

"I don't know. What gives us a right to anything?"

"Jielang didn't kill my parents. She stepped into the power vacuum after the accident. Someone needed to. It couldn't be me. And true, she may be an asshole for tossing me out on my ear but she's done a good job governing what my parents left behind."

It took me some time to figure out what Jak was getting at. "Are you giving up?"

"I think I am," Jak said, surprising himself so much he stopped walking. "Damn it, I am."

"The magic of the quest strikes again."

"I want to deny it but I don't think I can. It's because of the quest, it really is."

"You know I don't want to hear that."

"The more I think about it, the more I realize how true it is. That flaw of yours? It's mine too, thinking I can control something I can't, pretending to be something I'm not. I guess I'm ready to stop pretending. The truth is I never had a chance. No use pretending I did, what with my lack of magic. My parents thought my powers would come later on and I think that prospect blinded me. I always expected some deep wellspring of magic to appear. It's time to give up the fantasy and resign myself to the life I have."

"Well," I said after a while, "It's not so terrible, is it? At worst, you get to shake your head at my screw ups for the rest of your life."

268

"Not such a bad life," he agreed but the grief, a sort of unspoken horror at having let go of what constituted a life sustaining lie, hung about him. Were it me, Jak might have some words of comfort to offer. But I had nothing. So I stayed silent, letting Jak work through it on his own.

After a long time, during which we walked slowly across the empty landscape, Jak released a long sigh. "It doesn't seem real yet."

"It won't be for a while, I suspect. Hell, it's not even real to me yet. It's hard for me to think of you separate of your mission."

"Better get used to it then. It's the new reality."

"There's a lot we're going to have to get used to as a result of this quest of mine," I commented, thinking mostly of Realignment.

"I'm still not sure how any of this reshuffling of good and evil is supposed to happen."

"It seems no one does. Things will fall apart, some suckers will have to put them together again and I don't know if much will change. All we can do is live in the times and do our best to affect them for the better, quest or no quest."

"A venerable goal in these troubling times," Jak said, striking an actor's pose. He dropped his arms when I shoved him and said, "In all seriousness, I think this quest turned out alright."

"How so?" I asked with a laugh. "You didn't get what you wanted. We still don't know if Keran and Jazmin will get what they want."

"I suppose it could've turned out better for us individually. But for the world, I meant. We did good without taking ourselves too seriously and without believing we deserved to make these decisions. Not to give us too much credit but I have a hard time imagining anyone better to set the tone of this Realignment."

"I'm not going to go quite as far. I will say I don't have too many regrets. The Eigen States threw a lot of things at us and we did the best we could. We can be satisfied. But not too satisfied."

"I'll say," Jak said, with yet another sigh.

"You know what I really don't understand?" I asked after a pause. "Why did the fourth rule light up before the darkness swept us up? I didn't see any inviolable rule breaking."

"I don't know. Maybe it was something that had to be done. To fulfill the stages of the quest or something."

"Perhaps. I really thought someone was going to take our heads off and pop them back on to screw with us."

"I'm glad that didn't happen," Jak said.

"There's still time for it."

Rather unexpectedly, these words summoned a portal to take us home. The shimmering barrier rose out of the ring in the ground, revealing the fields not far from the capital.

"Already?" I demanded. "I agree with Keran. I'm not ready for this quest to be over. It doesn't feel complete."

"It's not complete. Even a fabricated quest like this one doesn't wrap up neatly at the end, as if we never lived before and had nothing to live out once it was over. There's plenty of work left."

"That's what I want to hear," I grumbled. "You're right though. I've got a feeling we'll be back. I don't know when and I certainly don't know why I would ever voluntarily return. But there's plenty unfinished and something will pull us back sooner or later."

"Later perhaps, if it must be. I'm sorry to break this to you Rahni but a road trip with you is a bit more eventful than anyone really likes."

"Myself included," I agreed as we passed through the barrier together.

ABOUT THE AUTHOR

Alda Yuan is an attorney at the Environmental Law and Policy Center based in Chicago, Illinois. She graduated with her JD and probably several complexes from Yale Law School in 2018.
She lives with her cat, an adorable orange menace who only occasionally answers to the name Artemis.
You can find her online. Seriously, she's extremely easy to find.

Made in the USA
Middletown, DE
29 December 2018